A Road Wanting Wear

Also by the author

A LINE INTERSECTED

Left Coast Lit   San Marcos, CA

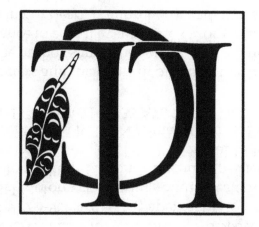

A ROAD WANTING WEAR

BY

DAVID GRANT URBAN

Publisher's Cataloging-in-Publication data

Names: Urban, David Grant, author.
Title: A road wanting wear / David Grant Urban.
Description: San Marcos, CA: Left Coast Lit, 2023.
Identifiers: LCCN: 2022911376 | ISBN: 979-8-9864070-1-2 (hardcover) | 979-8-9864070-0-5 (paperback)
Subjects: LCSH Motorcycle touring--Southwestern States-
-Fiction. | Motorcycling--Fiction. | Friendship--Fiction. |
Brothers--Fiction. | BISAC FICTION / General | FICTION /
Action & Adventure | FICTION / Small Town & Rural
Classification: LCC PS3621 .R335 A76 2023 | DDC 813.6--dc23

Names, characters and incidents depicted in this book are products of the author's imagination or are used fictiously. Any resemblance to actual events, locales, organizations, or persons living or dead, is entirely coincidental and beyond the intent of the author or publisher.

Cover "Open Road" photograph by Ken Kistler.

For Kim, of course. And for those who ride.

A blind man halted at a junction and compared by feel the two roads intersecting there. He thought, "The road well-worn and deeply rutted is surely the path of many. Therefore, I must choose the other, for the road wanting wear eases my steps and speeds my way."

Chapter I

If what Michael said was true—that tomorrow makes fools of us yesterday—then we were fools. But I'm sure that is too harsh. We were only young men. And most people would agree, I think, that the young deserve to be spared the harsh hindsight time bestows to our future selves.

At least I think so now. Life is a great arc, and on its downslope one can afford to be generous. Wouldn't you agree? Besides, we were different. We still wanted a connection with the world, to actually live in it and to learn something, and we did our best to understand what the world was telling us. How well we did you can judge for yourself.

I will say this: I'm not drawing anyone a map. I cannot do what life itself fails to do. No one can. And each man's journey is uniquely his own. But within the wildness, the adventure, and the eventual tragedy, it's all there if you look for it. So I'll just tell the story straight. You'll miss most of it at first, as of course we did ourselves. I think you'll come to it in the end. Or maybe not. But I hope you do.

It was the summer of Steven's final year at UC Santa Barbara, the last year of four he spent chasing a degree in chemistry. That's a tough major and sometimes Steven wanted to drop out, but I held him to his commitment and he grudgingly stayed in school. Although just one class short of graduating, Steven elected to

1

fulfill his last requirement in the fall and take the summer break instead.

Who could blame him? As his brother I was proud of him, he had a good future, and I looked forward to when he joined me in the business. The summer break gave him another chance to come down to San Diego and visit a while.

We were talking on the phone and Steven asked about the poker game I was planning.

"Is there room for another player, bro?" he asked.

"Of course," I said.

Steven had a classmate he wanted to bring down. His name was Derek Connor and he attended the university part-time. Steven told me Connor was the brightest guy in the class but barely passed. The professors liked him. He always stirred the class up, Steven said, but his assignments were absent or incomplete and out of class he had better things to do than study.

Steven seemed to like him quite a bit, as nearly everyone did, and they had some good times together. That was all I knew about Derek Connor then, although later I learned he had rolled out from Minnesota and that he rode a 929. He could ride, too, and I saw many times what he could do on that bike. Why he had come out west was something I learned about much later, and I wish my brother had told me sooner than he did.

"When will you be down?" I asked Steven.

"Early Friday night."

"You need a ride from the station?"

"I got it covered."

Steven rang off and I called Michael about the poker game. He said he would be there. That made four. I was glad Steven was bringing Connor. He sounded like a great guy.

It was late Friday afternoon with the sun just touching the horizon, and I was setting up for the poker game at the office. The office, where I worked and also slept, included a large fenced yard and that was where I had placed two 30-gallon barrels close together and then set a sheet of plywood on top to make a table. Next to that I set another barrel, this one filled with beer and ice. For lighting I used my portable halogen light stand, running the electrical cord back through the office door.

I was placing the deck of cards, the snacks, and the poker chip holder on the table, when I heard the motorcycle. The rider pulled up near the back of my truck, killed the motor, and removed his helmet. I saw it was Steven. Surprised, I walked to the chain-link gate and swung it open.

"What's all this?" I asked.

"Check it out, bro!" Steven said. He put his arm around my shoulders, holding the helmet in his other hand. He was smiling and happy.

"Good God, Steven. When did you get it?"

"Last week. Check her out!"

The bike was the Yamaha R1. It looked beautiful in the dying light.

"Why is it blue?" I asked. I had seen the new models. They had all been red.

"Champion's Edition. One of only five-hundred."

He had that proud look one gets with a first big purchase, so I walked around the bike and sat on it and asked questions to give him the satisfaction of my envy. The bike glistened with chrome and the tires still looked glossy black. The blue paint was waxed to a deep shine. It truly was a beautiful bike. It made me miss riding.

"Do you even have your license yet?"

"Permit. Got it today as a matter of fact."

"So that's why you didn't need me to pick you up at the station."

"No. I got it this morning and made the run down."

Steven normally took the Coaster down, the Amtrak that ran along the Pacific shore from Santa Barbara.

Steven was still smiling. He tried to hand me the keys. "Go on! It's a ride, bro."

I pushed his hand away.

"No way. I couldn't handle it."

Steven offered the keys again. "Go on! After all the riding you did? Take it."

"I'm too old for this bike."

"Nonsense."

"Besides, I rode a cruiser, not these crotch-rockets."

Steven locked his helmet to the bike. He was still smiling. He was careful in that new vehicle way, taking care not to scratch the paint or chrome as he locked the helmet. He walked with me into the yard, looking over the various barrels of chemicals next to the mixing tank.

"I can't believe you still sleep in your office," he said.

"Say what you want, no one bothers me here."

"I bet," he said. He walked to the barrel filled with beer and stooped down to read the label on the side.

"Hey, what used to be in this, anyway? Ethyl mono something?"

"Ethylene glycol. Butyl, for short."

"Is it dangerous?"

"Haven't you learned anything in class?"

Steven shook his head. He took off his leather jacket, reached into the ice water, and grabbed a bottle. His arm came back wet to the elbow.

"Man, these beers are cold!"

It was good to see Steven again. I had not seen him at Christmas. It had been since Thanksgiving, in fact. It was good to see him so happy. Steven walked to the table and pulled out one of the chairs I had set out. He draped his leather jacket over the wooden back and sat down. From his jacket pocket he removed several packages of cigars and packs of strike-anywhere wooden matches.

"Michael coming?" he asked.

"He'll be here."

Steven pulled out his cell phone and was thumb-scrolling the screen. "Derek is right around the corner," he said.

I heard the sound of another motorbike in the parking lot. The rider twisted the throttle and made the engine scream. Then the bike pulled up fast behind my truck and slid to a quick stop, the rear wheel rising off the ground. The rider swung one leg over the bike and jumped off. He removed his helmet and shut the bike off. He stepped around Steven's new motorbike, came close to the gate and looked through the fence. He spotted Steven sitting at the table.

"Hey!" the rider yelled. He swung the gate open and walked in. Steven stood.

"About time!" Steven said. They shook hands.

"So, what happened?" the rider asked Steven.

"Just a warning. He said if he ever caught me again, I'd be in jail and I'd lose the bike. What happened to you?"

"Kept going! He couldn't get us both, now could he?"

I couldn't follow what they were talking about until Steven explained that on their 200-mile run down from Santa Barbara a cop caught them speeding on the freeway. Steven pulled over and got off with only a warning. The other rider, the one I was meeting now for the first time, had ditched the cop by cutting across four lanes to the next exit.

So this must be Derek, I thought. "You shouldn't have left him," I said, annoyed.

He gave me a level look but before he spoke Steven moved between us. "Derek Connor, this is my brother, Jordan Wryte," he said.

"The great Jordan Wryte, eh? Steven talks about you a lot." Derek Connor reached out and we shook hands. I noticed Derek stood a couple inches taller than me, maybe six two or three. He had a good build. His grip was strong.

"Help yourself," I said. I let my initial annoyance go. It was just this: ditching a riding buddy wasn't done, especially a new rider. But what the hell, I thought. They'd gotten away with it. I waved my hand toward the barrel filled with beer. Derek took off his jacket. He followed Steven's example and placed it on the back of a chair. He reached deep into the barrel of ice and beer, pulled out a bottle and tossed it up, catching it behind his back. He pried off the top and some foam spilled out.

"Guinness! Your brother has taste!" he said to Steven. He took a long drink and then raised the bottle in my direction. I nodded as acknowledgment. I reached for one, too, then I sat at the makeshift table. The three of us drank beer and talked and waited for Michael.

A few minutes later Michael drove up in his car. He parked by my truck and waved at us as he opened the driver's door and stepped out. He came through the gate, glanced off-handedly at both motorbikes parked just outside, and joined us at the table.

My brother introduced Derek to Michael. Michael leaned across and shook hands with Derek.

"Michael Case. Pleased to meet you, Derek."

"Same."

"That your 929 out there?" Michael asked.

"That's it."

"That's a nice bike. Really nice."

"Thanks."

Michael looked at the two bikes by the gate. "Too bad that R-zero parked so close to yours. Ruins the picture."

"Yeah," Michael went on, "It's a real shame when some beat-up piece of…"

"You bastard!" said Steven. "You should get so lucky to own a work of art like that!"

Michael was laughing. "Oh, is that yours? It's a fine bike, I guess, except the color's wrong and no doubt the controls are backasswards."

I was laughing, too. The look on Steven's face was perfect.

"Well, I guess I should take a closer look before I judge, though." Michael stood, grimacing and feigning a most serious manner, and walked to the bikes. Of course we had to get up and take a look also. It's part of the ritual with motorbikes. Everyone stands around a new bike and stares at it and nods his head and asks questions of the rider, and this is what we did. Michael conceded Steven's R1 was a great bike and that meant a lot to Steven. Michael had been riding a long time and owned three motorbikes, including a late model Triumph Speed Triple, a 1994 Harley Fatboy, and the big Honda Valkyrie with the six-cylinder engine.

"You be careful on this," Michael said. He sat on Steven's bike, checking the balance and feel, something one would never normally do unless invited, but Michael had a certain license because of his knowledge.

Steven just nodded, happy with his new bike and bolstered by the respect Michael gave it. Michael leaned the R1 back on its stand and we went back to the table. There, all of us reseated, we lit cigars and smoked as the first few stars came out. It was a warm summer night and it felt nice to be sitting outside.

"All right, enough of this. Let's play," I said. I picked up the cards and dealt. We played draw or stud. I noted Derek played good poker. He bet a little wild but seemed to make out. He carried on well and he and Michael hit it off fine.

Derek looked at the poker chip holder and asked me about it.

"My grandfather's," I said. I passed it to him. The chip holder was a plastic cylinder the size and shape of a small cake. At the top was a round knob. When you turned the knob twelve columns turned outwards from around the edges. Each column held a stack of chips.

"Your grandfather still around?"

"No. Seven years gone. He died soon after our mom. It's the only thing I have from him."

Derek turned the knob, watching the columns with the chips stacked and sorted by color swing in and out. He passed the chip holder back.

"That's nice," he said, and he seemed to appreciate what it meant to me.

We kept playing. Each of us made regular trips to the barrel for more beer. During the game I held my own, Steven and Michael were losing, and Derek was up. We took a break and stood around the barrel drinking more beer.

"You got it good living here, bro," said Steven.

"It's all right," I said. "I get a little tired of it."

Derek looked at me, puzzled. "You live here? At your business?"

"I sleep in the office. I save where I can."

"What about showers and all that?"

"The gym."

"Every day?"

"Every single day. Sometimes I go twice a day." I shrugged. "When the business gets bigger I'll get a place. Sleeping in the office for now doesn't hurt me any. Like Steven said, it has its good points. There's no one around."

"That's for sure."

"I can play the music loud, have poker games, and no one complains."

Derek turned to Michael. "What about you, Mike? What do you do?"

"Oh, I'm a manager. Wal-Mart. Assistant manager."

"He lives in the belly of the beast," I said.

"Sure. Four-hundred billion a year…a million employees. I'm one of them."

"You like it?"

"It's a job, you know? It's what I do. It has its moments and then some."

I asked Derek what brought him out from Minnesota.

"Many things."

"School?"

"No. Not really."

Derek seemed hesitant to talk about it and I didn't press it.

Michael said, "That's quite a ride, though, from Minnesota."

Derek just shrugged.

We continued playing poker and Steven bet after he drew two cards. He tossed in a few chips and said to Michael, "You ever have an accident riding?"

"Never," said Michael. He knocked on the plywood table. Like many who rode motorbikes, he was superstitious. "You're not supposed to ask, you know."

"I don't think you did either, right, bro?" Steven said to me, ignoring Michael.

"I was lucky," I said. I knocked on the table also.

"Derek wasn't so lucky. Tell them about your wreck and what happened," said Steven, looking at Derek. As a new rider, Steven had a heightened fear of accidents. It takes a while to develop the fatalism veteran riders have.

"It's not that much of a story, really," said Derek.

"I'd like to hear about it, if you want to talk about it," said Michael. I nodded in agreement.

"Well, I'd just come out here. Didn't know a soul, I mean no one. I spent a lot of time just cruising the streets. This was up north in Santa Barbara."

He paused, calling Steven's bet, tossing a few red chips on the table.

"I wasn't sold on the place yet. I thought of maybe heading to Oregon. Or Mexico even. I was cruising down the boulevard one day and the light changed to yellow. I gunned it to beat it and there's someone turning left in front of me. I t-boned him and went over the car. A Volvo, of all things, you know, safety and all that, and the man jumped out crying, 'I didn't see you, I didn't see you'. People came running from out of their cars and I was there in the street in a pool of gasoline."

"Were you hurt?" asked Michael.

"Sure. I cracked three ribs, broke my wrist, cracked my pelvis, and ripped my balls open."

"No!"

"Oh, yeah. The tank split open on my bike, that made for all the gasoline. The metal edge sliced the old scrotum right down the center like a Ginsu knife."

Michael was cringing in his seat.

"I'm lying there, and all the time the man was crying to everyone, 'I didn't see him! I didn't see him!' And the thing was, that light turned red when I hit the intersection. The Volvo had hung out in the middle waiting to turn, waiting for traffic to pass. After the last car, he turned. He never saw me. I'm sure he figured he was clear."

"Weren't there any witnesses?"

"Sure. The usual bunch."

"Didn't they see the light?"

"No. You know how it is. They hear a collision, look up, and then they tell the cops what they guess they saw. The thing was, the man kept saying that he didn't see me. People just assumed he was at fault. But I think the light was red."

"Now tell them the good part," said Steven.

"Well, I healed up all right. Spent some time in the hospital and all."

"How'd the balls do?" asked Michael, unable to help himself.

"Balls are fine now. Thanks for asking. But a lawyer was on the scene. I mean, right there. I'm lying in the street, soaked in gasoline, and the guy's giving me his business card. Never had to go to court. I collected nice. I bought a new bike, the 929 you see there, and here I am."

Michael said, "That story is gonna make me quit riding. At least maybe wear a cup or something. Forget the helmet. Best to guard what counts."

"You don't have any brains to protect, anyway," Steven said.

"None of us do. If we were smart, we wouldn't ride the damn machines."

Michael tossed his cards onto the felt. Steven won the hand with three tens. Michael got up and walked to the beer barrel. Derek and Steven also got up. I joined them. We took turns reaching in to grab bottles of Guinness, our arms wet and cold as we reached down deep to grab from the remaining bottles. The night was still with no breeze. The poker chips looked colorful and the cigars smoldered in the ashtrays.

We returned to the table and played a little more. I think Steven and Michael were still down, maybe more now, and Derek kept winning. He had more luck than brains, or maybe I was just jealous over his winning, and meanwhile his pile of chips kept growing.

Derek folded on the next hand and watched the game go its rounds.

"Raise five," said Michael.

"Call you. Raise ten more," said Steven.

"Big spender," I said. "That's fifteen to me. I raise twenty more."

"Call."

"Call."

I tossed down a full house, jacks full of eights.

"I don't believe that crap," said Michael. He threw his cards in.

I dragged all the chips to my side and began sorting and stacking. Derek suddenly banged the table with his fist, making all the stacks fall.

"What the hell?"

"I'm just messing with you."

Derek got up for a beer and brought four back. He passed them around.

"You guys ever think about a tour? Take the bikes and maybe ride through the West?" he said, his question mainly directed to Steven and Michael.

"I'd love to," said Steven. "What do you think, Mike?"

"Could be fun."

Derek said to me, "I'd include you, but I heard you don't ride."

I said, "I don't ride *anymore*. I'm busy with my business."

"If you change your mind you could come."

"If I did I wouldn't need your permission."

"Easy, Jordie. Just trying to be friendly."

"Try a little harder. And the name is Jordan."

"Hey, come on, guys," said Steven. He wanted me to get along with Derek, I could tell, and for his sake I toned it down a bit. But I didn't like Derek treating me like that.

We kept playing and talk of a tour went on, but I couldn't see how to get time away from my business. Steven was keen on the idea though.

"At least consider it, bro."

"I'll think about it."

By the night's end we settled. Steven and Michael were the big losers, while Derek and I were evenly ahead. We counted out the chips and divided the pool of money. We sat around just talking and getting ready to call it a night when Derek counted out five twenties of his winnings and tossed them to the center of the table.

"Match it. We'll cut cards," he said to me. He shuffled the deck and set it down, then drew the jack of diamonds. He replaced the card and slid the deck over to me and waited.

"I'm not doing that. Why would I risk the whole night on one cut?"

"You might win it all."

"I might lose it all."

11

I looked at the deck. "Let's just see how it would have turned out, though," I said. I reached for the cards but Derek grabbed them first and tossed the cards high in the air. The cards fluttered down all around us.

"Now you'll never know," he said.

Chapter II

They had all left and it was late in the night. I began to clean up the yard. I thought I would hit the couch in the office but when I laid down the room spun round and round. It was better to stay on my feet. The yard looked like a riot. Cards were scattered on the ground and broken beer bottles lay everywhere. I had set an empty trash can for recyclables a short toss from the poker table, but it seems our aim had degenerated as the night wore on. A few bottles may possibly have landed on the roofs of adjoining buildings.

I dumped the water from the beer barrel. Only three bottles were left. I took a broom and swept the yard. All this at three in the morning. When I at last had things in order I went back to the office and locked the doors behind me. I turned off the desk lamp and I saw the envelope on the desktop with *Steven* printed on the front of it. I had forgotten to give it to him at the game. I found the couch and grabbed the blankets piled on one end and I lay down. The room had stopped spinning as I fell asleep.

I awoke at noon. In the office I had a small microwave and refrigerator and I made myself a quick breakfast. Out in the yard it was very bright. I saw that Steven's bike was gone. Michael had driven Steven home last night at my insistence. Steven must have come back sometime in the morning and retrieved his bike.

Derek refused Michael's offer and rode off, pulling a wheelie out the parking lot to the cross street and down the road. All that beer seemed not to affect him. We heard him get on the freeway ramp and accelerate. Steven and Derek, I had learned, were staying at some beach motel. I guessed they were probably soaking up the sun at the beach. My truck still sat outside the fence. I opened the gate and drove it in.

The parking lot had a few cars in it. Some of my business neighbors worked on the weekends. I was glad I had cleaned up last night. Most of my neighbors were nice, but there was one who suspected my business was actually a meth lab. I explained I was just a small chemical compounder, but he reported me anyway one night when I was working late. The police arrived in three patrol cars, along with some very hard-eyed DEA agents. I had to explain what all the chemical barrels were about. It took a while.

I knew people thought it odd for me to live at the office but I really didn't mind. Some people woke up weekends to mow the lawn or paint. I woke up to compound product so I had inventory for the coming week. It was nice not to have to go to work, I was already here, and, as I said, no one bothered me. Most of the time, anyway.

I needed to make a fresh tank of Laser Degreaser and so I began to prepare. I first half-filled with water the 500-gallon tank that sat outside in the yard and I turned on the mixer. I added the powders, about 50 pounds each of phosphate and metasilicate. I had to climb up a ladder with a pail to the top of the tank to dump the powders in. Once the powders dissolved I added a small amount of sulfonate. It served as a stabilizer. Next came 55 gallons of surfactant and 55 gallons of butyl solvent. I had an air-driven pump that I used to pump the surfactant and the butyl from 55-gallon barrels on the ground up to the tank.

I added the preservative last, which was just a very small amount of formaldehyde, then the dye, and then I let everything blend well. That finished the job except for topping off the tank to the 500-gallon mark with more water.

Laser was easy to make and had a good profit margin. I had

developed it myself, and I sold it to industrial accounts county-wide. It was a damn good degreaser and I was giving the big compounders a run for their money in this town. I did all right for a bathtub compounder, which is what the competition called me. In a few years, with Steven's help, I hoped to be one of the top chemical compounders in town.

After I made a tank I normally filled barrels and pails right away, but I felt a bit rocky from last night. I let the big tank of the scarlet-colored degreaser stand full and decided to fill the barrels and pails tomorrow. I lay on the couch in the office and fell asleep watching some old black and white movie based on the adventures of Bengal Lancers.

The mailman rattled the mail slot and the sound of Saturday's mail falling through the slot woke me up. I swung my feet off the couch, sat up, rubbed my eyes, then I went straight to the pile of mail. In a small business you live and die by the mail. I sorted it, opening first anything that looked like money. Today turned out to be a good day when I opened two big checks I had been expecting. Then the day turned into a grand day with the arrival of a much larger check I had not been expecting at all.

I saw the clock read four-ten. I would have time to get the three checks to the bank before it closed. I locked up, grabbed my bag with the gym clothes, and left the office through the door leading out to the yard. I drove to the bank and deposited the checks. I had a quick workout at the gym, showered and changed, and then I had a good meal at Janet's Café. It felt good to get those checks in the bank and I thought perhaps I would make a night of it. I drove to Dirk's Horseshoe Lounge and parked in the back. Near my truck a black Valkyrie leaned on its kickstand. It looked spotless and its polished chrome glowed softly in the early evening light. I knew Michael must be inside.

Chapter III

I found him sitting at the bar, facing away from the stage, looking down at his phone.

"Well, hello," he said. "Back from the dead?"

"What do you mean?"

"We came by this morning."

"Never heard you."

"Pounded on your door. You never answered. Saw your truck and tried calling. Got the answering service."

"I turn the phone off weekends."

"We thought so. Steven got his bike."

"I noticed."

I ordered a coke. Michael watched as the bartendress brought the coke.

"You swearing off?"

"After last night, maybe."

"That was fun. I had a great time, except for the money."

"Hey, don't worry about that. Tonight is on me."

"In that case," Michael said, and ordered another drink. The bartendress gave him a big smile. She was a pretty girl with bright red nails.

"That Connor guy seems all right, I thought," Michael said.

"Maybe."

"He and Steven have a nice room at the Sands, right on the beach. They went to the beach today."

"I thought they might. Must be nice."

"Derek's laying out the money for the room all week."

"He doesn't seem to be lacking it."

"Sure. I noticed you two seemed to be at odds."

"I don't know, Mike. Something about him. Too cocky."

"He's not a bad guy, Jordan. Treated me to lunch with him and Steven. Wanted to thank me for getting Steven to his bike."

"Really," I said. "Such a great guy."

"Give him a chance. Anyway, have you thought about the tour idea at all?"

"I can't, Mike."

"You couldn't get some time together?"

"No. I can't get away. You aren't going, are you?"

"Thinking about it. I've got time. It sounds like fun. We'd leave in one week. Next Saturday."

"Sounds like you've done more than thought about it. Is this a done deal?"

"Well," Michael said, a little embarrassed, I thought. "Why not? You ought to come, Jordan. Really. You ought to come."

"What did I just say? I can't go. You understand? I can't get away."

"Don't get sore."

"I'm not sore."

So we sat at the bar and watched as it began to fill. The extra help arrived to handle the Saturday night crowd. The bartendress with the red nails spent less and less time with each customer as she served the drinks. The daytime regulars surrendered their seats slowly to the Saturday night partiers. They went out the door and into the night, while inside the lights dimmed and seats became scarce and finally the band members arrived, all wearing leather jackets, the Beat Farmers, and they started to fool around with whatever they had to do to set up their gig.

The Beat Farmers had started out years ago at the Spring Valley Inn. I wandered in one night and found I was the only one there. It was the first night they had played as a band and the gig was more a practice session than a show. The Inn then was just a dive. It still is, really. Anyway, the Beat Farmers took off from there and recorded several albums. I'd gotten to know some of the band members.

Michael and I sat at the bar as Dirk's began filling up, and one of the Beat Farmers came by to say hello.

"This'll be wild tonight. I can feel it," he said to us, shaking my hand.

"I got the last CD, Jerry. It's damn good."

"Thanks, Jordan. Bring it in. I'll get all the guys to sign it."

"I will."

I bought the three of us shots of tequila. After we downed them Jerry went back to the stage.

"He's a good guy, isn't he?" Michael said.

"Good songwriter. Awesome guitarist."

We stayed at the bar talking, Michael noting my short ride on the wagon, and he lined up more beers until the band started. The first song was "Never Goin' Back," and the crowd poured onto the dance floor. Michael and I stayed at the bar and drank and then we found dance partners and got on the floor ourselves.

I danced with a thin redhead who smiled at me and didn't mind the crowd, both of us squeezed in so tight we could hardly move, which was fine by me since it hid the fact I can't dance. I could see Michael sweating hard a few dancers over, and the Beat Farmers blasting away song after song until they took a break and everyone cleared the floor and I walked back to the bar.

At the bar I set us up with another round.

"That's a blast, eh?" said Michael.

"Yeah, it is." I took a long drink. "I gotta get out more."

"Yes, you do."

"What's that supposed to mean?"

"Just agreeing with you."

A crowd three-deep pressed against the bar and swamped the bartenders with orders. I ordered from one of the waitresses passing by. She had to lean close to catch my order. Her hair brushed against my face as I spoke into her ear. She brought the drinks and we accidentally bumped faces as she leaned over to set the drinks on the bar. The bartendress with the red nails scowled since the waitress was poaching her territory, so I tipped the waitress and left another tip on the bar for the bartendress.

Michael and I toasted and downed the shots. As I put the shot glass down I saw Steven and Derek making their way past the doorman and into the bar. I couldn't raise their attention; it was too loud and crowded. They made their way to a corner and hung out in another part of the crowd. But a few minutes later Steven appeared next to me at the bar.

"Hey bro!"

"How you doing?"

"Great. Spent all day at the beach, had lobster tonight. We've been cruising the town since."

"On your permit?"

"I'm being careful. Come on, lighten up, will you?"

"You know they catch you at night you're done."

"This from the guy who rode a year without a license?"

"He's got you there," said Michael.

"Sure. Thanks, Mike."

Derek Connor walked up. "Well, well. Spending your winnings?" He shook hands with Michael, then me.

"The trick," said Michael, "is to go out after you lose with the guys who won. Guilt makes them treat you all night. Most times."

Derek laughed. He put a fifty on the bar and whistled loudly. The bartendress came over and he ordered shots and beers for all of us. "Drink up, me hearties!"

Steven and Derek left us after the drinks and roamed through the bar. The Beat Farmers started up again, the music loud and the crowd filling the dance floor once more. I lost track of Michael. I sat alone at the bar enjoying the scene until finally, with that sudden realization that several hours have somehow gone by, I got up to leave.

I looked over the crowd to say goodbye, if I could find anyone, and I saw them standing near the band by the small tables off to the side. I shouldered my way through the crowd across the dance floor.

"There you are," said Michael. He was sitting down. Sweat ran down his face and I knew he must have been out dancing again. I got Steven's attention.

"I'll see you tomorrow, eh? Maybe we can do something."

"Sure, bro!" Steven said. He grabbed my shoulder. "You're my brother, bro! Hey, come on the trip, bro! Come on the trip!"

His hand tightened on my shoulder as his legs gave way a bit. I steadied him up.

"Whoa," I said, searching the key pocket on his leather jacket draped on the back of his chair. "You're not riding tonight," I said. I was smiling.

"Leave him alone. He'll be all right," said Connor.

"No, he's not all right."

"You his mother or something?" said Derek Connor, and the smile left my face. Connor had grabbed my arm and I rotated it against his thumb side to break his grip. I found the keys and gave them to Michael. I turned and faced Connor.

"Sometimes it's best to keep your mouth shut," I said.

"You've got nothing to teach me, sport."

We stood a foot apart, just seconds from a go around, when Steven effectively broke things up. He vomited between us, covering the tabletop and making Michael jump up and back like someone yanked him with a rope.

"Jesus!" he said.

Chapter IV

Midnight came and passed. I was back at the office, sitting out in the yard. The office remained hot and stuffy until I aired it some. Meanwhile I had taken a chair and sat outside in the cool air. I drank one of the last three bottles of Guinness. Lord knows I didn't need it. By all rights I had no business driving home from Dirk's. Calling a cab would have been smart but I was not exactly feeling smart lately.

What the hell was wrong, anyway? That was a nice scene at Dirk's, the doorman hustling us out, and Steven angrily pushing me away. I said I would give him a ride, and he, pulling away from me, telling me to fuck off. Michael took care of him. Thank God he was there, but how many times had I been in his shoes? He's only twenty-one, for heaven's sake; of course he'll have that type of night. Does six years difference mean I have forgotten what it's like?

And what was Michael's problem? You should get out more. What did he mean by that? I mean, of all of us I had done more, been more places. They haven't done near what I've done. Get out more. Can't they see I'm trying to build something here? It takes hard work. It takes all I have.

And Derek telling me what to do? I wondered how much

Steven had told him? I had practically raised Steven after mom died, or at least got him through the rest of high school and then into college. Mom's dying wish: Take care of Steven, Jordan. And I had.

I sat out in the yard cursing the world and all the things in it, and then I walked to the far corner of the yard next to the brick wall and stood under the overhang. I pulled the cover off the motorcycle that had sat there for the last six years. I pushed the bike to the middle of the yard and looked it over.

It was a sad sight. The tires were flat, the paint looked dull, and the chrome needed polishing. Starting it was out of the question, the battery was surely dead, and the fluids were all shot, probably. Still, I sat on the bike and the memories of all those miles on the road flooded back to me.

So the sonofabitch suggested a tour. Everyone seemed up for it, no doubt. The bastard thought I wouldn't have the balls. Well, well, we'll see about all that, now, wouldn't we? I left the bike there in the center of the yard and went back inside the office and finally fell asleep.

The following morning I awoke at eight. Before breakfast I emptied the tank of Laser into six 55-gallon barrels and 34 pails. I applied labels, then rolled the barrels and stacked the pails where they belonged. That, and what I had already, gave me plenty of stock for the week. Still, I would have to make at least a couple more tanks to boost inventory if I planned to take a week off. But that was enough work for this morning, and as usual I headed over to Janet's Café.

One of the drawbacks of living at the office was having to eat out quite a bit. But then, what matches a hot breakfast served to you, along with good coffee made sweet with cream and sugar, and the Sunday paper to eat and relax by? The café waitresses all knew me from my daily visits, of course, and my coffee with the special vanilla creamer I liked was usually at my table before I even sat down. They could see me coming through the windows.

By the time I returned to the office I felt pretty good. I parked my truck and walked inside the yard. The bike sat there, still looking sad and neglected. I found my resolve wavering. Last night, angry and under the influence, it was easy to spout off on one thing or another. It didn't look so simple now. I would really have to work at getting time away. For a one-man operation it was nearly impossible. Some of my bigger customers might not like the idea.

And the bike, now that I really looked at it, was a mess. I would have to get Michael over to work on it. He would get it running, but I wasn't sure it would be ready in time for a tour. It was not going to work out. I grabbed the motorcycle by the bars and began to wheel it back under the overhang.

A motorbike pulled up and, since I had left the gate open, it came right into the yard. The rider removed his dark-visored helmet. I saw it was Steven.

I didn't say anything to him.

Steven looked at my old bike.

"You're bringing out your bike!" he said. Then he saw I was still angry about last night.

"Hey, I'm sorry, bro. I didn't mean any of that."

I looked at him and I felt bad about what happened also, and I knew I could not stay angry. Not with my brother.

"It's all right. How do you feel?"

"A little rough, to tell the truth."

"I'm sure."

Steven dismounted and walked to my old bike. "So you decided to come along?"

He looked so happy and I felt I couldn't refuse. I had that odd feeling of being drawn into something already written.

So I nodded and said, "I'm thinking about it."

Steven pumped his fist. "Yeah!"

"I have to arrange things. It might not work out," I warned him.

"You'll find a way."

"You have more faith than I do."

He put his helmet back on, lifting the visor so I could see his face.

"I'll check back later today," he said.

"We can have dinner if you want."

"That sounds great."

He rode off through the gate and out the lot. I heard him accelerate down the street.

I walked back into the office and called Michael. He came by later. He looked the bike over and pulled at some wires and cables and took off the side covers.

"You'll have to get it in the shop," he said. "There's too much here for me to do in one week."

He started ticking off the problems: tires, battery, fluids, timing, and so on. I kept seeing dollar signs, but we lifted the bike onto my truck and strapped it down. I planned to get the bike in the shop first thing Monday morning.

"I'll go with you," said Michael.

"You don't have to," I said.

"No, I'll go with you. I don't start my shift until eleven. I want to make sure it goes well."

Michael left and later in the day Steven came back by and we had a nice meal at the café. It was pleasant to talk about school, the business, and how things were going. He was excited about the trip.

"Bro, how do you want to go?"

"You mean the route?"

"Sure. Which way do you want to go?"

"It's a little hard to go west from San Diego."

"You think? The Pacific might be hard to cross on a bike," he deadpanned.

"So we have north, south, east."

"Not south. I'm not taking my bike to Mexico."

"We can go east through the desert, then. If you don't want the heat we can go up the coast."

"No coast. I'm tired of Santa Barbara."

"All right. How about east, then up past the Salton Sea? I still haven't seen Death Valley."

"I thought you had."

"No. I passed north of it. I ran through the gold country. Up to the Lost Coast, Eureka, Coos Bay. The Olympics, Port Townsend. That was some great riding up there."

"You went up the West Coast, right?"

"I did. I never saw such a wild coast. Beats the East Coast all to hell, except for Maine."

"You liked Maine, I remember."

"Beautiful state up there. All that color in the fall."

"You wrote about the Black Ball ferries at Port Townsend in Washington."

"Yeah, I hit Victoria, too. You really remember the Black Ball ferries?"

"I saved all your letters, bro."

I smiled. It was fun to remember those places. Our waitress came by with more coffee and gave us a smile. I watched her go to the next table where two couples sat quietly, each person thumb-scrolling a smartphone. The waitress had to get their attention. I shook my head.

"What are you looking at, bro?" Steven asked.

"Nothing," I said. We continued talking and it was a nice meal and after Steven left I was glad we'd had a chance to talk and just be brothers.

The next day, Monday, I got up at five a.m. and planned my day. Michael would be along by half past eight. By six I had all the messages from the answering service and I had a good idea of what the day required.

Before Michael came by I returned all the phone calls, made out my delivery route, and planned afternoon visits to my biggest customers. I couldn't load my truck with product since my bike sat in the bed, so I waited by the gate for Michael. When he showed he jumped in the truck and I drove to the bike shop.

"Be prepared to spend some money, you know," Michael said on the way.

"Sure. I just want a fair deal."

"It won't be cheap."

"I just want it fair. No attitudes."

"You've got six years to make up for. It'll cost you."

I was not pleased on the way to the Harley-Davidson shop. I had never bought in to the whole attitude that so many Harley riders adopted and I hated to deal with it. These guys, the mechanics, they thought they did you a favor working on your bike. The salesmen were worse. They always seemed to size you up to assess your worthiness as a customer. Even the damn counter guys had the attitude. Some riders turned themselves into walking billboards for the company, scraping and bowing to the almighty image. All their clothes and gear had the logo. Guys who didn't even own a Harley wore the stuff. Maybe it was because I was in business myself and I resented the whole marketing and manipulation angle, but I would be damned if I needed anyone to pass judgment on me because of what type bike I rode.

Michael must have read my thoughts because as I pulled into the rear of the shop he said, "Let me handle this." He was out of the truck and talking to one of the mechanics before I fully parked. I leaned against the side of the truck, listening.

The mechanic had one of those red rags they always have around and he was wiping his hands with it, talking to Michael. They walked to one of the bikes in the shop.

"That's got to be an early decker," I heard Michael say. "Nineteen sixty-one, sixty-two?"

"Sixty," the mechanic said, pleased. "I've got three years on it so far."

Michael said something else I couldn't make out and then he and the mechanic were walking back to my truck. The mechanic eyed my bike.

"What happened here?" The mechanic glared at the bike.

"Been in storage," Michael answered, before I had a chance to speak.

"No way to treat a bike."

"My buddy here wants to get it up and running again."

The mechanic turned to me and we shook hands. He had tattoos down both arms.

"Nice to meet you," I said.

"Name's Ed."

"Jordan."

Michael said, "Here's the deal. We're leaving on a tour this weekend. I'm bringing my ninety-four Fatboy..."

"Nice."

"Thanks, and my buddy needs this Softail ready to roll."

Ed looked the bike over. "Nineteen ninety?" Michael nodded. Ed shook his head. "I don't know. One week. Five days. That's cutting it close," he said, squinting at the bike as if it were on life support.

"Here's the problem," Michael said, putting his arm around Ed's shoulders, walking with him a bit, speaking in low tones now. "We're the only two real bikes. The rest is all rice, you know? And I sure as hell don't want to take any shit from them, you understand?"

Ed nodded. He set his face in a grimace.

"All right," he said. "Let's get her off the truck."

We lifted the bike down and rolled it in the shop. Ed looked at the bike again.

"Might have to order parts. Check back late Friday," he said.

"Anything you can do would be great."

We all shook hands like conspirators, and then Michael and I left.

On the road I turned to him and said, "Are you kidding me?"

He shrugged. "Better than you going in there and butting heads with the guy."

"I wouldn't have done that."

"Bullshit. You would have argued money and customer service and gotten nowhere fast."

"I'm the one paying for the work, aren't I?"

"You're missing the whole point. The man's an artist. Money has nothing to do with it."

I dropped him off back at the office and he left for work. I loaded up my truck, made deliveries until lunch, and then after lunch I visited three of my larger customers. None had any issues with me leaving for a week. In fact, I was surprised how nice they were about it. At the transit company I walked the bus yard with the maintenance supervisor.

"Sounds like a great time, Jordan," he had said.

"I can stock you extra product. Delay billing, you know."

"We'll be fine. Take the trip. Bring some pictures by when you get back."

"I will."

I spent the week this way. For my smaller customers I simply called and explained I was taking a vacation. Some of them placed orders to get by until I came back. It made for a busy week but I got through it. I saw Steven a couple times for a beer and once at a bike shop to help him pick out bags for the tour. He bought a nice set designed to fit his bike.

By late Friday I felt things were under control and I swung by the Harley shop to pick up my bike. I just made it before they closed. I had to walk through the front since all the rear roll-up doors were shut. The counter man pulled my invoice and presented the bill, sliding it across the counter. The bill was $1,459.03, less ten percent, since I had originally bought the bike from the shop, used, many years ago. I must have still been in the files somewhere.

I swallowed hard over the bill, paid it, and then followed the counter man out to the shop to get the bike. As we walked along I thought about the talk I would be having with Michael. The counter man opened the last of the three roll-up doors and I got a good look at my bike.

It was gorgeous. It was reborn, a rolling work of art, cleaned, polished, leaning on its kickstand, the pearl-colored paint glowing softly in the late afternoon sun, the chrome sparkling like polished silver before a fire.

"The guys really worked on it," the counter man said.

I was at a loss for words. I sat on the motorcycle and straightened it up.

"You mind if I turn her over?"

The counter man nodded. I pushed the starter button and the soft rumble echoed through the garage and reverberated from the walls and out through the roll-up door. I pressed down with my foot and clicked the shifter into first and eased out the clutch. I rolled slowly out to my truck. I shut it down and dismounted. The bike felt brand new.

"That's a good-looking bike," the counter man said.

"It is, isn't it? Tell Ed I'll come by after my trip, will you?" He helped me load the bike onto the bed of my truck and I strapped it down.

We would be leaving tomorrow.

Chapter V

Michael was the first to arrive in the morning. I let him in the office and he helped himself to coffee. He walked out to the yard to see my motorbike. I followed him out. I saw his Valkyrie parked by the gate.

"I thought you were riding the Fatboy?"

"Changed my mind. Hard to beat the Valkyrie on long trips." He looked at my bike, still sitting in the bed of the truck.

"You aren't even ready."

"I suppose I can levitate the bike down by myself?"

"How do you load and unload those?" he asked, indicating the fifty-five gallon drums of chemicals sitting in the yard.

"With a chain sling. And I am not using that on the bike."

We got the bike down all right, never easy since it weighed 600 pounds, although there is a trick to lifting it on and off. I went back inside to gather the saddlebags. I had them packed from last night and all I had to do was throw them across the pillion pad and strap them down. A smaller bag rode on the rack behind the backrest.

Michael was eyeing the bike.

"Looks good." He walked around it. "New belt, battery, I'm sure; tires, wheels trued, brakes, clutch, all fluids, timing, greased, lubed, polished. How about that."

"Yes, how about that."

He stood there, grinning.

"Sure, keep smiling," I said to him. "You didn't have to pay the bill."

"How much was it?"

"You don't want to know."

We heard motorbikes screaming off the highway, making their way to us.

"Christ," I said. "I hope the whole trip is not like that. We'll never keep up."

"I will, Jordan. You won't."

I must have looked surprised, because Michael said, "Don't worry. I'm cruising, not racing."

Steven and Derek Connor pulled up by the gate. Both of them jumped off their bikes and walked in, removing their helmets as they came into the yard. We shook hands all around.

Connor looked at my motorcycle.

"That's a nice bike, Jordan."

His comment surprised me. He sounded sincere and I did not catch any trace of sarcasm. That made a good start.

"Thank you," I said.

I had a couple more things to do in the office and when I came out I saw the three of them standing by their bikes, each thumb-scrolling their smartphones as they waited. I went back into the office and returned with a small cardboard box.

"Here," I said. "Ditch the phones."

All three looked up, not saying anything.

"Ditch the phones," I said again. "We're hitting the road. You don't need them."

"How we will know what's going on?" said Steven.

"Try looking around."

"Yeah?" Steven made a show of looking. "I see drums of chemicals, an office building, and across the parking lot a tall building with maybe three or four beer bottles on the roof."

"Very funny. I'm serious. We don't need those face-magnets. Ditch the phones and open your eyes instead."

Derek said, "I've got Facebook friends I want to update."

Michael said, "I like to tweet what I'm doing."

"Fuck Facebook. Have a party instead when you get back. And Twitter is the sewer-hole of society. You don't need any of that shit." I kept holding the box out. I could see the doubt on their faces.

Michael was the first to decide. He dropped his phone in the box.

"Fuck it," he said, smiling.

Steven and Derek looked at each other. Then they dropped their phones in also.

"Yeah," Steven said. "Fuck all of it. Bro's right. We're hitting the road!"

"Damn right!" said Derek.

I put the box in the office and locked up. The four of us fired up the motorbikes and rolled clear of the yard. The others waited for me to dismount and run back to the gate, swing it closed and lock it. We rolled out to the street together.

We decided to eat first before hitting the raised highway east. We rode to the café and the others teased me for the coffee and vanilla creamer waiting at our table as we walked in.

"You'd think he owned the place, the way they jump," said Michael.

"What do you expect? He must come here three times a day. When we had dinner he didn't even have to order. They just brought him a sirloin." This from Steven.

We each ordered steak and eggs for breakfast and we ate and talked over the proposed route. I had my map out with marked roads that took us east to the Salton Sea, then north to Death Valley. The others agreed, although we also agreed to keep our route loose. No sense in schedules and deadlines. I was pleased both Steven and Derek brought camping gear; not much, since you cannot carry much gear on sport bikes, but enough so that if we had to throw down bags somewhere they would be fine. It was nice sometimes not paying for a motel.

We paid the bill and in a few minutes more we were on the road, heading east on the Interstate.

We rolled along at a good clip. Michael and I rode side by

side, suicide style. Steven and Derek rode ahead with the sport bikes, jockeying for position with bursts of speed, but stayed in sight mostly. Traffic was heavy until out of town. We cruised towards the mountains that rose to four thousand feet and then leveled to a series of gentle summits. We passed turn-offs leading to backcountry small towns. The weather was clear and cool. We passed a few trucks loaded down with freight and the landscape on either side stretched away to more mountains. In the mountains we saw open valleys scattered over with big oaks.

We hit the last of the coastal mountains and suddenly the road dropped into a boulder-filled canyon. We leaned our bikes into long smooth curves as the road continued to drop several thousand feet until finally we escaped and nothing but flat sandy desert appeared.

We felt the temperature difference right away. The air had that warm oven feel that let you know it was going to get hot. Far off in the distance I saw smoke plumes. The smoke rose to a certain height and then flattened and blew south. We ran along the straight highway and found the town of Ocotillo. The town was just past the drop from the mountains and sat on the edge of the vast desert. It was just a gas station, some old empty buildings, and the Lazy Lizard bar. We wanted the bar and we pulled into the gravel parking lot and walked inside.

It was too dark to see at first, but after our eyes adjusted we found seats at a table. Michael said he would handle the first round. He got up to order beer. There were several other people who looked like regulars and they sat quietly at the bar. Michael returned with two pitchers and four glasses, a finger in each glass, I noticed.

"Some ride at the end there, eh?" said Michael.

"Coming out the bottom I hit one-thirty," said Derek.

"I saw you. If I tried the curves that way I'd scrape."

Steven poured the beer.

"Here's to the start of the trip!" he said.

We toasted and drank.

"Feel like the old days?" Steven asked me.

"It does. It feels good to be back on the bike."

"Where'd you ride before?" Derek asked me.

"Just about everywhere. I spent a year on the road. I don't think there's a state I haven't visited."

"Why'd you stop?"

"Our mom. Steven sent me a letter, general delivery. Lubec, Maine."

"Easternmost town in the United States," said Steven.

"Right. I had some silly idea about hitting the farthest points in the country. Something like that."

"Northwest Angle, Minnesota. Farthest north."

"I know that town," said Derek.

"Key West, Florida. Farthest south," Steven was counting the towns off on his fingers, "And for west ..."

"Ozette, Washington," I said. "I'm surprised you can remember all that. Anyway, Steven let me know mom was dying of lung cancer. So I came back. I took care of things, then I started the business. I never got back to the road."

"I'm sorry about your mom," said Derek.

It was odd about Derek Connor. We had not started off on the right foot, true, but it was not as though he was a complete asshole. We just did not mesh. Sometimes it is like that. But he could be nice, and I believed he truly was sorry about my mom and the cancer.

"Well, things happen."

"A year is a long time on the road."

"It wasn't all on the road. I stayed put in a few places. I spent a few months in Vancouver. New Orleans, also. Saw the Mardi Gras. Key West was good. But it was all a good time. When you're twenty-one you can't help it."

"Where was your favorite?"

"New Orleans, I think. It's pretty good there. Except for the bugs, the humidity, and the heat."

"Here's to that," said Steven, raising his glass. After the toast, he said, "He used to write me letters. Almost every week. He'd let me know where to send letters ahead so he'd get them general delivery."

"I got most of them, I think. Probably there's still a few sitting in small towns across the country. Waiting for me, still. I know for a fact there's one in Kansas City."

"You didn't make Kansas City?"

"I hit rain on the way like a fire hose. I picked another route."

"Why didn't you just telephone instead of writing letters?" asked Michael.

"No. It ruined it. Destroyed the sense of distance, time. You travel three thousand miles and talking on the phone made it seem like you were in the next room. Letters give you a sense of space and time. Distance."

"You must hate e-mail," said Michael.

"It's fine for work. But I'll tell you, it was nice to pull up to the post office in some town and go to the counter. The postman would go back to wherever they go and when he came back I'd see a letter in his hand."

"I saved all your letters, bro. I was like fourteen or fifteen, I think. I used to mark your progress on a map. I always hoped someday we'd travel the same route again."

"Maybe some day."

"Here's to some day." Steven lifted his glass and we all drank.

Across the bar, on the other side, the main door opened and a man on crutches came in. He sat by himself at a chair along the wall just past the door. He had a full black beard, gray streaked, and he wore a red and black cotton shirt. He looked like a lumberjack, except he was missing his right leg. A German Shepard dog had followed him into the bar. It lay down by his chair. The bartendress opened a bottled beer and gave it to one of the regulars. He carried it to the man with one leg.

"Thanks, Harry," the one-legged man said, as he took the beer.

"How you been, Fred?" the regular asked him.

"Good. Good. Gettin' by, you know."

The bartendress said, "Fred, I might have the Health Department coming by today. He comes in, you put on your sunglasses."

The regular walked back to the bar.

"Christ, Mary," he said, "it ain't enough he got but one leg, he's gotta be blind, too?"

"The dog, Harry. I can't have no dogs in here."

The banter made us smile and Michael raised his beer in a toast to the Lazy Lizard. We clinked glasses and drank.

"You certainly find some interesting places," Michael said to me.

The man with one leg was setting up some kind of wood box. He took out what looked like leather necklaces and laid them carefully on the table in front of him. Each one had a stone fastened to it. The dog stayed by his side, watching the man lay out the necklaces.

I said to Michael, "Let's go see what he's got."

Michael stood and we walked to his table. Up close we saw the man was older than he had appeared at first. He had flat eyes like roofing nails.

"You boys have the bikes out front?" he said.

We said we did and explained the trip.

"What do you have here?" I asked.

"Stones I find."

"You prospect out in the desert?" Michael asked.

"I get out there a bit."

"What do you get for these?"

The old prospector paused and said, "Well, I ask two for each one." He sounded shy about the money.

I looked the necklaces over and as I handled each one the prospector named the stone each one featured.

"Obsidian."

"Malachite."

"Bloodstone."

"Azurite."

I had four necklaces in my hand. "I'll take these," I said. I got out my wallet but I didn't have the right combination of bills. I walked to the bar and asked for change. Mary changed a twenty for me and I placed another twenty on the bar and slid it across to her.

"Use this for any beer the old guy wants, but don't say a word, all right?" She smiled and nodded. I went back to the old man's table and gave him eight dollars.

As I handed him the money he placed one hand on my arm and said, "Let each man choose. Each will be drawn to a stone."

I nodded solemnly as though we now shared some ancient secret and I walked back to the table. Michael had already sat back down. Of the four necklaces I liked the malachite best, so I kept that one back and spread the other three on the table.

"Here you go, mates. The old man said you'd be drawn to a particular stone, so choose."

Steven picked the azurite and Michael picked the bloodstone. That left the obsidian for Derek. He picked it up.

"I really didn't get a chance to choose, now did I?"

"The decision was made for you," I said, smiling.

As we put the leather necklaces on the door opened again and a man walked in wearing a white shirt with a silver badge pinned on it. I saw the one-legged man put on sunglasses, and I elbowed Michael. The man with the badge walked to the bar and talked to Mary. Then he walked around behind the bar, looking at various glasses and the sinks and checking bottles. He walked to the back area with Mary leading and talking. When they returned he went into each restroom. Finally he had Mary sign something and she seemed relieved. The man left. He glanced at the blind man as he walked out the door. The dog watched him go.

Michael looked at me. "It doesn't get any better than that, does it?"

We sat there smiling and drinking and Mary walked over with a pitcher of beer.

"On the house, guys. Thanks for staying quiet."

"Hey. All right!" said Steven. He began to top off our mugs.

"So how'd your inspection go?" I asked.

"The same. I got to dump some bottles is all."

"Why?"

"Some of the opened ones. Sometimes those little bugs get in there."

I saw Michael wince.

"Do you really dump them?"

"I do."

"How much does that cost you?"

"More than I want to guess. But what can you do?"

Mary walked back to the bar. Michael was inspecting his beer.

"I think the beer's all right, Mike," I said.

"Just drink it, you big baby," said Steven, smiling.

We were laughing and we finished the beer and left. But as we left an odd thing happened. The old man's dog got up and blocked Derek's path. It just stood there, staring at him, until the old man called it back to the table.

Outside in the bright sunlight we put our helmets on and prepared to leave.

"What was with that dog?" said Derek.

"What? You're afraid of a dog?" said Steven.

"Did you see it? It looked like it wanted me for lunch."

Steven shook his head. "Some crew we've got here. One man afraid of bugs, the other afraid of dogs. I guess we're the only real men here, hey bro?"

"Damn right."

We mounted the bikes, turned them over, and left the gravel lot. Steven led, spinning gravel behind his wheels.

Chapter VI

The highway ran long and straight. Steven, Derek, and Michael snapped their wrists and their bikes accelerated like rocket sleds. I had no chance to keep up. I lost sight of their bikes and resigned myself to a leisurely cruise the next few dozen miles to El Centro. I was sure they would be waiting at the off-ramp for me to catch up and then we would take the surface road north from there, as we had planned. But when I arrived they were nowhere in sight.

I circled the ramp keeping an eye out, but they must have flown past. There was a fast-food place just off the highway and I decided to wait there. I walked inside after parking and ordered a coke from the clerk. I asked him how hot it was. He replied he didn't know.

"I didn't go outside today," he said.

I settled down at a table to wait. I looked out the window towards the road in case they rode past.

A truck pulled up in the parking lot. It blocked my view of the road, so I stepped out and sat on the wooden bench outside the building. The heat made me drowsy and I must have fallen asleep. I dreamed I was balancing high above an endless fall and I fell, falling forever through space. As I fell I heard the sound of motors whining and roaring and I awoke with a start, jerking awake, sweaty in the heat, and Steven, Michael, and Derek were sitting on their bikes in front of me, revving the engines and laughing.

"Real funny," I said. I stood and began walking out to my bike parked in the lot.

"Hey, come on, bro," said Steven. "We just missed the exit."

I got on my bike. "I'm not playing this game the whole trip. We either stick together or not. It's bullshit sitting around waiting. I don't plan to do it every few hours. I didn't think you guys would be ditching me."

"Maybe you need a little more bike," said Derek Connor.

"Maybe you need to keep your mouth shut."

"Calm down, sport."

I got off my bike and stepped towards Connor. "Go fuck yourself," I said.

Steven and Michael got between Derek Connor and me.

"Hey. Come on, guys," Michael was saying.

"The heat getting to you two, or what?" said Steven. "Come on. Let's go."

Connor and I stood there facing each other. Then he just shrugged and got back on his bike. Michael and Steven waited for me to get back on mine, then they mounted their own bikes and the four of us left the parking lot. We headed north on the surface highway a few miles before veering to the northwest and the Salton Sea.

We passed through the truck-stop town of Brawley. From the road I saw farmers burning their fields. That was the smoke I had seen coming down the canyon. The town was hot and humid. Large trucks rumbled through loaded with produce. A brown haze spread low through the sky and it became darker and the wind picked up.

We left the outskirts of the town after stopping for gas and we approached the south end of the sea. The wind pushed us around so that we all rode single file. Off in the distance I saw a yellow wall of dust quartering its way towards us. I pulled over and the others followed me.

"That's probably going to get a little nasty," I said. I pointed towards the approaching wall. I dug through my bags and found the handkerchief I wanted and tied it on so the lower half of my face was covered. I found an extra one and gave it to Michael. Steven and Derek had full-face helmets and would not need them.

I pulled out onto the highway once more. The others stayed behind me. The wind increased and the sky dimmed to an ocher color. The wall hit us just as we reached the Salton Sea.

I had the lead, keeping my head ducked behind the windscreen, and the wind pushed and knocked me from side to side on the road. Wind-driven sand flowed across the blacktop, the leading edges moving like long sidewinders. Strong gusts hit and I heeled over like a boat spilling wind from its sails. I saw the dim outlines of everyone behind me, each bike heeling and rising to the gusts, then it became darker and all I saw were the headlights staggered behind me. I could not tell who was who and I just counted three lights to know we were still together.

My handkerchief protected my face from the worst of it, but the dry sand still managed to sting like rain against any exposed part of my face. Small black dots rolled and bounced across the road, I think they were dates from all the date palms in the area, and they sometimes hit my ankles. They stung like scorpions if they bounced just right. From the Salton Sea itself rose a smell of dead and rotting fish.

I concentrated on getting through the wind storm and kept my eyes fixed on the immediate road in front. A bike pulled up alongside me and I saw it was Steven. He was signaling to stop. I rolled into a parking lot of some store, I couldn't tell what in the darkness. Steven wheeled up close. Michael was behind him.

Steven lifted his visor. "Let's head back!" He had to squint against the sand.

I looked around. "Where's Derek?"

"He already turned back!" Steven dropped his visor and began circling in the lot. I followed, with Michael behind, and Steven led back down the road we had just come up. After several minutes I saw Derek stopped on the side of the road and as we passed by he joined us. Steven led us back to Brawley. The wind quartered us from behind now and it was easier to ride. When we hit Brawley again we were out from the worst of it.

Steven led us into the parking lot of a 7/11 store. The four of us went inside.

"Damn! What the hell was that?" said Derek.

"Sandstorm. They get them pretty regular out here," I said.

The clerk overheard me and said, "Should have been here last week." He said it with that casual nonchalance locals use to impress tourists. "This is nothing. It was a lot worse last week."

"And what the hell was that stink?"

"The Salton Sea," I said. "It gets these weird inversions. The air leaves the water. All the fish die and rot on the shore."

The clerk said, "Hasn't been too bad this year."

"You don't call that bad? It stinks like shit," said Derek. He paid for a soda and walked out. We joined again outside. It was still gusting with a warm wind, but nothing like we had just escaped.

"Well, what's the plan now?" said Michael.

I pulled out my map and began looking at it. Everyone crowded around me.

"I'd planned a clockwise trip through the West, but we can reverse it," I said.

"Counter-clockwise," said Steven. "Like reversing time."

"We've kinda wasted time," I said. "With this sandstorm," I added, because I didn't want to bring up the time we had wasted getting separated in El Centro. "Let's head back to El Centro and head east through Yuma and into Arizona. We can make Gila Bend easy."

"What's in Gila Bend?"

"Not much, I'm afraid."

Everyone agreed, though, and so we finished the sodas, got back on the bikes, and backtracked to El Centro. We hit the highway once more and we stayed together on the ride east through Yuma. We hit Gila Bend before dinner.

There is an odd motel in Gila Bend called the Space Age Motel. It is covered with neon lighting and has a spaceship mounted on the roof. I knew about it from the Frommer's Guide I had brought. This was the motel we picked to stay. We paid for two rooms, one for Michael and me, and the other for Steven and Derek. Before we ate, we spent time at the hot tub and pool. It felt good to relax and be away from work. We were all in a good mood. We switched between the warm water of the hot tub and the cool, clear water of the pool. We watched the sky settle down overhead. It changed from blue to twilight purple and then to a dark indigo that gave way finally to a deep and endless black. The stars came out slowly and we sat in the shimmering pool lit by underwater lights, until hunger drove us from the water and we hit the road looking for dinner.

The desk clerk had warned us there wasn't much to do on a Saturday night in Gila Bend, which was something we had pretty much figured out on our own. There was, however, a little bar close by we might enjoy. Some nights, she added hopefully, they had a dance.

We cruised up and down the main drag looking for a place to eat. We felt free and loose without the gear strapped across the motorbikes. We were not wearing helmets, as Arizona law did not require them, and the four of us rode side-by-side in two lanes.

Gila Bend had the feel of a deserted movie set. The buildings sat dark in alternating shades of brown and gray. Streetlights threw dim cones of yellow light on the asphalt. The whole time we saw only one person out walking. We found a badly-lit restaurant off a side street and we pulled into a dark parking lot. We walked in and ordered dinner. It was a quiet meal and when we left the employees began to close the place down.

Before we rolled back to the motel we decided to have a beer. We found the small bar the desk clerk had told us about. There were cars in the lot and that let us know it might have some life, so we parked the bikes and walked through the door. The place was nothing special, just a small room with a low ceiling and a plastic-topped bar, some booths upholstered in red fake leather, and a small dance floor. Maybe twenty people were inside, mostly men. There was no band. There was a karaoke machine and a host up front was singing in Spanish.

We ordered beer and drank from the bottles. Our leather

jackets made us seem out of place. Everyone else, at least the men, wore plain shirts with pockets. Most of the shirts had long sleeves.

The host, the one who had been singing, came to our table. He asked us something in Spanish.

"Estoy apesadumbrado. No hablo español," said Michael. "I'm sorry. I do not speak Spanish."

"Cante?"

"He asked if anyone wants to sing," Michael said.

Steven and Derek looked at each other and decided to give it a shot. They walked to the small stage up front and dropped a couple dollars in the tip jar. They picked out a song. The music played and the two began a raucous duet of "Wild Thing."

Michael and I watched from our table.

"I didn't think you were going to stop," said Michael.

"What do you mean?"

"Through that sandstorm. You weren't going to stop, were you?"

"No. Why would I? All we had to do was keep going. We'd had gotten through it."

"Sure. Did you see Steve and Derek?"

"I could only see their lights."

"They were taking a beating. Their bikes are much lighter than ours. You sure you weren't getting a little payback for El Centro?"

I considered that a moment.

"Maybe. Why'd you take off like that past El Centro?" I asked Michael.

"I'm sorry about that. We were just flying along, you know?"

"Flying, hell. You know my bike can't keep up."

"We were cruising at 120 miles per hour. I haven't unwound it like that in a while. Next thing we knew you were gone."

"Thanks."

"Don't sweat it. I'll stick with you from here on out."

"Me and all the guys in Milwaukee would appreciate it."

Michael looked around the bar.

"Do you see some of these women? Not bad, eh?"

"I wouldn't be looking too hard here."

There were only a few women in the bar, but they were quite pretty.

"I'm just looking. I see what you mean, though."

One of the women had smiled at Michael and the two men nearest her had followed her look with some hard-eyed stares.

We clinked beers and Steven returned to the table. Derek was at the bar. He was shouting out, "Cervezas en la casa! Estoy comprando!"

"What's he saying?"

"I think he's buying for everyone," said Michael. "I hope he knows what he's saying. Here comes the beer."

The bartender was setting bottles on the bar and Derek was pulling bills from his wallet. The bartender kept reaching down and bringing up more bottles. The other customers were passing the beers around and nodding to Derek as they drank. He was surrounded at the bar. We got up and joined him. We were very popular. Steven and Derek hit the karaoke a few more times. Michael and I were content to just relax. Michael taught me Spanish words: dos and cervezas. He had me practice on the bartender and each time it cost me money. By midnight I was tired.

"Mike, I think I'll head back."

"Hold on," said Michael, "I'll ride back with you. Let me tell Derek and Steven."

He caught them with another group, talking half English and half Spanish, and let them know we were leaving.

"They're staying a while," Michael said to me. We left for the motel. Sometime late in the night I heard two motorbikes pull up outside the motel and I knew Steven and Derek had come back.

Chapter VII

The morning was not kind to Gila Bend. A low haze gave the town a washed out look. The buildings we had seen last night still looked drab. They had a dull adobe color that made them look thick and squat. The buildings all faced the street fronted with tiny parking lots, and between some of the buildings were billboards advertising farm equipment and trucks and trailers for rent. One billboard, old and faded, featured pomade. Wires looped from pole to pole along the street. Gila Bend had the comfortable look of a used furniture store.

Gila Bend sat on a bend of the Gila River. The town began only because this was where the stage stopped to rest the horses. When the railroad came through, the town served as a watering stop for the steam engines. I read that in the Frommer's Guide.

Michael and I sat outside our room in chairs placed under the cover of an overhang that ran along the front of the motel. We had coffee from the coffee maker in our room and we sat drinking from paper cups, watching the morning traffic come alive. We compared notes on the town, talking softly to not disturb anyone. We agreed that we liked Gila Bend. It seemed to us to be a working town that was solid, a town that would last.

Steven and Derek walked out from the next room. They moved slowly—they must have had a night of it last night—and

46

we walked to the diner for breakfast. We took seats in the corner booth and ordered our food. The waitress was thin and young and had a cold sore on her lips. When she came to take our order I asked her what people did for fun in Gila Bend.

"Well," she said, "I'm married. My family comes first." She added, "I spend time with my husband and children." She wore glasses and after she spoke she fixed her gaze steadily on me, as though she had just made a point.

"That's nice," I said, nodding. She turned and walked away primly.

Michael said, "Did she think you were going to ask her out?"

Derek saw a display of gifts and he was looking at an odd two-foot tall stuffed figure. It had a purple rooster-like comb on its head. It was hunched over as though playing an attached flute. Derek was quite taken with it. He walked to the counter and inquired. We saw him paying money and he came back with the stuffed doll in his hand.

"Meet Kokopelli," he said, holding up his find. "He's known as the trickster. He'll be our mascot."

We took a liking to Mr. Kokopelli. We passed him around while we ate and asked him questions. One of us would hold Mr. Kokopelli up solemnly, asking, perhaps, "Is Michael the ugliest person at this table?" Mr. Kokopelli would turn slowly to each of us and then back at the question's originator. He gave his answer by slowly moving his head side to side for no and up and down for yes. In the question just asked the answer was yes. Three of us agreed that Mr. Kokopelli was remarkably accurate.

Steven had the stuffed figure.

"Kokopelli," Steven asked, "which motorcycle is best?"

Kokopelli did not answer.

"It has to be a yes or no question," said Michael.

Steven looked at me and winked, then tried once more.

"How hot will it get today?"

"Give me that thing!" Michael said.

"Now, Kokopelli," he began to ask, pronouncing it cocoa-belly, "will Steven keep the rubber side down today?"

We all groaned at the question and I knocked on the table.

"Sorry," said Michael, knocking also on the table.

I asked the final question.

"Will the four of us finish this trip together?"

Mr. Kokopelli looked at each one of us in turn, then back at me. He shook his head yes. He was wrong, but none of us knew that then.

We paid for breakfast and walked outside. The morning sun was bright. It was going to be a hot day. I suggested we tour the railroad tracks and we walked behind the motel and explored the empty boxcars linked to nothing. We balanced on the steel rails, played a game of horseshoes with some loose spikes we found, and Steven climbed up into one of the cars and hid from us. We admired all the junk lying around and looked at a large pile of metal. We took turns guessing how many pieces of metal track holders the pile held. No one cared about the answer. I took a picture of Kokopelli sitting on the track.

The morning had that wonderful feel of nothing to do. Today we would be off the highway and onto the back roads. We were in no hurry. There were miles of open road ahead. When we tired of the tracks we walked back to the Space Age Motel, checked out, and we hit the road once more.

It took only minutes to leave Gila Bend behind. We took the road straight south to Ajo. The land on each side of the road was flat and arid and the yellow-orange soil looked burned and scorched from the sun. It looked very hard and unforgiving. Mesquite shrub rose from the hard soil and mixed in with the mesquite a few creosote bushes appeared. The leaves of the creosote looked small and shiny green. The mesquite looked dry and dead. We saw neither birds nor rabbits and the sky was clear. Nothing ran across the road, not even a lizard. The road ran south without traffic and we had the road alone. It seemed as though the living world had vanished except for the road, the desert, and us.

We glided along, sometimes passing each other just for fun. It made no difference what lane we traveled, nothing else was running either way, and the motorbikes rolled smoothly along the flat road. The long straight stretches of road played tricks with our depth perception. Except for the pavement just in front of the motorbikes it seemed we were in a still-life painting. The road in front of the wheels blurred, but all else was still. Motion was only the blurring and the wind in our faces.

The rising sun warmed the air quickly. The air was dry. It blew across our faces and felt hotter as the sun rose. Halfway to Ajo small raised mesas appeared and farther on we could see a large rock outcropping. On the small mesas we saw the first saguaro cactus. We recognized the tall shapes right away. The bent arms of the giants made them look like sentinels. The road changed from its straight line and curved toward the rock, running through a narrow pass that split the rock outcropping. The road curved through the pass and straightened out once again. We continued south to Ajo. The giant saguaro retreated to the dry hills far back from the road. On the hills they looked like small men standing with their arms up.

We made Ajo forty minutes after leaving Gila Bend. It was hot and we sweated in the sun. The chrome on the motorbikes was blinding and hurt our eyes. It was hot to the touch. We found a gas station just before we came into town. We stopped to get off the road and to get out of the sun.

The gas station doubled as a convenience store, and all of us went inside to get sodas. Inside the store it was cool. I filled my cup with ice before I added cola. As I topped off the cup Michael said, "Well, I'll be damned!" and walked outside. I followed him back out to the heat.

"I don't believe it," he said. He was looking across the two-laned road at an old building sitting by itself. He began walking across the street. I followed him and we walked up to the old building.

The building was deserted and had once been painted a bright red. The red paint was faded and it peeled away from the wood. Old lettering across the building facade read Ben Franklin 5 & 10. Michael stood in front of the building, staring at it.

"You know what this is?"

"No," I said.

"This is where it started. Not right here, of course, but this was the original chain Sam Walton worked for. He left Ben Franklin and started Wal-Mart. I never knew any of the old Franklin stores still stood."

"Should we kneel or something?"

"Wise guy."

We stood silently in front of the building. I felt sweat running down my back. It wet my shirt and made it stick to my skin.

"There's not a Wal-Mart anywhere near here," I said.

"No," said Michael.

"Maybe this old building is a talisman of sorts."

From back across the street we heard Steven yell at us, so we came back to the gas station and started the bikes again. All of us had our leather jackets off, either packed in the panniers or strapped across the bags. Michael and I had our helmets off, too, but Steven and Derek had no place to secure their own and so they kept their helmets on. It had to be suffocating in the heat.

We slowed as we followed the main road through town. The road doglegged a bit and we passed a large plaza filled with people. They were all dressed in nice clothes. The men had white shirts and ties and the women wore skirts. It was too hot to wear a suit jacket. Two old churches, large and white in the sun, sat in the middle of the plaza surrounded by green landscaping. I had forgotten that it was Sunday. The people must have been going to morning services.

The road led us past the town and we accelerated again on the desolate road, still heading south. We passed a talus pile built from the mines in the area. The mines were not visible. All we could see was the brown talus pile and it ran parallel to the road blocking our view. I thought of the clean white churches we had just passed, with the courtyard between them green and well manicured, and I had a sudden memory of something I had seen on the East Coast. We passed the talus pile. Derek and Steven were out ahead. I could see Kokopelli strapped onto Derek's pillion pad, his head bobbing and the little purple comb fluttering madly in the wind. We came to a junction and began to head east. The road banked, dipping and rising through the desert, and after a few miles of no traffic we came up behind another group of riders.

For a while we rode behind this other group. They were five riders, all of them on Harleys, and they rode in a staggered formation; the proper way, actually, staggered so that if one had to stop the group could collapse on itself without colliding. Derek and Steven still led our group and I could tell they wanted to pass. They were crowding the group from behind. The other riders didn't acknowledge us and didn't give any signal to pass. Suddenly, Derek twisted the throttle and pulled a wheelie, this at sixty miles per hour, and he weaved through the Harley group. Then Steven pulled out wide and passed, both their bikes screaming with that high-pitched sport bike revving sound. In a second they were gone. The lead rider of the Harley group and one of the others raised one hand and they gave the departing sport bikes the finger. That was all they could do. Catching them would have been impossible. Michael and I stayed behind. I glanced at Michael and he just grimaced, but the other riders didn't seem to connect the two sport bikes to us. When finally they signaled, we pulled out and passed and left them behind. I saw the lead rider, fat and big with muscular tattooed arms, and I noted his red beard, long and braided into two leads that fluttered back from his face in the wind. He would be hard to miss if we ever saw him again. The Harley group was not bothered by Michael and me. They thought Steven and Derek did not belong with us.

The road ahead was empty and we cruised along. A few miles farther on I pulled into a dirt turnout. There was a small building that sat off the road. It looked like a school, although there was no one around. Michael rolled up next to me.

"What's up?" he said.

"Nothing. I just wanted to enjoy this."

We shut down the motors and stayed quiet and looked over the landscape. Beyond the school building I could see the flat desert running to low mountains that looked blurred in the bright sun.

"What did you think of Derek's little stunt?" asked Michael.

"Not much."

"He nearly hit that lead rider."

"I saw that. It must have scared the crap out of him."

51

Michael nodded. "Have you been seeing all those tiny shrines on the side of the road?"

"I have. Any idea what they're for?"

"No."

"Next one, let's stop."

"Give me a signal if you're going to stop. Don't surprise me."

We started the bikes and pulled out to the road. After a few miles I saw a shrine set back on the left. I gave a low hand wave, slowed, and doubled back. I parked maybe twenty yards away on firm soil, so my bike would not fall, and I walked across soft sand and through the mesquite shrub. Michael was just parking his bike next to mine. As I approached the shrine, thinking I was alone, something rose from the ground and turned toward me. I froze, my heart beating fast, then I saw it was only an old woman dressed in a shawl. She could not have worn a better disguise. She blended so well with the desert she had startled me when she stood.

I had interrupted her. There were fresh flowers placed at the shrine and I guessed she had just set them there. There were other objects placed around the shrine: small bottles, old flowers, a few tiny crosses, and other items I didn't recognize, and I felt I should not come any closer. The old woman looked me in the eyes and she stepped towards me. She held something in her hand and made as though to offer it to me. It was some type of woven cloth with a pattern on it. She held it out. I took it from her and examined it. The pattern was a maze. It was a maze pattern showing a figure of a man at the top with the maze below him. I understood her to mean I should buy it from her. Maybe it was the only way she earned money, I thought. So I reached for my wallet and pulled out a few bills. But she drew her hand away and shook her head. I stood there with the woven cloth in one hand and money in the other, and she only looked at me for a moment and then walked away. To where, I couldn't guess. I had not seen any sign of a town or house, besides the school building, for miles.

I walked back to my bike. Michael was standing there.

"What was that all about?" he said.

"I'm not sure." I showed him the woven cloth.

He looked at it. "You know, that's not really a maze. It's a route that leads to the center." He handed it back.

I looked at the weaving again.

"You're right. The little man only needs to stay on the route. He'll find the center." I traced the route with my finger. I looked back toward the shrine but the old woman was gone. I packed the weaving in one of my bags.

"Odd seeing her out here."

"It's too hot to be out walking."

"Let's get out of here," I said.

We thought Steven and Derek might be waiting for us at a town marked Sells on the map, but they were not there. We gassed up the bikes at the Sells gas station and cruised all the way to Tucson with no luck. At Tucson we rode the busy interstate east a short distance to Benson, and from there we dropped south down a pleasant road lined with big trees that led us to Tombstone. Our plan, discussed at Gila Bend last night, was to meet at the OK Corral if we split up. As we hit the outskirts of Tombstone a Circle K store appeared. Standing out front by their bikes were Steven and Derek. They yelled at us as we came by and so we u-turned and joined them.

Michael pulled up first and shut off his bike. I heard him say to no one in particular, "The OK Corral is a Circle K now?"

Steven walked up to my bike, in good spirits, holding a cup of soda.

"Bro, what took you guys?"

I explained about stopping at the shrine. I asked, "Couldn't you find the OK Corral?"

"It's all boarded up. Nothing to see, so we waited here. You had to pass by sometime."

"We have to find a motel."

"We didn't see much in town."

"Better get the guide out," said Michael.

I began rummaging through my panniers for my Frommer's Guide. Another motorcyclist pulled up. He was riding a BMW K100RS with hard-shelled saddlebags. He saw our bikes and walked over.

"Looks like you all are touring," he said to me.

"Second day out from San Diego. Where are you riding from?" I asked.

"Moab." He held his hand out to me. "Kevin," he said.

Kevin and I shook hands. Michael was looking at his bike.

"You've got a classic there," he said.

"Thanks. It's an eighty-five. I bought it used. It's been a good bike. Nothing like a Valkyrie, though."

"I've been happy with mine. Takes a while to get used to it. It's a big bike."

Kevin explained he was alone and had simply wanted to take a ride.

"Some ride," I said. "That's got to be 600 miles."

"I take two days. I used to do it in one."

"Have you been to Tombstone before?"

"Several times," he replied.

Then I said, "I'm sorry. This is Michael, Derek, and Steven."

All of them shook hands.

"Did you find a place to stay yet?" asked Kevin.

I held up my Frommer's Guide that I had dug out of my baggage.

"Not yet. This is our first visit."

"Don't waste your time. Try the Trailriders. It's right down the road on the left. Only place to stay. It's cheap and clean. Close to town."

"How big can the town be?"

"I mean the old Tombstone." Kevin went on to explain that Tombstone had an old part laid out parallel to the main drag. The Trailriders Motel was close to this, he said.

I thanked him for the information. He took off and said he would see us around.

"Nice guy," said Michael.

"Let's go get the rooms," I suggested.

Steven and Derek finished their drinks and threw away the cups. We rolled out in single file. A mile down the road we found the Trailriders Motel. Our tires crunched through the gravel parking lot and we parked next to the office. I saw Kevin's bike outside one of the rooms. In the office the manager gave me the room rates. I paid the going rate for two rooms, mentally calculating how much the others would owe me. Then we moved our motorbikes next to the rooms. I figured Michael and I would take the end unit. Steven and Derek would take the adjoining room. In the end room I threw my gear on the bed farthest from the door and flopped on the mattress.

"That's a deal for these rooms," said Michael. He pulled out some bills to pay for his share. He tossed them towards my bed. I let them fall to the floor.

It felt good to be in Tombstone.

Chapter VIII

Michael showered first and I cleaned up next. Our clothes were wrinkled from being stuffed in the panniers, so we hung them on hangers in the bathroom while we ran the showers. We hoped the steam would help. Michael was shaving.

"It's been a good trip so far," he said through the open door of the bathroom.

"It has," I said.

"Steven and Derek seem pretty tight."

"That's the college thing, I guess."

"You know they're planning another trip this year."

"Really?"

"I heard them talking about it. Across the country. Coast to coast."

"Steven hasn't said anything about it to me."

Michael poked his head out the bathroom door. "He's worried you'll be angry."

"You're kidding?"

"No. He told me you'll be disappointed he won't join you in your business right away."

"I wouldn't blame him for wanting to travel. I did it."

"Maybe you ought to talk to him."

Michael resumed his shaving. I got up from the bed to find

my shoes.

"I will," I said.

I walked to the bathroom entry.

"Nothing will help that face of yours, you know."

Michael was wiping the shaving cream off his face with a towel. He tossed the towel on the floor. He leaned in close to the mirror.

"I've had some luck with it. Not much, but some," he said.

"You do all right. And thanks for telling me about Steven."

"Sure."

We pulled our shirts off the hangers, they were more or less wrinkle-free, and we dressed.

"You know, Jordon, you never really told me the story about your mom," Michael said.

"I told you she passed away."

"I knew that. But not about the cancer, or that you cut your trip short to come home." Michael finished buttoning his shirt. "When you mentioned that at the Lazy Lizard that was the first I'd heard."

We were about ready to leave the room. I stopped at the door, thinking that Michael sounded hurt. I hadn't meant to exclude him. It was just that sometimes one just bears what comes along without making a show of it. I turned and faced him.

"I was traveling across the country," I said. "Ever since dad passed away I'd been getting social security checks, or at least my mom had. She had put them away for me and when I turned twenty years old I bought the bike. I traveled all across the United States and Canada."

"Not Mexico?"

"Never went there."

"You could go there now. You speak some Spanish. Say cerveza."

"Funny."

"You must have had a nice bank account if she saved all that money for you."

"Dad died when I was six. Mom was pregnant with Steven. It was a nice amount and I blew it all, almost. Then I got Steven's letter and everything changed. I came back home. Mom lived six weeks more. I handled the funeral, the will. The rest of it."

I made to leave, placing a hand on the doorknob.

"The rest is simple," I said. "I sold the house and got an apartment. Steven lived with me. I set money aside from the house for him and I used my share to start the business, Steven used most of his for college. When he graduates he'll still have some left."

"You had an apartment?"

"Before Steven left for college. I moved into the office after. It was either that or start dipping into his money."

"Your mom's will split things up between you and Steven?"

"No. It all went to me."

"Really?"

"Yes. Really. Now, you happy?"

Michael was looking at me, smiling. "You bet," he said. "I got the great Jordan Wryte to talk. Mark this day, o brothers. We have been blessed."

I just shook my head. We walked outside.

We saw the next room had the door open and so we looked in and gazed on the disorder and general mess one might see in a college dorm room. Steven and Derek were getting ready to join us. They came out of the room. The four of us sat on the bikes and we rode out from the gravel lot. It was still warm, no one wore a helmet or leather jacket, and it felt good to cruise the boulevard.

Two blocks over and in there was a dirt road running through town surrounded by the oldest buildings. This was the heart of old Tombstone. Wooden posts blocked car traffic through the dirt street, but we threaded our way through. No one seemed to mind. We parked near a red and white building with a sign that read Big Nose Kate's. We backed the bikes to the wooden sidewalk in unison, which can be challenging when people are watching and they have no way to judge you except by how well you handle your bike. We walked in the saloon and joined the rest of the tourists inside. A raised section of floor near the front windows held a round table. We sat there and ordered beer and when the waitress brought it we raised our glasses to the trip.

Michael added, "To us!" and we raised our glasses again.

It was pleasant to sit and watch the other tourists. We could see people walking by on the street. Our four motorbikes were lined up outside. Kokopelli was still strapped onto the back of Derek's bike.

"I'm getting hungry," said Steven.

Michael caught the waitress and asked for advice where to eat. We followed her directions and walked to a place called the Longhorn, but it was closed. It would not open for an hour yet. In every direction were signs and posters advertising the OK Corral. We walked by it, but there was a tall fence we could not see past.

"Why would they do that?" asked Derek.

"They want you to pay to see it."

"Well, I've seen corrals before."

We walked around and saw a place off Allen Street that served ribs and hamburgers. It was crowded inside but we found a table near the piano player who was doing his best to play over the noise the crowd made.

"Did you notice the small piles of white powder we kept passing?" said Michael.

"I did," I said. So had Steven and Derek.

"I wonder what they mean."

The waitress took our orders and came back with beer. While we waited for the food we drank the beer and watched the crowd. Michael heckled the piano player.

"Play something you know!" he yelled at him.

The piano player took the heckling good-naturedly.

"Where are you guys from?" he asked.

We replied, San Diego.

"Nice town," he said. "I've been there. Have you been to Tombstone before?"

"First time for all of us," I said.

Michael leaned over to me and whispered, "You should say you're Wyatt Earp's distant cousin or something."

He was trying to raise our status, but it couldn't be done. We were mere tourists. First timers, the lowest of the low.

"This town's all right," the piano player told us. "There's

more here than meets the eye."

We nodded solemnly.

"I only play here for fun, you know. I've had bigger gigs. In fact, I know Billy Joel. I went to high school with him."

We asked him where we should go next. He made a show of thinking, as if Tombstone could not be walked up and back within 20 minutes, and said, "Try the Crystal Palace. There's usually something going on there."

We saw a woman dressed in a period piece walking through the crowd. She looked like a saloon girl from an old western. She was talking to people and enjoying the attention. I thought that maybe she belonged to the restaurant. Our food came and it was good. We finished eating and said goodbye to the piano player.

It was a short walk to the Crystal Palace. We liked the place. There was a high ceiling lined with copper. There was a long bar of darkly polished wood where we found seats. A long mirror ran behind the bar. Wood tables and chairs were arranged on the floor. The floor was wood planked. It was not hard to imagine Tombstone notables filling the place. A small plaque that hung behind the bar stated that Virgil Earp had used an office upstairs when he was Tombstone's marshal.

The Crystal Palace had a fair crowd and up front there was a karaoke machine. Several people tried singing and some almost succeeded. Derek signed up and in a few minutes someone called him to sing. Steven didn't like the bar stools and he moved to a table in front of us.

I moved my bar stool to get a better view. I noticed a woman standing a few feet away. She had on black-framed glasses and wore bright red lipstick. She caught my eye.

"Is that your friend singing?" she asked.

"Yes," I said.

"He sings well."

The woman told me she lived in town, and she and I went through the assessment. When she was satisfied her resident status impressed me, the mere first-timer to Tombstone, she settled in to give me the town lowdown.

She began with the smoke-shop man.

"They fired him, you know," she said. "It's not fair, because John knows who took the money, but she's Big Tom's daughter. She's such a bitch, but everyone's afraid of her father."

I tried to be polite, but she tested my patience. I have little tolerance for strangers who monopolize my time. But she caught my ear with the band story.

"Last night, though, that's what they're all mad about," she said.

"What happened last night?" I could not help myself, sadly.

She looked at me. "The band was playing."

She looked at me hard, making sure I knew what she meant. Her facial expression suggested a shared confidence was lurking. She moved closer.

"Every Saturday night they have a band here. I know most of them. There's always parties and stuff. After the bar closes. It's no big thing."

It was understood she ran with a fast crowd. She leaned into me.

"They think I did it with the bass player."

It took me a moment to catch on. Her expression made her meaning clear.

"Oh?" I said.

"On the stage, they said. They're just jealous 'cause he's the best looking one, but we're just friends. So now they're saying things about us."

"Bastards," I said, looking for Michael. I maneuvered my bar stool to make some room. I thought, with some degree of horror, that her closeness made it appear she was my girl. Derek had finished his song and he walked back to his chair. He saw me and at once assessed my predicament. He elbowed Steven, who was sitting facing away from me. Steven turned his head. He gave me a big encouraging smile, then turned back around. I could see his shoulders shaking with laughter. This left me no other choice.

"What's your name?" I asked her.

"Susan." She smiled and held out her hand.

I shook it.

"Susan, meet Michael."

Michael, who had been sitting at the bar minding his own business, looked at me oddly, his alcohol-dimmed brain slowly taking it all in.

"Michael is with us. We're taking a bike tour of the Southwest." I stood up.

"Susan, have a seat. No need to stand there." I was so gallant it hurt.

Susan settled heavily onto the bar stool, looking at Michael with interest, while Michael tried hard to keep the panic from playing about his face. I saw there was some commotion when a group of women gathered around Derek. His singing had impressed them. They wanted him to join their table. There was tugging and pulling going on and during the interruption I made an excuse to talk to Steven. I left my seat at the bar and joined Steven at his table.

"You are a cruel man," he said.

We toasted to Mike and his new girl.

"Serves Mike right. On general principle," I said.

"No doubt. Should we move our bikes over here?"

"They'll be fine where they are."

Steven nodded. "I'll check on them later," he said.

It was still noisy and the crowd had grown. Derek carried on with the same group of women. I saw Michael was alone at the bar. I walked up to him and asked where his friend had gone.

"She's in the ladies' room."

I sat at the bar and ordered a beer. The bartendress brought it and took my money as she set it down.

I took a long swallow.

"So, Mike," I asked him, "do you think maybe…"

"There's not enough beer in the world," he said.

I laughed. Susan was coming back from the women's room. She moved straight through the bar. Everyone else had to move around her. I had taken her seat. She pulled another bar stool close and rejoined us.

The same woman in the period dress walked in. A small man wearing polished black boots and black denim pants followed her. Tucked into the denim pants was a crisp long-sleeved white shirt partially covered by a black vest. He wore a black hat that shaded a face with black eye-brows, sharp clear eyes, and a silver-grey waxed handlebar mustache that extended a couple inches past his chin. He looked like a pint-sized version of Wyatt Earp. I asked Susan about the couple.

"They're part of the Tombstone actors," she said.

"What do they do?"

"They give shows and mingle with the tourists." Susan scowled at the woman. "She's a little old to be a ceiling expert."

"What's that?"

"She's supposed to be one of the old 'ladies of easy virtue' in Tombstone." Susan made a face. "I don't think any man would have paid for that."

"Oh, I don't know about that," said Michael.

As so often happens, the woman and man looked our way as we talked about them. I was curious and I stood from my bar stool.

"Mike, I'll be back. I'm going over to talk to them for a bit."

The two characters seemed to be expecting me.

"Hello, I'm Jordan. I saw you over at the rib place," I said. I put out my hand.

"Nice to meet you. I'm Lucky Lacy," the woman said. She shook my hand, then handed me a business card.

I looked at the card. It read:

"Lucky Lacy" (Black Heart)
The Boothill Gunslinger Ladies
P.O. Box 300
Tombstone, AZ 85638
"The Town Too Tough To Die!"

The 300 was crossed out. Number 126 was handwritten in. There was a handwritten phone number across the top.

"I'm Jimmy the Shooter!" the man with her said. We shook hands. I noticed how short Jimmy was; Lucky Lacy towered above him.

Jimmy was smiling. "How do you like Tombstone?" he asked.

I replied I liked it just fine so far. I gave a quick speech about our trip. Jimmy's eyes lit up.

"You say San Diego? That where you're from?"

"El Cajon, actually."

"I grew up in Lakeside!"

Lakeside is just a few miles from El Cajon.

"What brought you out here?" I asked.

Jimmy scowled. It seemed so out of place on his face. "You know how it's getting out there. Getting all built up."

"I agree. How about a beer for you and Lucky Lacy?"

"I'll take a beer, partner!" said Jimmy.

Lucky Lacy said, "No, thanks. I don't drink." She looked over my shoulder. Then she asked me, "Do you know her?"

I followed her look, which led to Michael and Susan. Susan was elaborating something to Michael. She was making a point. He looked depressed.

"Only just met her," I said.

"Watch out for her. She's..." Lucky Lacy let her voice trail off.

"My friend will be very disappointed."

I winked at Jimmy, who smiled even more.

"I'll be right back," I said.

I rejoined Michael and caught the eye of the girl behind the bar. I ordered four beers. Susan heard me order.

"See. That's what they want you to do."

"What do you mean?"

"You have to pay to talk with them." She was looking at Lucky Lacy and Jimmy the Shooter.

"See how old she is?" Susan said. "A little ridiculous, if you ask me."

The girl came back with four bottles of beer. She set them on the bar. I paid and picked up all four bottles, two in each hand. Susan made a motion to grab one but caught herself when she realized I was not sharing with either her or Michael. I walked back to Jimmy. Lucky Lacy had walked off. I gave two beers to Jimmy and kept two for me.

"Thank you much, friend!" said Jimmy the Shooter.

I asked Jimmy about his outfit. I told him what Susan had

said.

"No, it's nothing like that. We just have fun. Tombstone's different. No one pays us. We just like to bring some color to the town."

"You do this for free?"

"Why not?"

That made me laugh and we clinked beers. Jimmy continued.

"Tourists tip us, sometimes, but mostly we just have fun dressing up. What can be better than this?"

We toasted each other again with the beers. After a long swallow, Jimmy the Shooter looked around the bar and then looked back at me.

"I grew up to be a nine-year-old kid!"

I liked Jimmy. I invited him over to meet Michael and posed with him while Michael took a picture. Jimmy shook my hand again and excused himself. I saw him mingling with the crowd, posing for more pictures. The crowd loved him. Lucky Lacy stood by a table with one foot on a chair. Someone was kneeling near her and pulling off her garter while the crowd cheered. Derek was still carrying on with the table of women. Michael and I drank. Susan said she had to go home and left.

"Well, that was something," said Michael.

"I thought you two might leave together."

"She tried, believe me."

"I saw."

The Crystal Palace was filling up, surprising for a Sunday night. Michael and I were content to watch the crowd. Steven and Derek sang a few songs and wandered around the bar.

"I thought Ajo was a nice town," I said to Michael.

"It looked nice. You never can tell, though."

"I liked those churches in town."

"They were pretty, all right. One of them was a Roman Catholic Church. The mining outside the town was ugly, though."

I remembered what I was thinking about while passing through Ajo.

I said to Michael, "When I was traveling on the East Coast I saw this small Bristol yacht. It had tied up alongside a garbage scow."

"What's a garbage scow?"

"A big flat barge. They pile the garbage on it and dump it at sea."

"I've never seen one."

"They don't do that in San Diego. Anyway, this pretty little yacht was tied up alongside this scow. Strange looking sight."

"What made you think of that?"

"I guess Ajo and the churches hard up by the mine, maybe."

"I'll take the mine over the church," said Michael.

"I thought you were Roman Catholic?"

"Used to be. My mom and dad would drop me off at the church, then go off protesting something or another."

"I was never one for the church."

"I suppose the church didn't touch you the way it did me." Michael was staring straight ahead. He became quiet.

I said, to get him talking again, ""I recall you told me your parents were activists."

"Yeah. They'd be out some place carrying signs and protesting one thing or another. They used to give me books like Orwell's 1984, or Animal Farm. Books like that."

"So? What's wrong with that?"

"For birthday presents? Come on, Jordan. Most kids get games, or even cars. I got social essays."

"Where are your parents now?"

"San Francisco, saving the world probably."

"I had no idea you were such a cynic."

"I'm not a cynic. I was just a small boy, Jordan."

He got quiet again and I let him alone. He never told me what was on his mind. Not then, not ever. And I never asked. The talk about the Ajo churches seemed to have affected him. As a child I attended Sunday school and I had a certificate or something that said I was baptized but it meant nothing to me. After my father died we never went anymore. Religion for Michael seemed to be a closed door, and for me it was a door never opened. It was only years later when the scandals came out that I guessed, but then, sitting at the bar at the Crystal palace in Tombstone, I missed it.

So I changed the subject.

"How far you want to go tomorrow?"

"I have an aunt and uncle in Truth or Consequences. We can stay there. At least two of us."

"What about Steven and Derek?"

"Maybe they can get a motel, if they don't mind."

"Sounds fine. They'll be fine with that."

Some of the early people we saw in the Crystal Palace were wearing running shorts. They seemed to know each other. Then a whole mass of men and women came in together. They wore running clothes, too, laughing and yelling and the Crystal Palace was now packed bar to door with people. The crowd swamped the bartendress with orders. Pitchers of beer slid along the bar top and were passed from the bar to the tables. Someone handed me a pitcher of beer, laughed, and walked off. I looked at Michael and shrugged, and then I asked for two glasses and began pouring from the pitcher.

Steven and Derek shared their table with many in the crowd and everyone at their table kept raising their glasses for a toast. Someone across the room caught my eye and he walked over, pushing his way through the crowd and freeing himself from the hugs of several women.

"Well, mates! Hope we haven't ruined your party," he said.

"Who's we?" said Michael.

"The Hash Harriers, we are! Running group and all that. Maybe you saw our hare out today with the flour?"

"Those little white piles?" I said.

"Right, mate. Shows us the track, you know. Follow the marks and try to catch the bugger." He stuck out his hand. "Name's Harry."

We shook hands and introduced ourselves.

"Well," said Harry, "let's get a proper introduction. Here now"—he was gathering people around—"let's say hello to Michael."

A crowd pressed around us, everyone holding glasses of beer. Harry led a chant: "Here's to Michael. The man's a genius, he sucks a horse's penis! Down, down, down, down!"

At the "down, down" part the crowd indicated Michael was to chug his beer to the bottom without stopping, which he did to applause and yells. The crowd turned to me next, singing the same obscene song, and I also chugged a beer to the cheers of "down, down."

Harry said, "What do we say to Michael and Jordan, girls?" and the women in the crowd raised their voices and shouted, "Hi, boys! Wanna go to bed, boys?" and Harry then asked the men, "What do we say to the boys, men?" and all the men yelled, drowning out the women with a deep-throated roar, "Fuck you, boys! Go home!" and once more Michael and I chugged our beers and people slapped us on the back. I saw Steven and Derek near us, and Derek slapped me on the back and then went off somewhere in the crowd. I thought I saw Steven head for the door.

Harry faded into the crowd and Michael and I were left alone.

"I think this is really a drinking group that runs," said Michael.

"I think you're right. Look at those two."

Two members of the running group had climbed onto tables and were trying to speak, but as they spoke, in Australian or perhaps New Zealand accents, the crowd began chanting, "Sheep fuckers!" They drowned out the speakers and forced them off the tables.

At the bar it seemed our money was no longer accepted. Pitchers of beer were piling up, so Michael and I kept filling our glasses and any others that came near. We noticed that when anyone wanted to speak, that is, speak to the crowd as a whole, they made a fist with one hand and placed the fist on the top of his or her head.

There was a young woman near me who seemed part of the group. I asked her about the fist-on-head pose.

"You must place your fist on your head if you want to speak!" she said, laughing at me.

"But why?" I said. I liked the way she smiled.

"No one knows why. But if you don't, you end up like him," she said. She pointed to a man a few tables away. He was wearing a large bra over his shirt.

"I see," I said. I did not see, of course, but I liked talking to her.

"My name is Jordan."

"I'm 'high and tight'," she said, her eyes crinkling at the corners at my surprised expression.

"My running name," she said. "That's the only way we know each other." She pointed out other people in the bar.

"That's 'unlawful entry', 'gag and shag', 'alotta vagina', and that poor guy over there is 'two angry inches'."

"No!"

"Unfortunately, yes."

There was a man sitting down next to her. She introduced him as her husband. He barely raised his hand in acknowledgment. I didn't think he could stand.

"I'm going to have trouble calling you 'high and tight'," I told her.

She was standing next to me and she turned her back and then backed into me a bit, looking over her right shoulder, and she said, "Really?"

I was very conscious of her husband sitting just a few feet away. She turned again so she was facing me and she whispered into my ear, "Holly." Her lips brushed against my ear and her blond hair fell across my cheek. The crowd was tight and she remained pressed against me and we kept talking. My arm found its way around her slender waist.

At some point Michael had merged with another group and from across the room he saw my situation. He raised his glass in salute. I saluted him back, but I knew nothing was going to happen. I had met dozens of Hollys. All they wanted was the attention their husbands failed to give them. I was being used as a means to make Holly's husband jealous. As long as I didn't get out of line Holly would play her part. But if I tried to push it she would run back to safety.

The door to the Crystal Palace opened and a man ran in, out of breath. A roar rose from the crowd.

The crowd chanted, "Dead fucking last! Dead fucking last!"

Holly leaned into me again, speaking into my ear.

"The last runner. D F L. He gets the prize."

The crowd had the runner up on someone's shoulders and they carried him through the bar. He leaned down from the height and they placed a necklace strung with a huge rubber penis around his neck.

"Some prize," I said. Holly had both her arms around me. She looked up at me and smiled and did not turn away.

The door opened again and I saw it was Kevin, the rider we had met at the Circle K coming into town. He made his way through the bar. I caught his eye. When he saw me and headed my way I knew something was wrong. Kevin finally came near enough to speak to me.

"Hey, your buddy's hurt," he said.

I could see Michael across the bar, and Derek was up front singing, so I knew it had to be Steven. I followed Kevin out and managed a signal to Michael to follow us. Kevin led us across the dirt street to Big Nose Kate's.

The motorbikes were still parked in a row. I had assumed Steven had tried to ride drunk and hurt himself but instead I found him sitting on the edge on the wooden sidewalk. Blood flowed from his nose and he was holding his side. He looked up as I approached.

"Hey, bro. I had a problem here."

Some people stood around making comments and Michael scattered them away. I sat next to Steven.

"What happened?"

"Those riders we passed." Steven paused, catching his breath. "We had a little scuffle."

Kevin said, "I came outside and either four or five guys were beating on him. I pulled one off and said I was going to call the cops. They left and rode off."

"What were they riding?"

"All Harleys."

I stood and put out my hand and Kevin shook it.

"Thanks, Kevin. I owe you."

"No problem," he said. He turned to leave and then stopped. "They were beating him pretty good. You might want to have him looked at."

Steven heard him. "I'm all right," he said.

"We'll see about that." I helped him up. Steven could stand but it obviously hurt. His nose kept bleeding.

Michael was looking at Derek's bike.

"What the hell?" he said. "Check this out, Jordan."

I looked closely at what Michael pointed to and I saw the stuffed figure, still strapped on the back of Derek's bike. It was dripping wet.

"They were all pissing on him," said Steven.

"You saw them?" said Michael.

"I came out to check the bikes. They were all standing around pissing on our bikes."

So that's what started it, I thought.

"So you were defending Kokopelli's honor?" I asked Steven, trying to make a joke, but neither Steven nor Michael smiled. Michael surprised me. He looked angry. I suppose I was angry, too, but at the moment I was just glad Steven had not been more badly hurt.

"They got both the sportbikes," Michael said. He looked at Steven. "I'll help walk him back to the motel." He took Steven's other side. I let go of Steven's other arm.

"You coming?"

"I'll be back in a while," I said to them.

Together they walked slowly down the road. I watched them go. After they left I walked inside Big Nose Kate's and then down the street the other way. I crossed several blocks. There were other bars I entered and then left. Finally, I went back to the Crystal Palace.

The noise still blasted inside and the crowd had not decreased any. Harry saw me and pressed a mug of beer in my hand and would not leave me alone until I finished it in one draught, the crowd around me chanting again, "Down! Down! Down!" Then another mug appeared and I finished that, too. Finally I had to push through the crowd to find Derek but he was not inside.

I went out the front door and turned down the street I needed to return to the motel. It seemed so quiet after the Crystal Palace.

71

I passed an alley and heard noises and I stopped. I looked into the shadows and saw two figures. I stepped closer to see and I saw a man and a woman, the woman bent over with her blonde hair loose and her hands placed on the edge of a large planter that held a palm tree. Her running shorts were pulled down to her ankles and the man was thrusting into her from behind. With each thrust the woman gave a small cry of pleasure and for a moment she looked up and our eyes met. It was Holly. Her lips were parted slightly and she gave me a smile, then put her head down again. The man was Derek.

I left the alley and walked back to the motel.

Chapter IX

Iunlocked the door to our motel room and stepped inside. I sensed more than saw Michael asleep in the near bed. His silhouette made a dark shape. The room glowed with a flashing red light. I peeked out the curtains but I could not see anything. The walls pulsed red and I opened the door again and looked out, but there was nothing. I heard Michael stir.

"Jordan."

I shut the door softly and peeked out the curtains again.

"Jordan! That light is coming from you."

I reached over my shoulder and found a small flashing red light pinned to the back of my shirt. Someone must have pinned it on while I was in the bar. I took off my shirt and threw it on the floor. The shirt diffused the little red light and it glowed softly in the corner.

"Where have you been?" asked Michael.

"Out walking. How's Steven?"

"He took a pretty good beating. His eyes are clear, though."

"Should we take him somewhere?"

"I stayed up with him a while. I don't think he took any real hits to his head. He's just going to be very sore tomorrow."

"Thanks, Mike."

"Sure."

"Mike?"

"Yeah?"

"What's that smell?"

I heard Michael getting up. He walked to a corner of the room and picked up a plastic bag. I heard it rustle as he picked it up. He opened the door and put the bag outside.

"Sorry. That's Kokopelli. Maybe we can wash him at my aunt and uncle's."

"You went back and got it?"

"Seemed wrong to just leave it like that. And I took a wet towel and wiped down their seats."

"Throw the damn thing away."

"No. We'll wash him and clean him up and we're all going to finish this trip together."

I was too tired to argue. I lay down on my bed and the room started to spin. I had to sit up again.

"You all right?" asked Michael.

"I'll be fine. Go back to sleep." I heard him roll over on the bed. In a few minutes his breathing became deep and regular.

I sat on the bed a while longer. Then I undressed. When I could lie down without the room spinning, I lay back and tried to sleep. I could recline but I had to keep my eyes open, even in the dark, just to keep steady. I lay there and kept thinking.

How could they have known Steven had been on one of the two sport bikes that had passed them? Of course they could not have known. The bikes had passed too fast. Besides, they had full-face helmets on. It was stupid what Derek had done, passing like that. That went against the code. He had missed the lead rider by inches. It must have scared him pretty good. He wouldn't forget. It was the stuffed figure. They saw it and they remembered it. They recognized it on his bike and showed their contempt. Funny. Until Steven walked into it. That was way beyond the line. And what was Steven doing? It was five against one. And for what? It was all so stupid. But still, maybe I would get a chance sometime to even it out.

And what was Michael's problem lately? Keeping the damn doll. Maybe his aunt can clean it. Sure, I would like to see her face. Michael getting all sentimental and symbolic on me. What did he care? If he had seen those guys pissing on the bikes he would have walked the other way. Hell, he might have joined them. No, that wasn't fair. He would have done something.

I would have done something too, but it would have come out different than what happened to Steven. Much different. But damn that it had to happen at all. And Derek. What was the problem with Derek, anyway? He took it too far. But that didn't give those riders any right to beat Steven. And what exactly is my problem with Derek, anyway? He thinks he is superior to me? Is that it? Or is it I'm afraid of him? No, I'm not. That isn't it. It's because he doesn't care. He doesn't care about what he does or how it affects others. He's the type that makes everyone else pay a price. He's the drunk driver who walks away from a fatal accident. That's not fair. He couldn't have foreseen any of this. I'm thinking too much. I just don't like him. Not from the first time we met and I like him less now. There's something wrong there. And me, pretending to get along for Steven's sake.

Good God, I drank a lot. Those runners. They had the right idea, all right. Drink it all away. Down, down. Harry was nice. He would be a good traveling buddy. And the fist on the top of the head, whatever that means. That girl, she was pretty. What was her husband all about? Forget the husband, what was she all about? Did she take advantage of his drinking? Or did he drink because of her? But I don't want to think about that, now do I? No, I don't. No, I'll forget that if I could. Come on, Jordan, admit it. It hurt, didn't it? It hurt to see her in the alley. Be honest, it hurt because she was with Derek. Sure, it hurt. Yes, it hurt. And so what? Is this jump on Jordan night? Why not, you bragging sonofabitch. I came home, took care of things. That's what you told Michael. Like it was nothing. You took care of things all right. Mom looked you in the eyes, didn't she? You'll know what to do. That's what she told you and you watched her die. And when the final day came you removed the rings from her fingers and you witnessed her cremation and not once did you cry. You loved her very much and you never cried. You took care of things, you bastard. And what is it you can't admit? That you were scared? All right, I was scared. You were terrified. There was nothing you could do. You saw it in her eyes. Time running out before she was ready, a last conscious thought that everything had been squandered away, a full harvest of regrets. And there was nothing you could do. And sure, you were scared.

Those were the thoughts I spent the night with. I sobered up slowly and I felt better, and I could close my eyes at last. My mind quieted down and nothing seemed so dramatic now. I lay on the bed and sleep came creeping around at the edges. It had just been a wild night, nothing more.

In the morning everything would be fine.

Chapter X

Michael awoke the next morning and flung open the curtains. Sunlight began to crawl across the room. I had been comfortably half-asleep, and I rolled over with a handful of blankets. He bounded through the room cheerfully, singing songs he knew half the words to, and showered and shaved. He brushed his teeth, checking on me every few minutes. I sat up finally. The brass headboard looked as shiny and bright as I felt dull and haggard.

"Shut up," I said to the floor.

"Good morning!" said Michael. "Good to see you alive. You stumbled in last night like you'd been plugged by the sheriff."

I grunted something and headed for the bathroom to shower. There was one small hand towel left from the clean supply. The rest lay in sodden piles. I managed to get fairly dry and I came back into the room.

"What's the plan today?" I said.

"Hey, you're calling the shots."

"Then let's eat and see the graveyard before we leave."

"The graveyard it is. Boothill, here we come."

"And by the way," I said. I balled up the hand towel and threw it at him, but he ducked out the door.

I was the last to get out from the motel. The others were

outside, waiting. Steven was wearing sunglasses, but it was easy to see he was bruised up good on one eye. His nose was swollen and his lower lip was cut pretty good. I asked how he was.

"Sore," he said. He didn't seem to want to discuss it. I could tell Derek knew all about it already. They must have talked last night when Derek got in, or this morning.

"You want to just walk to breakfast? We can pick up the bikes on the way back."

"Sure."

We walked a few blocks to a café. It had a sign that read Best Coffee in Tombstone. Breakfast was quiet. No one talked about Steven getting beat up and he seemed grateful for that. Derek would not meet my eyes. I'm sure my anger showed, but I didn't care. The cafe served emu, ostrich, and buffalo burgers. We stayed with eggs and toast but Michael, still in high spirits, started a running commentary about the food.

"How big is an emu? Not as big as a buffalo, surely. So how many burgers from an emu? Or an ostrich?" Michael was gesturing with his fork. "I wonder if emu burgers are cost effective? Who would have thought Tombstonians like emu burgers?"

He called for the waitress and she came to us.

"Let's have an ostrich burger."

"For you, sir?" she said.

"No. For this gentleman right here." He pointed his fork at Steven. "Just the thing this gentleman is wanting. One ostrich burger. Rare, please."

Steven tried to object but we could tell it hurt him to speak, so the waitress left with Michael's order. She came back in a few minutes. She set a plate down in front of Steven. He made a poor effort at it, but I took a knife and cut it and ate one half so it wouldn't go to waste. It was pretty good. Michael stayed in high spirits until the bill came and he saw the charge for the ostrich burger. Even Steven had to smile.

We walked back to Big Nose Kate's and picked up the bikes. Derek's bike was not there. He had ridden his back last night. I didn't know how he did it with all that beer in him. There was a note on Steven's bike. It read *Please do not park here!*

"At least they didn't tow it," I said.

We rode back to the motel. Derek rode on the back of Michael's Valkyrie. We packed our clothes and strapped on the panniers and bags. Michael had Kokopelli double-bagged in plastic trash bags he found in the room and he stashed him deep in his panniers. We checked one last time through the rooms and once outside again we agreed it had been a good place to stay. We rode from the gravel parking lot and back up town to Boothill Graveyard. We had passed it coming into town yesterday.

Boothill was less a hill and more like a gentle rise that overlooked the far mountains. The view stretched across a quiet valley. We walked among the rock-covered gravesites landscaped with cactus and ocotillo, reading the short inscriptions. The markers read either "Shot," "Killed," Hanged," or "Murdered." One marker said, "Hanged, legally." Farther down the rise there was a Jewish section, but there were no markers we could find. There was only a plaque. Steven moved easier and he enjoyed the walk through the graveyard.

We left after an hour under a clear and bright sky. We put the town behind us and we rode through brown hills and rocky canyons. We leaned into the curves and passed through a tunnel. I could smell the sage in the air.

We stopped in the town of Bisbee. It was getting hot and we ordered sodas at some place called the Stock Exchange Bar. We spent time walking through town and admiring the cosmopolitan architecture. There was a grand old hotel named the Copper Queen.

"This reminds me of parts of San Francisco," Michael said.

"Or it could be along an Italian coast," said Steven.

"You've been to Italy?"

"I saw pictures. Or it could be on a Greek island, too."

"Let me guess. You haven't been to Greece, either."

We did not stay long. When we left we passed the huge copper pit that sits just outside the town. The water at the pit bottom—over a thousand feet down, the sign said—sparkled like a blue-green jewel.

The road led us east and south, down to the flat land by the

Mexico border. At the border town of Douglas we turned north. We passed a monument that marked the spot where Geronimo surrendered in 1886. Just past the monument we entered New Mexico. Interstate 10 took us seventeen miles east along its massive lanes. We got off the interstate at Lordsburg. From Lordsburg we began to travel northeast to the mountains and Silver City. We thought Silver City would be a nice lunch stop and we looked forward to the run up.

But the road to Silver City was not what we had hoped. We thought it would be a pleasant ride through the mountains but for most of its length the road was multilaned and heavy with traffic. Although we were climbing we had little sense of being in the mountains. Somewhere we crossed the Continental Divide but we didn't see it.

As we neared the town it got much better. There were green meadows and deep woods stretched out on either side. I saw a few deer grazing. Beyond the trees I saw distant blue mountains. The sky remained clear and cloudless and we escaped from the heat bearing down on the desert. We hit Silver City and it was greener everywhere with thick forests of juniper, pine and spruce.

We pulled into some burger place to eat. Inside, we ordered and sat at cheap plastic tables with plastic trays and ate our food. The waitress who brought our food flirted with us, I think the job bored her, and she checked back several times to see how we were doing.

A cheap newsprint flyer was on every table. I leafed through a copy.

"It says here Silver City was the place to come if you had tuberculosis," I said.

"Wonderful," said Steven.

"That's a nice draw for a city," said Michael. "Come here if you're sick. You'll fit right in."

"In the old days the weather was thought to be a cure. People slept out on the porches."

Michael brought up his aunt and uncle.

"I don't want to bring the whole gang to the house," he said. "You guys mind getting a motel for the night?" He spoke to

Steven and Derek.

"That's fine," said Steven. "I wouldn't want four bikers clomping in either."

"I'm sure they'll have us all for dinner. There's just not room for all of us overnight," Michael said.

I think he felt bad asking Steven and Derek to stay at a motel while he and I stayed at his aunt and uncle's, but it didn't seem to be an issue.

We finished lunch and walked out to the bikes. Michael said he wanted to use the restroom and went back inside. Steven had left his keys on the table and went hunting for them. He seemed to be distracted today. I couldn't blame him. It always feels out of sorts when you have been hurt and it takes time to get the rhythms back. In the meantime Derek and I waited awkwardly by the motorbikes, each of us shuffling around and not speaking. He finally spoke.

"You know I never meant Steven to get hurt," he said.

"Maybe not. But that was stupid to antagonize those other riders. What's the point?"

He was looking out towards the mountains.

"Sometimes I just need to break out."

"That doesn't mean someone else has to get hurt," I said. I saw that my words stung.

Derek looked at me and then said, "Pain spreads."

I didn't know what to make of that. I sensed he wanted to tell me more but couldn't, and his eyes looked unfocused and confused. He looked away and left me hanging and I only thought: here was a guy who had money and time and no worries, and as far as I could tell he was pretty set. He could leave anytime and travel, or stay in school, or do any number of a hundred things that most of us couldn't do, and yet he still tried to push the limits. There was something there and yet I did not think he cared about anything.

We waited until Michael and Steven joined us, then we turned over the motors and pulled onto the main road through town. Silver City had a pleasant feel of contentment, as opposed to the rugged garishness of Tombstone. We passed through a few stoplights, moving easily in light traffic, until the road opened up again. Outside town huge strip mines appeared. The mines ran in long striated ledges of tan earth. They were ugly to look at. It felt good to leave them behind. We saw signs that announced the Black Range and the road began working its way through deep forest filled with spires of red-colored stone. We wound our way through dark canyons and high passes. As we passed one overlook I saw a stream rushing white down a steep gorge. All around us were rolling blue-green forests under a cloudless sky. The air was clean and smelled of fresh pine. Michael and I rode side by side and he nodded at me as we passed the overlook. We hit a summit marked at 8,228 feet. From there we began dropping down the other side of the range. An abandoned truss-and-girder style bridge spanned a narrow canyon and we traveled across a new bridge that paralleled it. I guessed the engineers left the old bridge as a monument of sorts. Near the end of the downhill run we rode past the ghost town of Kingston and then past a small town called Hillsboro. A sign read Population 225.

Only Michael knew where his aunt and uncle lived, of course, and he took the lead when we hit the interstate leading north to Truth or Consequences. I missed riding over the winding two-laned blacktop, but Michael kept the speed down to eighty-five so I could keep up easily. Steven and Derek had no choice but to stay with us. The interstate ran due north and we cruised along until signs announced the town and Michael chose an exit. We followed him through some plain looking streets, turning here and there in random fashion, until I began to think he was lost. We rolled along a residential street, then he pointed at a house with a small front yard and kept going, leading us out of the maze and back to the commercial part of town. He found a parking lot of a Motel 6 and pulled in. We followed him, rolling up tight.

"Are we supposed to find our way back to the house?" said Steven.

"If that's the right house," I said. I mimicked Michael's vague pointing gesture. "Was that supposed to mean something?"

"That was my aunt and uncle's house. I just wanted you to know where it was. I'm sure they'll invite all of us to dinner."

"You'll have to come get us and show us the way back," said Derek. "We'll never find it."

"That's fine," said Michael. He rolled out, leaving Steven and Derek to get a room at the motel, and I followed him back to his aunt and uncle's. It seemed we took a different way back. I was lost by the time we pulled up in the driveway.

Chapter XI

Michael's aunt opened the door. She looked surprised, but her eyes were bright with friendliness and welcoming. I liked her at once.

"Come in, come in!" she said. She held the door for us. I followed Michael into the house. His uncle stood by a chair, one of those types that recline, and watched us come in. Michael introduced me and we shook hands. His skin had the feel of a cantaloupe. He sat down only after Michael and I sat on the sofa. Michael's aunt sat on a chair set to one side. The room seemed quite full and I saw now why Michael was not keen on all of us staying there.

His uncle addressed us. "You made it all right!" He looked at each of us in turn. Michael's aunt also looked at us, still smiling. I said nothing. Michael stayed quiet. I wished he would say something.

Finally, Michael spoke.

"We rode in from Tombstone today."

Michael's uncle took note.

"Took you a while, did it?"

"Well, we left kinda late."

"Oh."

Michael's aunt said, "Would you like something to drink?"

"Do you have sodas?"

"Of course!"

Michael's aunt went to the kitchen. We heard her pour the sodas and she came back with two glasses filled with soda and ice.

Michael's uncle watched us drink the sodas. He was older than what I imagined. From what Michael had told me I knew he was the brother of Michael's dad, but there must have been some amount of years between the two.

"You'll like this town," said Michael's uncle. He asked where else we had been and we told him about the trip so far. He seemed knowledgeable about the West. Somehow we got to talking occupations. Michael's aunt was a nurse.

"Twenty-five years," she said. She sat on the edge of her chair, ready to spring up should Michael or I want something. Michael's uncle was a retired fireman. He had retired early with a disability but he didn't elaborate.

Michael's uncle said, "I don't do much now, of course. I write articles."

"Really?" I said. "What subjects?"

"All types. I research history, local events. I've had a few things published."

"He's being modest. He gets published all the time," said Michael's aunt.

"Well, I don't know about that."

"Of course you do! Tell them about your book."

"I'm sure they don't want to hear about it."

"No, please. I'd like to know," I said.

"Well," Michael's uncle began to speak, moving himself in his chair. I thought he was uncomfortable talking about his writing. "I'm writing a history book about Don Maguire. He was a trader who traveled through the Southwest about eighteen-eighty or so. Quite a character, really."

"Sounds interesting," I said.

"He left a journal of his travels. He met some fine characters. He was in Tombstone during its early days, actually. I'm trying to write the book as though he was writing it himself. Through his eyes, you know, as though he were still alive."

"I bet it will be great."

"Great might be stretching things, but I think it'll be worthwhile to read. Shame, actually, that so little history gets read. Hell, I was reading that most Americans can't even find the United States on a map, let alone know its history."

Michael looked at me and winked.

"I saw that, Michael. Keep it up and I'll start quizzing you to prove my point."

Michael laughed, and he and his uncle talked about his parents. I was surprised Michael had so little contact with his mom and dad. He could not answer most of the questions his uncle put to him about where they were and what they were doing.

"You really ought to stay in touch, Michael."

"I'm sure they're too busy marching and protesting somewhere."

"Well, regardless of their politics, they are your parents. I'm sure they care."

Michael did not say anything.

Michael's aunt had gone to the kitchen and came back with something for Michael's uncle. She put several pills in his hand.

"Your water is on the table, dear," she said.

He swallowed the pills and took a long drink of water. When he finished, he asked if we had made plans to stay the night somewhere. I glanced at Michael. Plainly, the only ones who didn't know we were spending the night at Michael's aunt and uncle's house were his aunt and uncle themselves.

"Well, we hadn't really thought about it," Michael answered, masking the fact that only a few hours ago he was promising me a nice house to spend the night in.

Michael's aunt and uncle looked at each other.

Michael's aunt said, "Why not stay here? There's plenty of room!"

She sounded so enthusiastic I felt guilty for Michael's play.

Of course we agreed to stay and while Michael's aunt bustled here and there and made preparations we stepped out to grab our bags.

Outside by the motorbikes I said to Michael in a low voice, "Smooth, mate. Swindling your aunt and uncle out of a night's lodging now, are we?"

Michael was unstrapping his bags. He stopped a second.

"My uncle knew. He just wanted to make me sweat."

"You two are close, aren't you?"

"He's more my dad than my dad. I wish he lived in San Diego."

We carried the bags inside. Michael's aunt already had two rooms set up for us. It felt like luxury to have my own room. The bed was one of those extra-thick affairs with lots of blankets and a soft white quilt covered with maybe twenty pillows. I hoped the rooms were not too bad over at the Motel 6.

Michael came into my room.

"Not bad, eh?"

"Not bad at all."

"My aunt and uncle want to have us all for dinner, Steven and Derek too. I thought we'd go get them. Pick up some wine, maybe."

"That sounds great. I'll buy the wine."

"My uncle already gave me cash. We won't be able to spend our money here."

I saw Michael was carrying the doubled-plastic bag.

"You're not serious?" I said.

"You don't understand. My aunt and uncle are big on all the Southwest lore. Look around you."

I saw on the shelves covering one wall some brass figures. When I looked closely I saw they were miniature Kokopellis. On the other wall were some western paintings and an Indian tapestry.

"Still, Mike, artwork is one thing. A piss-soaked rag doll is another."

"You'll see."

I followed him out the room and he tracked down his aunt. He explained most of the story, though how he did it with a straight face is beyond me. His aunt grabbed the bag and exclaimed, "Of course!" She moved into the utility room and opened the bags.

She pulled out Kokopelli and threw him in the washing machine, added soap and twirled some dials around, then shut the lid.

"That's sacrilegious, what they did! We'll get him all fixed up in no time."

Michael and I went back to the living room and found his uncle reading the paper. The news was on. He read the paper and glanced at the television whenever something interesting caught his ear.

"Have a seat, boys," he said.

He had a drink beside him. He saw us look at the glass.

"I'm not supposed to drink, of course. Not with all the pills I take, but what the hell." He called out for Michael's aunt. She came out from the kitchen holding a towel.

"See if these boys can handle two of our specials."

Michael's aunt smiled at us and went back to the kitchen. We heard her clink some bottles around and she returned with two glasses. She set them near us. Michael and I each took a glass and tried a sip. The drink was strong and burned, but it was good. I thought I might be able to handle no more than three of them, on a good night.

"Not bad, eh?" said Michael's uncle. "My specialty. Combination of wine and whiskey."

"What?" I said. I looked at the drink again.

"Sure. Learned about it in England."

"Uncle backpacked there one summer," Michael said.

"And had a great time, too. Travel, that's the thing. Just what you boys are doing now."

Michael asked about dinner and his uncle called out once more, bringing Michael's aunt from the kitchen again. It embarrassed me the way he kept calling her, but she seemed to enjoy it. It seemed on the surface one-sided but I suspected there were few things they wouldn't do for each other and I was sure it all evened up. She said dinner would be in forty-five minutes. She went back into the kitchen. Sounds came from there suggesting she was busy with what she needed to do to serve six people on short notice.

"Let me call Steven and Derek," Michael said. He reached for his cell, then caught himself.

"We'll have to ride back the motel they are staying at," Michael said to me.

"Can't you call them?" Michael's uncle asked.

"I made everyone ditch their smartphones for the ride," I explained.

"Good man. I totally agree. In my day it was beepers," said his uncle. "Slide-rules, beepers, calculators. Then computers, digital this and that and so on." He shook his head. "I'm not complaining, mind you. It's all fine until you can't live without it."

"Oh, listen to you!" said Michael's aunt from the kitchen. "Don't mind him. Take his Internet away for one day and see what happens. All fine until you can't live without it! You'd think the world had stopped, no Internet."

Michael's uncle had a big grin. "My retirement spans the world, it seems. When the net goes down things sure stop. You two probably can't remember it never existing."

"No, I remember when it came out. I'm not sure about slide rules. I read about those in history class. Along with the Greeks, I think," said Michael.

"A comedian, now? Well, well, the young ones certainly know it all." Michael's uncle put down his paper, folding it in half, and he turned down the volume on the television. "You can tell me some of the latest books you've read, perhaps?"

Michael slouched a bit. "Come on, now, you're embarrassing Jordan."

"Not at all," I said. "I'm fine. I'd like to know myself." I was enjoying the banter between the two.

"Thanks," said Michael. "Well, let's see. I just finished some Hemingway, and I'm working through Chandler right now."

"Hold it right there. What Hemingway?"

"The Sun, and For Whom the Bell Tolls."

"All right, you're fine there. Just know that all Hemingway is not good Hemingway. It got so he was imitating himself in his later stuff. But, the Sun is good. He called out the year he'd die in that book."

"He did?" I asked.

"Sure. He has the Jewish character say 'in thirty-five years we'll all be dead.' He wrote the book in 1926 and shot himself in 1961. I think some of the others he wrote about had died by then, too. Have you read it?"

"I have, but it's been a while," I said. I wasn't sure if I had ever read it or not but I didn't want to let him down.

"Of course, you did. They rammed it down your throat in school and you hated it, I'll bet. I've always tried to get Michael to read and appreciate literature. I am failing miserably." He looked at Michael. "Tell me about Chandler."

"So far I've liked it all. I like mysteries."

"Don't be so quick to dismiss them as mere mysteries. Chandler was as good as they come. He could write as well as anybody. Fitzgerald, Faulkner, Hemingway, even Steinbeck. The poor guy got typecast as a mere mystery writer and the critics never gave him real credit. Not here, anyway. They respect him much more in England."

"I suppose you have some more recommendations?" said Michael.

"I," said his uncle, "will make you a list."

I heard Michael sigh.

"The state of things these days," Michael's uncle said. "Some flash-in-the-pan writes a tell-all and it sells millions, but good, honest-to-God literature goes begging. What's happened to this world?"

"It's the same world, Uncle. It's just us."

"Perhaps. But you don't have to be ignorant. Not in this day and age. But maybe it's easier, eh?" He winked at us and looked at his watch. "Better collect your friends. And we prefer merlot but get a few bottles of what you like."

We stood and Michael's uncle saw us to the door. Before we left he took my arm and said to me, "I don't mean to say you're ignorant, you know. Michael tells me you're a chemist, and I'm sure you have a good education."

He seemed worried I had been insulted and I liked him immensely for it.

"Of course not," I said. "I haven't been much of a reader, though. I've traveled some, but I haven't read too much."

He was relieved. "Well," he said, "that's the great part about books. They're always there, waiting for you when you're ready. All the characters, the issues, their entire world, waiting for you to join them anytime."

"I'll remember that."

"We'll be back in twenty, Uncle," said Michael, and we walked out to the bikes. The sky had that falling blackness look and stars were beginning to show. It was still early evening and I imagined the skies really lit up in the New Mexico nights.

I followed Michael out and once again became hopelessly lost as he turned here and there with Hollywood stops at every stop sign, until at last he ran into some main street. After a few stoplights we turned into the motel parking lot. We saw Steven and Derek's bikes.

"Good thing they hadn't gone somewhere," Michael said.

We figured to ask at the office for the room number and we headed that way, but as it turned out they saw us from their second story room. They stepped out on the landing.

"Hey guys! Up here!" Steven yelled.

"Come on down!" Michael yelled back. "We're all having dinner at my aunt and uncle's."

We saw them go back into their room. They came out a few minutes later and we met at their bikes. Both of them were in a good mood. Steven told us about the motel.

"It's filled with those Shriner guys!"

"Every room has Shriners and bottles of liquor," added Derek.

"Once they knew about us and the trip, they had us go from room to room trading stories and shots. It was great, bro."

"We were a hit, no doubt."

"Our motel is better than a bar," said Steven.

I filled them in about Michael's aunt and uncle's place.

"You'll like them," I said. "Just mind your manners." Steven seemed a bit high to me and I didn't want him to embarrass Michael. Or me.

Michael said there was a liquor store just down the road and we rolled into its parking lot. The front of the store had bright blue and purple neon lighting. We walked in and wandered through the wine aisle. I found some Napa Valley merlots with what I hoped were good labels and I grabbed two bottles. Michael picked out two bottles of whites, a chenin blanc and a sauvignon blanc, and one more merlot. Steven grabbed a bottle of tequila, which I made him put back, and he then found a bottle of Yellow Tail, from Australia, which made six bottles of wine total. Derek selected a large bottle of Bailey's Irish Crème, after checking with Michael first. He wanted to pay for it on his own, to thank them for the dinner.

"I think that's enough," said Michael. He had seven twenties his uncle had given him rolled up tight in his hand. We got in line and waited while some old drunk dug change coin by coin from his pocket to buy a fine bottle of rotgut. That's what Derek called it under his breath, anyway.

The clerk watched as the drunk dropped the coins on the counter. He slid them across the counter and flipped them into the open cash register tray. He was watching the coins and counting them and we were watching the drunk and none of us saw the two men enter the liquor store, both of whom were armed.

We heard the first gunman shout. He had a short-barreled shotgun and he leveled it at us. The four of us stood there and stared. It did not seem real.

"Get down!" he shouted again.

The second gunman had a black pistol and he went quickly around the counter and grabbed the clerk by the back of his shirt. He threw him down hard. I heard him fall behind the counter somewhere. The second gunman started pulling cash from the still-opened register. When he emptied the tray he pulled it out and threw it against the clerk on the floor. There were a few more bills that had been lying under the tray, probably the larger bills, and the second gunman grabbed those also. He yelled at the clerk, "Where's the fucking rest? Where's the rest, motherfucker!"

The first gunman stepped closer towards us.

"You think I'm fucking kidding? Get the fuck down!"

We stood there, Derek and me in front, Michael and Steven

just behind us. No one had said a word. I think if one of us had made a move to get down the others would have followed, but no one did.

The gunman with the shotgun put the barrel up against Derek's neck.

"You feel like dying, bitch?" he said. He hissed the words. The second gunman was kicking the clerk behind the counter. The clerk was making noise but he was not telling him anything.

Derek said nothing. He stared back at the gunman with pure hate in his eyes. I knew I would have to go for the shotgun. I didn't have a choice, I thought. At any moment the gunman was going to kill Derek and the second gunman would open up on us as well. I felt oddly very calm.

The second gunman, from behind the counter, yelled, "Let's go!" He hopped the counter and slid across the top, knocking off small displays of merchandise, and landed in front of us. "Let's go!" he said again.

The first gunman stared hard at Derek and then pushed the shotgun barrel viciously against Derek's neck. Derek staggered back, grabbing his neck and choking. I remained still and the gunman turned and ran out the door with the other. It was very quiet. From behind the counter we heard the sounds of the clerk moving. From outside we heard a car squeal its tires.

The robbery had taken less than one minute.

Michael was the first to react. He went behind the counter and helped the clerk.

"There's a phone back here. Call 911! Tell them to send an ambulance," he said.

I made the call and then helped Michael with the clerk. He had him sitting on a stool behind the counter. His face was a mess. His nose was smashed and there was a deep gash above his eye. His mouth was bleeding and he was holding his side. Michael asked him where the restroom was and then he told Steven to get some paper towels. Derek was rubbing his neck and standing on the other side of the counter.

We heard sirens coming.

Chapter XII

The police pulled up in three patrol cars. They had the lights flashing and two officers entered with pistols drawn. The others took positions behind their opened car doors. The two officers who entered took no chances. They trained their pistols on us and told us not to move. One officer covered us and the other checked the place out. The one checking things out asked the clerk if there were any firearms behind the counter. There were. The clerk pointed them out and the officer ordered us out from behind the counter. The officer found a shotgun and one small caliber pistol. He was not pleased. The clerk was dripping blood on the floor.

The officers separated us and patted us down and had us pull out identification. We stood there, not talking, until the police were satisfied everything was under control and finally they relaxed, as little as cops do. The ambulance had arrived and the paramedics received permission to enter. Two paramedics attended to the clerk. He did not look good. They strapped him onto one of those rolling gurneys with the snap-down wheels and lifted him into the back of the ambulance. It left the parking lot with flashing lights but no siren.

The police kept us apart and asked each of us to make a statement. I was surprised at how little I could describe the gunmen. I could not recall the color clothing or give a good physical description. I remembered mostly the nastiness that dripped over each face, the flat eyes and the cold demeanor that read they didn't give a damn.

Michael asked one of the cops if he could make a call. The cop shook his head. I saw Derek giving a calm account of the robbery. He spoke slowly, in detail, and waited patiently for the cop to write it down. Of all of us he seemed the least affected by the event, even though he had been the one with the shotgun pressed against his neck. Steven was using his hands as much as his voice to describe what happened.

When we finished the statements the police brought us together for a quick briefing of what to expect next. We were told a detective would be contacting us. Being from out of town didn't seem to be an issue. I asked what would happen if we needed to come back for a trial or something and the officer said it would be worked out. Nothing would happen for months, since the whole process might take a year or more once they caught the gunmen. The officer told us there had been a string of robberies the past few weeks and they expected it was just a matter of time before they caught the perpetrators, as he put it.

The cop speaking to us said to Michael, "Say hello to Treehouse, will you? Tell him Officer Franks says to get on down sometime."

"I will. Okay to borrow a phone? I'd like to call him before he sees this on the news."

The cop let Michael use his phone. After he called I asked him what the cop meant.

"He knows my uncle. He saw my name and I told him I was his nephew."

Two of the police cars left the parking lot. The remaining two officers had secured the whole area with yellow barricade tape that read: Police Line-DO NOT CROSS. There was a white van in the parking lot. The van had the call letters of a local news station on it. A man stood near with another man who carried a video camera and one of the police officers was talking with them. He pointed at us. The man raised his hand to the cameraman as a sign to wait and walked over.

"KNDS News 14," he said, putting out his hand and shaking ours in turn. "You guys were in the store when it all went down? I'm going to be taping here in a second. Anybody want to be on the air?"

I looked at Derek and Steven. We shook our heads, no. Michael came back. He had gone to his bike for something.

"How about you?" the newsman asked him.

"Me what?" Michael said.

"An interview on camera about the robbery."

"No, that's all right."

"How about off-camera? Can anyone give a good description of the perps?"

"I can," said Derek.

The newsman wrote on a small pad while Derek gave a precise and detailed description. I had not caught half of what he saw, and I could tell by Steven and Michael's expression that they had not either. Derek had the gunmen down cold. If a detective contacted us, Derek was the one to give details.

When Derek was done the newsman thanked him and asked again if any of us wanted to be on camera. No one did. We just were not interested. I couldn't say why except that maybe we felt we had said our piece to the cops and that was enough. There was no need to make a show of it now for some news station.

The newsman walked back to the cameraman and they stood together with the neon lights of the liquor store behind them. The newsman had the microphone in his hand. The cameraman raised his camera and the newsman began to speak.

"Moments ago this liquor store behind me was robbed and the clerk brutally assaulted by two armed men..."

We watched him launch his report.

"Bro, you believe that shit?" Steven said to me.

Derek looked at me.

"You were going to go for the shotgun, weren't you?" he said.

"I was thinking about it."

Derek grimaced and then he said, "Before or after he blew my head off?"

"Wouldn't have done much good after," I said.

We stood and faced each other. He knew if I had planned to make a move it would have been to save his life as well as mine. And the others, of course. Some words don't have to be said. But he knew, and it was the first time I felt we had any understanding.

"How's your throat?" I asked.

"It hurts."

The four of us walked to our bikes. Steven and Derek were talking. Derek straddled his bike and he had a far away look in his eyes. Steven walked up to me.

"Hey, bro. You mind if maybe we don't go to Mike's house?" he said.

"You don't want to come to dinner?"

"Well, no. Do you mind?"

"You should ask Mike, I think."

I looked at Michael and he looked at Derek, and then Michael said, "No, that's fine. They'll understand."

"We'll meet up in the morning, bro."

Steven and Derek started their bikes and rode out of the lot. I watched them go.

Michael said, "Let's get back to my uncle's." He started his bike and waited for me. We rode out into the street and went the other way from Steven and Derek. As we rode along the lane side by side Michael yelled at me, "My uncle says it's on the news already." We arrived at the house again after many streets and turns.

Michael's aunt and uncle heard us pull up and they walked out the front door. Michael's uncle had a big smile but his aunt looked worried.

"I gave you money," Michael's uncle said. "You didn't have to rob the place!"

"Oh, shush!" said Michael's aunt. "They've had a scare." She fussed over us and Michael's uncle kept smiling, but I think he had been worried, too.

"The wine!" I said. "We forgot all about the wine."

Michael reached into his panniers. "No, we didn't. It's right here." He was pulling out five bottles of wine one by one from the panniers.

"I'll have to go back in the morning and pay for these. I left the rest behind. Wouldn't all fit." Michael said.

He kept three bottles and handed me two to carry. I followed him towards the front door. For some reason there was no porch light on and it was dark and hard to see. Before we reached the porch steps I looked up and I saw thousands of blue stars in the black sky. Michael's aunt kept asking if we were all right and we told her we were and we walked into the house. Michael's uncle had the television on and he waved us past the living room to the dining room table. Six plates were set out. There were bowls of green beans and corn on the cob, and two roasted chickens sat on a large plate in the center of the table. Another bowl held mashed potatoes. Michael explained to his aunt that Steven and Derek were not coming and she looked disappointed.

"Oh, that's a shame," she said. She picked up the two extra plates and went into the kitchen.

There was something on about the robbery and Michael's uncle moved to where he could see. Michael and I did the same. On the news station a live report was running. We saw the reporter recapping the event, then a tape ran. The tape panned over the front of the liquor store. In the background we could see the four of us standing with one of the cops.

Michael's uncle chuckled over the way we looked.

"Those leather jackets make you look like the bad guys."

The reporter was going on with the story. Michael's uncle turned the television off.

"So what happened?" he asked.

Before we could answer, Michael's aunt insisted we come back to the table. Over dinner we told them the story. Michael's uncle listened quietly and his aunt gave a few gasps. Michael told most of it.

"Those stupid m..."—he paused, because of his aunt, and went on—"punks never saw I had more money in my hand than was in the register," said Michael.

"You boys were lucky," said Michael's uncle. He said this with gravity and I knew he was not just passing the whole event off. His earlier manner had only been relief with the fact we had come through unharmed.

Over dinner we had several glasses of wine. The dinner was good and Michael's aunt brought out pie for dessert. It would have been nice if all of us were together and I wished Steven and Derek had come to dinner. While we finished our pie Michael gave his uncle the message from Officer Franks.

"Treehouse? That's what he called me, eh?" said Michael's uncle. Michael's aunt and uncle exchanged looks. I thought Michael's aunt looked sad.

"Why did he call you that?" I asked.

"Well, that kinda goes back to why I'm on disability."

"I'm sorry. If you'd rather not talk about it," I said.

"No, no. It's fine." Michael's uncle pushed his dessert plate away. "It's not too much of a story, really. We'd pulled up to a house fire. We were told there was no one inside, but then we heard screaming. I went in, you know, the fireman's job, rushing into a burning building and all that, but it was empty. The screaming came from the back of the house. There were two kids in a backyard tree house, of all things. They'd started the fire in the house playing with the stove and ran outside and up into the tree house. They were scared to death. I went up and I got them down, but I fell pretty hard. That was that."

"He always tells it that way," said Michael's aunt. "But that's not the story." I looked at her and I could see her eyes were wet.

"The tree was on fire when he went up," she went on. "There was no way to get the ladder back there, and there was no time, so he climbed up. He climbed up and brought each kid down one by one. The second child he had to drop to his crew. Climbing down he fell twenty feet and hit the brick patio. His crew dragged him away before he burned to death."

"Well," said Michael's uncle, "I don't know if it was as exciting as all that, but that's how I got the name. Of course, that was my last run. Hell, I was due for retirement anyway."

He stood and grabbed a few dishes and carried them to the kitchen. When he passed his wife he gave her a squeeze on the shoulder. She patted his hand. When he came back he ordered Michael and me out to the living room. "Bring the wine," he said.

Michael's aunt busied herself with clearing the rest of the table.

In the living room Michael's uncle sat in the recliner. I sat on the sofa and Michael sat on the chair opposite. Each of us had his glass of wine. I felt full from the meal. From the kitchen we heard the sounds of Michael's aunt cleaning the dishes.

"Tell me about that business you have, Jordan," said Michael's uncle.

"Oh, it's not much. I mostly manufacture a degreaser and sell it to industrial accounts," I said.

"Just the one product?"

"That's the simplest way. Keeps my raw inventory down."

"It seems to me there could be some money if you developed something new on the market. Have you ever tried?"

"I have some ideas. There's a man I know who makes a powder absorbent from kelp waste. I wanted to go in with him and try adding a new enzyme to his powder. This enzyme eats oil."

"And how would this be used?"

"Marine oil spills. You'd throw the powder onto the spill to absorb the oil and biodegrade it at the same time. It would break it all down naturally. You wouldn't have to suck it all up, the way they have to now."

"That could be something now, couldn't it?"

"It could. The other guy is a bit difficult, though. He says he has no interest in the idea, but I think he's working on it by himself."

"One of those types, eh? Any other ideas?"

"Elmer's glue—something to remove it easily. Janitor's hate it. They have to scrape it off desktops and cut it out of rugs at all the grade schools. The kids drip it and squirt it and it dries into hard lumps. The janitors have to clean it all up. I tried to develop something that would dissolve it instantly...make it easy to clean up. So far, no luck."

Michael's uncle looked thoughtful. Then he said, "Screw the janitors. I like the oil spill idea. There's some real money in that." He turned to Michael. "How's your job going?"

"Fine," Michael said. "I just transferred to another store."

"Perhaps you'll get your own store sometime?"

"Who knows. It'll either happen or it won't."

"Well, well. Such fatalism. In my day we made things happen. We worked hard for it. Don't give me that look."

"It's different now," said Michael. "Everyone's on their own. Companies will cut you loose in a heartbeat. There's no loyalty anymore."

"Oh, I can't believe that," said Michael's uncle. "You show them what you can do. Companies value that."

From the kitchen we heard Michael's aunt call out, "Don't you be giving those boys a hard time! You leave them alone. How it used to be and all that!"

Michael's uncle winked at us. "I suppose I can't blame you or anyone else. I know things change. It's all gotten so big now, so complex. All anyone cares about now is being famous. Fame for fame's sake. Not for what you do or accomplish, just fame. You can be despicable, but if you're famous you're forgiven. Hell, you're idolized." Michael's uncle sipped from his wine glass, then set it down again. "But I'm just getting old, I guess," he said.

Michael's aunt emerged from the kitchen holding a hand towel in one hand and another bottle of wine in the other.

"Here, boys. Finish this off. And don't let him monopolize the conversation. He'll get going and you'll regret not getting a motel for the night," she said.

"Get back in the kitchen, woman. This is man's talk," Michael's uncle said, trying to look stern. Michael's aunt stepped up to him and began slapping him all over with the towel.

"You want man's talk? Here, have some more!" She was hitting him with the towel while he covered up, laughing. He grabbed her and pulled her onto his lap. She stopped striking him with the towel and gave him a quick kiss. She got off his lap and returned to the kitchen. In a moment she returned and sat near me on the sofa. The four of us talked about odds and ends until a late hour. We finished all the wine.

Chapter XIII

It was the next morning and I felt good and well rested. The bed had been soft and comfortable and with the wine I had fallen asleep soundly. It was luxury to have a room alone. Compared to my office couch it was heaven. I dressed into shorts, then opened the door and went down the hall. I found the bathroom and took a hot shower. When I finished I heard someone knocking softly on the door. I opened it, still toweling my hair dry. It was Michael.

"Come on," he said. "I need in."

I returned to my room and finished dressing and combing my hair.

I left my room again and walked to the kitchen. I kept quiet, thinking that Michael's aunt and uncle were still asleep, but I need not have worried. I saw them out the kitchen window in the back yard. I walked out the back door to say hello.

They turned to look at me when they heard me coming.

"Well! Up from the dead, I see," said Michael's uncle.

"It can't be that late," I said.

He checked his watch, smiling. "Seven a.m."

"I'll start breakfast!" said Michael's aunt. "You boys will be hungry."

She started for the back door.

"No, you don't have to bother. I'm sure we'll eat on the road."

"Why do that? Here, it'll take just a minute."

"Now, let them decide what they want to do," said Michael's uncle.

"We're fine. Really," I said.

Michael appeared at the back door. He was barefoot, shirtless, and his hair was still wet. He called out, "I expected breakfast in bed, but I'll settle for it now if I have to!"

Michael's aunt walked happily towards him and entered the house. Michael disappeared after her.

"I guess we're eating here," I said to Michael's uncle. He smiled.

I looked around and saw there was a small garden. They had been working on it before I awoke. There were some tomato plants and what I thought to be carrots, maybe, along with a type of squash. The small patch of garden was the only greenery in the back yard. There were a few granite boulders set here and there, glittering with specks of mica. Among the boulders were smaller quartz rocks that seemed to glow and had black lines running sharply through the stone. Flowing around the rocks were pools made of white pebbles. Each pebble looked clear and distinct in the morning sun. In some of the pools thin metal poles were planted. The poles supported copper chimes, tarnished green and hanging motionless in the still air.

I liked it. It all looked good under the bright morning light. I took a deep breath and looked up. Above us the sky was endless.

Michael's uncle saw me noticing the garden.

"We grow a few plants, not much. It is a desert, you know. Let's go inside."

I followed him back to the house and to the kitchen. Michael was drinking coffee and reading the paper while his aunt cooked breakfast.

"Michael, someday you'll make a fine husband for some poor girl. Heaven help her," said Michael's uncle.

"Oh, you leave him be," said Michael's aunt. She served pancakes, thick and large, and she placed a glass pitcher of ice-cold orange juice on the table. She had two types of syrup. The pancakes were hot and tasted wonderful. She kept serving more every time I cleared my plate. I finally had to surrender and hold my hand over the plate to stop her.

Michael passed the paper to me. A small article described the robbery last night. They had the full suspect descriptions. The police must have given them to the newspaper. The hospital, the paper said, expected to release the clerk today. I put the paper aside and finished my coffee.

"I got a hold of Steven and Derek. I said we'd be at the motel just after eight," said Michael. He had used his uncle's landline to reach the desk clerk at the motel.

"I'll start to pack."

I thanked Michael's aunt for breakfast and went to my room. It only took a few minutes to get the bags ready. Then all of us were by the motorbikes as Michael and I prepared to leave.

Michael's uncle was curious about the bikes. I gave him the rundown and of course Michael, who really knows bikes, told him a lot more. Michael's uncle sat on both bikes and declared he liked my Harley best.

"Sure, for sitting. For riding you'd want mine," said Michael.

"Don't listen to him," I said.

"I haven't. Not since he got here," said Michael's uncle.

"Oh! Wait!" said Michael's aunt. She hurried to the house and came back with Kokopelli. He looked clean and all fluffed out. She handed him to me. I held him close and took a whiff.

"Much better," I said.

"You couldn't leave without him!" she said. I strapped him to my bike, on the short bar rising from the pinion pad.

"You performed a miracle," I said. I gave her a hug goodbye. Then I shook Michael's uncle's hand.

"I enjoyed your company, son. Stay with that business. Sounds like you could have something there," he said. "And you two be careful. Don't fall off those bikes."

"Actually, it's all about falling," said Michael. He straddled his bike, putting his feet down. "It works like this. When you start a turn, you move the front wheel away from how you want to go"—he turned the handlebars slightly—"and that causes you to start falling to the opposite side. Then it's just a matter of balance as you turn the wheel back."

"Show me that again," said Michael's uncle. He was intrigued by Michael's explanation.

"Interesting," he said, as Michael showed him once more.

"I've studied the physics behind it. You aren't the only one who knows a thing or two."

"Well, well. I take back what I've said about you all these years. Sounds complicated."

"No. It comes natural. If you had to think about it you couldn't do it. But you're always falling on a bike and balancing against it. It's a lot like flying, in a way."

"Well, I don't care what you call it! You be careful on those awful things!" said Michael's aunt.

Michael hugged his aunt. She started to cry and wiped away at her eyes. Then Michael and his uncle shook hands. I started my bike and Michael started his and we glided out the driveway and down the street. I looked in my mirror and saw his aunt and uncle standing close together, waving goodbye. We turned a corner and that was the last I saw them.

Once again I followed Michael out of the neighborhood. The streets began to look more familiar, but still, under the big open sky and the lack of any one dominant feature, I lost my bearings again. Growing up in San Diego there was always the ocean to the immediate west and I always felt an innate sense of direction. But here it was just so wide and spread out. When I had been traveling across the whole country it didn't matter if I knew my way around or not; one place was as good as any and I never cared where I was going as long as I was moving. Now it bothered me not to know. Maybe, I thought, as we grew older it became more important.

Michael found a main street and we turned onto it and rolled a couple miles. He waved to his right and I saw the motel where Steven and Derek were staying. I pulled up alongside Michael and he yelled that he was going to the liquor store first and would join me in a minute. I nodded and turned into the motel parking lot.

I had not learned what room Steven and Derek were staying

in, but it was all right since they were standing by their bikes in the parking lot. It was eight o'clock on the nose. Steven waved to me as I pulled in. Derek nodded hello. They were just putting the last of their belongings into the panniers.

I rolled up, shut off my bike, and jumped off.

"Hey bro, where's Mike?" said Steven.

"He's paying for the wine we never paid for last night. You two go out last night?"

"Damn right, bro. Damn right. We hit every bar in town, I think."

Hearing this irritated me because I wished they had joined us at Michael's aunt and uncle's instead, but then, remembering what we had gone through, I could not blame them. I might have done the same if I hadn't known Michael so well and hadn't just met his aunt and uncle. So what the hell, I thought.

Michael pulled into the lot and cruised over slowly. He turned off the motor and kicked out the stand for his bike. The bike leaned over and Michael remained seated on it.

"Well, boys, we're a hundred forty dollars richer this morning."

"What do you mean?"

"They wouldn't take my money. No one at the liquor store knew what to do. I slid the money across the counter and they kept sliding it back. They didn't understand me and I couldn't understand them. I think it was the clerk's relatives, his mom and sister, or wife, maybe. But they wouldn't take the money. They let me use their phone and I called my uncle. He said to keep it and have a good trip. He said he'd square things up later with the store."

We high-fived each other in the parking lot at the news.

"You two eaten?" I asked Steven and Derek.

"Hell, no," said Steven. "We got to bed about two last night. Woke up thirty minutes ago."

"We've eaten," I said, "but I don't mind going somewhere for coffee."

"I know a good place," said Michael.

"Let's do it," Derek said.

Steven noticed Kokopelli strapped on the back of my bike.

"Hey!" he said. "The little guy is back!"

"Courtesy of Michael's aunt," I said. We started the bikes and motored out of the lot. Michael led the way since he knew the town. For the first time it felt as if we were traveling as a group. A chain restaurant appeared after a mile and Michael pulled in. We followed him and parked the bikes. Inside, the hostess showed us a booth and Steven and Derek ordered steak and eggs from the waitress, while Michael and I just had coffee. The waitress should have been a model and her repeated presence at our booth added to our good spirits. Michael talked about the dinner at his aunt and uncle's, and we talked about the robbery.

"You looked pretty calm with a shotgun pressed against your neck," said Michael to Derek.

Derek put down his coffee. "I thought that was it. I was surprised myself how I felt."

I was watching him as he said this and I saw for a moment how he left us, almost literally left us to go somewhere else, his eyes becoming blank then coming back to life. He looked at Michael and smiled.

"Ask Steven about later."

"He got the shakes. Really got them bad," said Steven. He looked at Derek, as if to ask permission.

"Go on. You can tell them," said Derek.

"He started to cry."

"I couldn't stop. I sat at some bar shaking and crying."

"You weren't that bad, Derek," said Steven. To us he said, "He was quiet about it and it didn't last long, really."

I thought Steven was worried Michael and I might think less of Derek for his admission, but I silently thought it took a tremendous amount of confidence to be so truthful. I looked at Michael and saw he felt the same way.

"Bro, why'd you step towards the guy with the shotgun like that?"

"I didn't realize I had."

"You did. When he put the shotgun on Derek you stepped toward him. Michael and I stepped back."

"You're goddammed right I stepped back," said Michael.

"I don't know," I said. "I just did."

"Both of you are nuts," said Michael, meaning Derek and me.

"That newsman was persistent," said Steven.

"He sure wanted us on camera."

"Mike, you weren't so bad yourself with the clerk and all."

"You were the first one to move," Steven said, agreeing with me.

"You know where that comes from? Working retail. You'd be surprised with all the weird stuff we have to deal with. Just the return desk alone will toughen you up."

"Not quite like last night though, I'll bet."

"No, not quite like last night."

Michael used part of his uncle's money to pay the bill and we left. Michael asked the pretty waitress about the town's name on the way out. I think he just wanted to chat her up. She said the town was named after some game show broadcast way back in the nineteen fifties. It seemed to me a silly reason to name a town. I noticed Michael left a nice tip, which is easy to do when it's not your money.

We left the parking lot and Michael led us in a direction I saw wasn't going to lead to the interstate. I pulled up alongside him and yelled, "Where you going?" He just pointed and motioned to follow him. In a few minutes we rolled down a frontage road that paralleled something we could not see, and then he rolled down a dead-end side road after that. He pulled up to a small rise fronted by willow trees and tall brush and shut off his bike. He dismounted and took a dirt path leading through the trees. We followed and in a moment he stopped. We were standing in front of a slow-moving river. The water was green and flowed quietly around sand bars and each bank was thick with tall reeds and cottonwood trees.

"That's the famous Rio Grande," he said.

"That?" said Steven. He was not impressed.

"Don't kid yourself. That's the third longest river in the United States."

"It can't be more than two feet deep."

"At least it reaches the ocean. Even the Colorado doesn't do that any more."

We stayed a few minutes longer, letting Michael enjoy the river. It meant something to him, we could tell, but Derek and I had to agree with Steven. It was not much to look at.

Michael turned away and got back on his bike and we followed him at a fast clip to the raised interstate and we hit it going north.

The interstate held little traffic and it ran straight to the horizon as far as we could see. We rolled along through miles and miles of open space. On either side of us were brown and black hills covered with sparse shrub. There were mesas cut through with narrow canyons, out of which flowed orange-brown sand in large alluvial fans. In the far distance we saw tall buttes and strange gray mountains. Somewhere off to our right the Rio Grande tracked its slow course but it was impossible to see. The interstate ran smooth and straight through it all and we ate up the miles.

A wind began to blow across the landscape from the east. It buffeted us and made it hard to ride parallel in one lane. We stayed single file, Derek leading, Steven behind him; then Michael and me. The traffic stayed light.

The wind shifted and began to quarter in from the northeast and the stronger gusts pushed me nearly across a full lane. I could see the others were having the same trouble. A small town named Socorro was coming up and I was relieved when Derek pulled off an exit and rolled into the parking lot of an Arby's Restaurant. We parked the bikes and went inside.

"Options?" said Michael, once we were seated at a table by the window.

I had brought in the map. I spread it on the table, moving aside the four sodas we had ordered.

"We can continue seventy-five more miles to Albuquerque, or we can go west on Highway Sixty."

"How far have we gone so far?" asked Steven.

"Only seventy miles."

"Then that's it," said Derek. "Let's get out of this wind. I vote for Highway Sixty."

Michael was tracing the map with his finger to Taos. He was

measuring the miles.

"Damn. I was hoping to see Taos someday," he said. Taos was close to one hundred fifty miles north of Albuquerque.

"If you really want to, it's all right with me," said Derek.

"No. You're right. Let's get out of this wind. It'll be like this for the next two hundred miles."

Steven looked at the map, tracing the shaded green that indicated the forested mountains to the west, and said, "Let's get to the green area."

"I agree," I said, and that settled it.

We raised a toast with our sodas, "To the green!"

I folded the map away and stuffed it into the inside pocket of my leather jacket. Michael was talking about his other motorcycles to Derek. Steven was looking out the window. We relaxed and drank the sodas.

Most riders would have felt the same way about the wind as we did. The wind made riding tiring and after a few hours your shoulders ached from the strain. It wore you down having to anticipate and react to all the strong gusts. If you had no windscreen it could be really bad, your body felt like a sail catching the wind, or if you had a large windscreen, like some of the big touring bikes, it could be pretty bad, also.

I was thinking back over some of the rides I had taken across the plains country, where the wind had blown hard enough to lift my bike it seemed, when Steven spoke.

"That's not good," he said. He was still looking out the window. He had been idly watching a woman walk down the sidewalk on the other side of the street.

The rest of us followed his gaze. I saw the woman down on the sidewalk in front of an auto garage, sitting up awkwardly and rocking back and forth. It looked as though she was crying.

"She fell down," said Steven. He stood from the booth.

"What are you doing?" said Michael.

"I think she fell down," Steven said. "Let me see what's wrong."

He walked out the Arby's, with Michael, Derek, and me following, and all of us crossed the street. The woman on the ground was being helped by a man wearing a gray shirt that had "Al's Service" written on the front.

"Looks like she cut her knee," he said.

The woman sat on the ground and held one leg bent up to her chest. She was crying. Steven knelt beside her. She was bent up somehow and it made everything wrong. Up close we could see she was deformed. Nothing looked right.

"Should we call an ambulance?" I asked the gas station guy.

She was still crying, holding her leg up.

"She'll be all right. She comes by regular," the gas station man said. "It's a shame. They sometimes just fall like that."

When he spoke the woman started crying louder. She was shaking her head and trying to say something. I could not understand her. She was rocking forward and back. Steven tried to comfort her.

"I don't think she just fell," he said. He looked back. "I think she tripped."

"Tripped, fell. Doesn't matter," said the service station man.

I noticed the raised edge of the sidewalk a few feet back. It was sticking up just an inch or so where the ground underneath had buckled. Michael and Derek took a closer look.

"Right here," said Derek. "She tripped over this."

Michael tapped his toe against the raised lip.

"It's hard to see, actually," he said.

The woman heard them talking. She started nodding her head, her eyes wide, nodding her head and all the time looking at Steven. She kept nodding and trying to say something.

"We know," Steven said. "We know you tripped."

"Do you have some paper towels, maybe?" I asked the service station man. He led me to the rest rooms and I wet some paper towels. He did not come back with me. I handed the paper towels to Steven.

"Here," Steven said to her. "Let me wipe off your knee." He gently cleaned her knee. Michael ran across the street and came back with the first aid kit he packs in his panniers. He pulled out an antiseptic wipe and an adhesive bandage and gave them to Steven. Steven cleaned the cut, dried it, and applied the bandage.

The woman had stopped crying. She watched him work.

"Dr. Steven to the rescue," said Derek.

Steven asked the woman if she wanted help up and she did, so he helped her to her feet. We escorted her half a block to a bus stop bench. In a few minutes a bus came along and pulled next to the curb. The lady bus driver opened the folding doors and stepped down, saying, "Well, Linda, I see you have some handsome young men around you today!"

She helped the woman up into the bus and into a seat. She was very kind to the woman. The bus left and we could see the woman looking at us through the glass. We waved to her. We walked back to our bikes.

"That settles it," said Michael.

"Settles what?" said Steven.

"That I'm handsome. The bus driver said so."

"She said that about all of us."

"She meant me. She was just being kind to the rest of you."

Michael repacked his first-aid kit and we left the Arby's and ran due west on Highway 60. The two-laned road gently climbed away from the desert landscape and trees began to appear on either side of the blacktop. Where the trees stopped, rolling meadowland appeared. We kept rising and for a long stretch no other car passed us in either direction. We stopped once to look at the view, sitting in the lane and not bothering to move to the shoulder. It was nice to leave the desert behind. The wind remained gusty but once we reached the mountains it died down to nothing.

On the ride up I thought about what Michael had said about motorcycle physics. I paid attention as we wound along the curves and he was right, actually. He was right about the other part, too. Thinking about it made it much harder to ride and it was easier to let it flow by and not try to analyze it.

And wasn't that something, I thought, about Steven and that woman. He had seen immediately what was troubling her. It had not been the cut, not so much, but the fact we had assumed she had merely fallen. She needed to know that we knew; that we knew she had tripped the way anyone might have tripped. It was a small thing, really, but it was important. It was important to her.

We hit the ranch and mining town of Magdalena, population 913. It was a pleasant and rustic looking town surrounded by pine forest. An elevation sign read 6,573 feet. I did the math in my head and figured we must have climbed over 2,000 feet in the twenty-seven mile run from Socorro. The green area of the map delivered; up here it was forested, cool, and much nicer than the rugged land we had just escaped. I was thinking that the early pioneers coming west must have thought they had reached paradise after the desert crossing.

We saw signs advertising Kelly, a ghost town three miles back into the mountains. Michael voted to explore it, so we followed the signs to the Kelly turn-off.

After rolling down a smooth dirt road we found a parking area. From there we hiked and explored the old site. The kiosk at the parking area said that in its prime Kelly produced millions of dollars of lead, zinc, copper, silver, and gold. It also said, as Michael pointed out, that there was a fee to see the site but none of us saw how we could pay. There was no one else around. So we just began hiking up the abandoned mining track and figured that if a ranger found us we would pay him then.

But except for the wonderful view there was not much left to see. We saw some foundations and a fifty-foot high brick tower I guessed was used for smelting. There was a deep shaft that we could not see the bottom of, and some abandoned machinery of the time. We dropped rocks into the shaft and heard water splash after a long wait. Derek took a dare and climbed high across some rusty framework.

I wanted to get a picture like the one I had seen once on an old rock album cover, so I spent some time positioning Derek and Michael and Steven. I had them spread out and facing away from the camera, in front of the old brick tower overlooking the forested mountains. Months later I had the photo blown up to a black and white poster and framed it. It was the last picture I had of the three of them together.

We left Kelly and took the dirt road down the hill again to

Magdalena. Steven saw a bar with a shake-shingle roof and he led us into the parking lot. Inside the bar it was cool and dark and we sat at stools arranged around the L-shaped bar counter. The bartendress was every bit as pretty as the waitress in Truth or Consequences. I nudged Michael and told him he had better match the tip he had given the girl at breakfast or word would get around.

"I'll tell you," he said softly so she could not hear him, "these small-town girls are growing on me."

The bartendress brought two pitchers of beer. Derek and I poured the beer into four glasses. Michael handed over more than enough money to pay for the beer.

"Keep the change," he said. She rewarded him with a dazzling smile.

Steven said, "Easy with our money, eh?"

"My uncle's money. Enjoy your beer and shut up," said Michael. He didn't want the bartendress to hear Steven.

I said, "Well, the least you can do is get her over here and talk to us, Romeo."

Michael waited for a chance to catch her eye. She was serving the other few men in the place. They looked like locals, dressed in jeans and long-sleeved wool shirts, and they teased her with that inane joking that passes for wit in small bars. Michael finally got her attention and she walked back to us.

"Need more?" she asked with that wonderful smile. She leaned on the counter from her side of the bar. I thought Michael was tongue-tied for a second but he recovered and asked some question about the road ahead.

"Oh, no, it's a nice road. It's a pretty drive. Just watch out for the elk."

She put out her hand to Michael. "I'm Maggie, by the way."

Michael took her hand. "I'm Michael," he said. "These are my friends. Jordan, Derek, and Steven." We all said hello.

"What about the elk?" asked Michael. The other three of us were all ears but mostly eyes. We didn't care what Michael asked about as long as he kept her talking.

"We've had some accidents. The elk come out at dusk along

the side of the roads. Early mornings, too. One of our deputies crashed his cruiser into one last night, actually."

"Was he hurt?"

"I don't think so. But last week a family hit one and they had to airlift someone out."

"We're on motorbikes," I said.

She looked at me and said, "Those elk can be over seven hundred pounds." She winked at me.

One of the other men at the bar was eavesdropping and he called out, "You hit one of those elk on a goddammed bike and you can kiss your ass goodbye!" He didn't like us talking to Maggie. He had long hair pulled back into a ponytail and wore a beard. He called out again, "Hey! A little service over here." He tapped his empty glass on the bar top. Maggie smiled and said softly, "I'll be back in a moment." She walked over and placated the ponytailed man with a beer. He and the others glared at us, trying to intimidate us since we were not locals and had no right to be talking to the town beauty.

Derek leaned forward so he could see past Michael to me and said, "Shall we have a little fun with the locals?"

Before I could answer, though, Michael shook his head.

"I'll get her back," he said.

And he did. She spent the next hour ignoring the others, only serving them when she had to. She always returned to us. She told us about the area and the way she talked and smiled and sometimes laughed kept all of us enchanted. One or two of the other customers threw a few low comments our way. We could tell from the tone nothing nice was being said, but we just ignored them. I thought Michael was falling in love.

"If there's a Wal-Mart near here, I'm transferring," he said, when she had walked away for a moment. I think he meant it, too.

When it came time to leave, Maggie wished us all luck and Michael lingered behind while the rest of us went outside the bar to our bikes. He came out from the bar after a few minutes. Maggie was with him. They talked briefly and then Maggie smiled and touched Michael lightly on the shoulder. She waved goodbye to the rest of us and went back inside. Michael walked over to his bike.

"Well?" I said.

"You never mind," said Michael, smiling.

We motored back onto the road and traveled west from Magdalena to the town of Datil, population 621 a sign said, and along the way we passed a large meadow filled with huge dish-shaped antennas. They sat in the meadow and pointed at the sky. Listening, I supposed.

From Datil we dropped south through an area described on the map as the Plains of San Augustin. We were still in the high country, around 7,500 feet, and the road was in perfect shape as though it had just been paved. It was wonderful motorcycling country. There were mountain views and open areas surrounded by woods. The road was uncrowded and we had all the time in the world. We rode together and passed through small towns named Old Horse Springs, Aragon, and Cruzville.

It was late in the day when we rolled into Reserve, population 394. Derek suggested to Michael that we find a place to eat before camping somewhere. We agreed, as we'd only had breakfast and, except for the drinking with Maggie in Magdalena, we hadn't had any lunch.

There was a bar right in the center of town, meaning the middle of the three or four buildings that made up the business district, and we backed the bikes to the curb in front and walked in. Maggie had told us about the place, actually, so we expected the food to be good.

The bartender was the man who took our orders and he passed the order slip back through a serving window to a small kitchen behind the bar. Through the serving window we could see someone in a white apron cooking our food. After a few minutes plates appeared. The bartender brought them to us. He lingered at our table. He wore, like the locals at the Magdalena bar, one of those long-sleeved woolen shirts. I think they used to call them Pendletons. Maybe they still do. At any rate, it was a style they favored in this part of the country.

"You boys touring the state?" he said.

"Part of it," I said. "It's a big state." I gave a quick rundown of where we had traveled so far.

"Well, good. We don't see many tourists. Damn town is dead."

There were three men sitting at the bar drinking beer, pretending not to hear us talking, but when the bartender said the town was dead one of them turned around and said, "Dead, hell. Dead, autopsied, and buried is what it is."

"What seems to be the problem?" said Derek.

The man who had turned on the barstool now fully turned around and faced us.

"The problem? The fuckin' enviro-geeks and other assholes coming in here and telling us how to run our fuckin' town, that's the fuckin' problem."

"Fuckin' right!" said Steven, knocking his beer mug down on the table.

Steven's animated outburst made us laugh and this caused the man at the bar to get off his stool and stand. The bartender said, "Take it easy, Johnny. They don't mean nothing by it."

"What the hell, man. Calm down. We're just passing through," I said. I thought the man wanted to fight all of us. He sat back down and one of the other men pushed a beer his way and said something too low to catch.

"He used to work at the mills. Hell, we all used to," the bartender said. He seemed a bit embarrassed about the man at the bar.

"So what happened?" asked Michael.

"Environmentalists, like he said. Came in here and shut down all logging. Protect the owls and all that." He paused a second. "Tell me, what did you see when you rode into town?"

"Trees?" said Michael.

"You're damn right. Trees and more trees. This county alone is bigger than some whole states, and it's filled with forest. More trees than there were one hundred years ago. Know where our lumber comes from now?"

We looked at him, waiting for him to make his point.

"Canada," he said. "It comes from Canada. They truck it in and we sit here on welfare or unemployment. You figure it out."

We just nodded in sympathy. None of us knew a thing about it. But I wanted to know about camping somewhere and I asked him where we could camp. I had seen a campground sign riding into town.

"Don't camp there. That's for trailers, mostly. Go up the road a few miles and turn in anywhere. You'll find places to camp for free," he said.

"Free works for us," Derek said.

I thanked him and ordered more beer. We ate our food—it was good, like Maggie had promised—and every now and then one of the men at the bar turned and glanced at us. When we finished the food and beer we got up and left. As we walked out the door the same man at the bar yelled after us, "Yeah, go camp in the fuckin' forest. Might as well use it for something, assholes." We ignored him.

Outside, by the bikes, we were putting our leather jackets on. The sun had just set behind a mountain and daylight was running out. Steven had a big smile on his face.

"Nice friendly bar, eh?" he said.

"Good of Maggie to recommend it," I said, to needle Michael.

Derek, picking up the thread, said, "Mike, you take the lead, won't you? I hear there's elk on the roads at dusk. You can block for us."

"Funny," said Michael. "Keep it up and I'll go inside and announce you all belong to Greenpeace."

But he was smiling.

Chapter XIV

The road headed north from Reserve and began to climb. We passed through thick forest, the trees dark and tall, and the road worked its way up through the trees and sometimes it leveled out through ranchland and open meadows. We looked for a place to camp and a dirt road appeared to our left. There was a turnout on the paved road to ease turning and so we thought the dirt road had to be for something important. We turned and saw a sign that announced a campground ahead. We rolled down the dirt road a short distance and found ourselves led to a large clearing with campsites and a wood and brick privy. It was perfect.

We parked the bikes and walked a bit, looking for the best campsite. Along a footpath we found a stream that flowed way back in the woods, but we agreed it was too much trouble to get the bikes that deep into the trees. We found a site close to the cleared area where the privy stood. It did not matter, as there was maybe one other small group camping and they were far enough away. Other than that we had the place to ourselves.

At our site we unpacked our gear. We broke out the tents and sleeping bags and we pitched the tents around the fire ring, centering the fire among the four tents. Michael, Derek, and I had tents with clip-on support poles that we set up in seconds. We set them up and moved gear inside until we were satisfied all was proper. Then we watched Steven set up his Boy Scout affair of a tent he had picked up who knows where. He was pounding in stakes, arranging and tensioning guy ropes and whatnot. After fussing around a while he had it set up. Then he opened the front flaps and crawled inside to lie down. He popped out a moment later, smiling happily, and said, "I'm all set!"

The four of us set off to gather deadwood for the fire ring. We brought back armloads and we had a good fire going just as night fell. Steven left the fire ring for a minute and walked to his bike. When he came back he carried a six-pack of beer, which he had bought at the bar unnoticed by the rest of us.

"Here we go, men," he said, still in good spirits.

It became cool quickly, as we were over 7,000 feet in altitude. Despite the fire all of us put on warmer clothes.

"I wonder where the road leads to," said Steven, meaning the dirt road that passed by the campsites. All of us peered into the darkness, but of course nothing could be seen. We looked into the fire ring and stared at the fire. Then Michael said, "To Maggie!" and we clinked beers and drank.

"Your uncle is quite a guy," I said to Michael.

"It was good to see him doing better."

"He was worse?"

"He used to be on a walker. When I saw him last he was in a convalescent home."

"There was some get-together at the home," Michael continued. "All the residents went to the main hall. It was crowded, so after everyone got seated they moved the walkers outside. There were these walkers all lined up in a row outside the door. It was spooky. Everyone was inside talking, having a good time."

The fire blazed and crackled and kept away the cold settling through the dark trees. The firelight made our shadows flicker. I looked at our motorbikes, all lined up in a row.

"Anyway," said Michael, "He's really improved. He used to keep a police radio on all the time, listening to the emergency calls across town. I didn't hear it this time."

Steven and Derek were listening and Michael filled them in with the story about the tree house.

"Pretty amazing," said Steven.

Derek agreed.

"Yeah. I guess we have our own story now." He meant the robbery.

"I don't know," I said. "We didn't exactly do anything."

"We survived, bro. That's good enough."

"The clerk almost didn't. He was damn good through it all."

"For getting the shit kicked out of him?"

"You know what I mean," I said.

"Think they'll ever catch those guys?" asked Michael.

"They'll catch them. Then we'll testify to the truth, the whole truth, and nothing but the truth, and they'll be convicted," I said.

"Sure," said Derek, quietly. "Like the fucking truth matters."

He said this with such bitterness that we remained quiet a moment. I wanted to ask him what he meant and it must have showed on my face because Steven suddenly interjected and asked me to join him to get more wood. I looked at our pile and saw we had plenty, but he was insistent so I walked off with him.

Away from the fire it was cold and I zipped up my jacket. Steven followed the dirt road and stayed quiet until we were out of earshot. There was no moon and it was hard to see. The road was just a flat darkness that led between the tall trees, and overhead the stars gave just enough light to show black outlines. Steven walked along and I could not see his face but I sensed he was upset. We were perhaps a hundred yards up the road when he stopped. I waited for him to speak.

"I wanted to let you know about my plans after my last class," he said.

"It's some secret we have to be out here to talk about?" I said. I wanted to lighten the mood, but Steven remained serious.

"I won't be joining you at the business."

I did not say anything. Then I asked, "What do you plan to do?"

"Travel. I'm going on a long bike tour."

"I take it this is something you'll be doing with Derek?"

"Yes."

I gave it a moment before I said, "Well, it's something I did myself. I can't blame you. Hell, I wish I could do it again."

Steven did not say anything.

"Is there more?"

"I don't know about the business. I mean, me ever joining it. I don't know it's what I want."

"Steven, every other day I feel like that. But at least it's something. I've always counted on you as a partner. Together we can build it up, you know? You'll have that degree. Who knows what we could do?"

"Jordan, that's your dream. It was never mine."

Steven surprised me by calling me Jordan. It was usually "bro." We stood in the road and faced one another, although in the dark I could not make out his face. I did not know what to say.

"I can't help but feel Derek has something to do with this."

"Don't get angry."

"I'm not getting angry. I just don't see why everything is changed."

"Life changes, bro."

"Don't give me that bullshit. Life is what you make of it. You work at it."

"And what happens when it all gets taken away? Then what?"

"Live life on the edge? Is that what you're going to tell me? Derek's brilliant philosophy, I suppose? You have a future, Steven. Don't think of throwing it away."

"There's a reason Derek is the way he is. You've got him all wrong."

"I don't think so. He's irresponsible. He doesn't give a shit how his actions affect others."

Steven said nothing. Then, "He says you're arrogant and superior. I had hoped you two would get along. You're so much alike."

"Not true, Steven."

I could feel that there was more Steven wanted to say. He stepped away and turned towards the trees. Then he took a deep breath and exhaled.

"Jordan, two years ago Derek was engaged to be married. He was twenty. His fiancée was nineteen. I saw a picture of her. She was beautiful, Jordan."

I did not say anything.

"Derek's mom planned a wedding shower, or whatever they call it. All her friends showed up. There was a party. Then the friends left and later someone came to the door. Derek's fiancée opened the door and three men barged in. It was just Derek's mom and his fiancée there. The men tied them up and robbed the house."

Steven paused, and then went on with the story.

"They raped his mom and fiancée. It went on for five hours. They found the video camcorder his mom used to tape the party. They used it to record what they did. They taped everything."

I stood there in the dark and listened to Steven tell the story. I felt a cold sweat running down my back.

"They strangled his mom to death. One of them strangled her while another raped her. They laughed while she struggled. The one raping her joked how it excited him. After they killed Derek's mom, one of them made his fiancée get down on all fours and face the camera. He made her say goodbye and then he shot her in the back of the head. It was...on the camera.

"They caught the three men who did it. They had been showing the tape around and someone finally turned them in. They got attorneys, who claimed it was impossible to get a fair trial. There were activists, Jordan, advocating for the accused. Derek had to walk through them every day of the trial.

"The papers downplayed the crime. Barely covered it. The tape couldn't be used at the trial. The judge said it was too prejudicial. The prosecutor had to use a transcript from the detective who saw the tape and described what he saw. Derek attended every day of the trial."

"They were all convicted?" I asked quietly.

"They were all convicted. The jury voted for death sentences. The judge overturned the death sentences and gave life sentences instead. They can be out in twenty years."

We stood there, and off in the distance I could see our fire ring glowing with flames and sparks floating up to the sky. The small silhouetted figures of Michael and Derek were moving about and I supposed they were throwing more wood on the fire.

I turned to face Steven.

"I'm sorry," I said.

"That's all you have to say, bro?"

I just stood there. Steven turned and began to walk back. I stayed where I was. I felt sick to my stomach. I was not in the mood to return to the fire ring.

"You coming?" said Steven, over his shoulder.

"In a while," I said.

"Sure" said Steven. He kept walking, but then he stopped and turned.

"Jordan, I wish…" he started to say. His voice trailed off and then he walked back to the others.

Under the faint starlight I walked along the road some distance. The dirt road was uneven in spots and in the dark I stumbled a few times. I reached a small clearing off the side of the road and stopped. I wanted to be alone. The air was cold and I put my hands in my jacket pockets. I could not see back to the fire ring.

Under my jacket my shirt was wet from sweat. I stayed where I was, thinking about nothing. I looked into the darkness around me and up above at the stars gathering overhead. It was very quiet. After a while I walked back to the fire ring. The others had gone inside their tents. I knocked down the fire some more and then crawled inside my tent. I undressed and slipped into my sleeping bag and tightened the drawstring that gathered it close. I felt the warmth build and it felt good to lie that way and let sleep with slow degrees overcome me.

Chapter XV

All of us were awake before the sun came up. I moved around in my sleeping bag and unzipped it halfway. I sat up. I felt stiff and I missed the soft bed I had the night before. There was a small flashlight I had placed near my bag and I found it in the darkness. I clicked it on and with the small beam it threw I found the zipper to the tent door. Still half in my sleeping bag, I unzipped the tent door and looked out. Someone's dark shape was up and moving and the sound he made was probably what had awakened me. I flashed the light on Michael's tent and I heard him say, "You'll need a proctologist to shut that light off if you don't kill it." He spoke in a mock-angry voice and I knew he was also awake and getting dressed inside his tent.

The dark shape approached me and I saw it was Steven.

"Hey, bro," he said softly.

"Derek up?" I asked him.

"Yeah. He's using the head."

I slid out from the rest of my sleeping bag and climbed out of my tent. I was dressed in only underwear and a t-shirt. The morning air was chilly and I saw the first light of false dawn in the east. The western sky was still black and filled with stars.

"Nice out here, isn't it?" I said.

"It's great."

We were talking softly even though we were all up. I didn't think any other campers, or at least the ones we had seen last night, could hear us even in normal tones but it seemed natural not to disturb the early morning.

There was the sound of crunching footsteps approaching and Derek came towards the fire ring. He squatted down and palmed some toilet tissue he must have grabbed from the privy and placed it into the ashes. He poked the tissue and ashes around and I saw red embers flare. Small flames appeared as the tissue caught fire. He nursed the fire into shape and we had a nice campfire going again.

"Sleep well?" Derek said to me.

He seemed friendly and with no change in attitude. Steven must not have told him about our talk, I thought.

"Like I was dead," I replied.

"Me, too. We must have crashed before eight. I'm wide awake." He poked at the fire some more. "Want to find a town and get breakfast?"

I looked at Steven.

"You bet. I'm starved," he said. Then he said, louder, "Get that fire away from that tent. It'll go up in flames if we're not careful." This was directed at Michael's tent. Michael had not yet emerged.

Steven grabbed the cool end of a narrow branch, the other end which was burning, and began waving it back and forth in front of Michael's tent. From inside the tent we heard, "Knock it off! That's not funny!"

Derek and I were laughing.

"Come on, you slouch. We're all hungry," said Steven. He tossed the branch back into the fire and sparks rose and died away.

It didn't take long to break camp. We worked on our tents, removing the poles and rolling up the nylon. In only a few minutes the bags were packed and properly secured. Each of us checked a final time that nothing had been left behind and we mounted the bikes.

There is no quiet way to start four motorbikes and in the pre-dawn stillness the bikes sounded very loud. We motored out the dirt road and to the main highway. There was no traffic on the road and each of us twisted the throttle and accelerated smoothly up to speed. The air felt cold against my face and we cruised along under the first few rays of the real dawn. A sign read we were leaving New Mexico and entering Arizona. We rolled into a small town named Alpine and there was a breakfast cafe with lights on inside. The parking lot was full of pick-up trucks. We pulled into the lot and found space to park and then walked inside.

It was perfect. It was wood-paneled, plank-floored, and it smelled of bacon and bread and fresh ground coffee. There was sawdust on the floor, wooden captains' chairs at the tables, and it was busy enough to let you know it was a good place but not so crowded that we had to wait. The waitress smiled and said her name was Sarah. We ordered hot coffee with plenty of cream and sugar to start. The cafe was called Bear Wallow. The place was perfect.

Derek lifted the glass sugar container and poured sugar into our coffee cups.

"Nothing better than the first sip of hot coffee, is there?" asked Derek.

"Especially in places like this," said Michael.

"You must not ever have been here before," Steven said, meaning me.

"Why is that?" I said.

"No vanilla creamer waiting on the table."

The place was full of ranchers and locals. No one paid much attention to us. We ordered steak and eggs, with home-style potatoes and wheat toast. Sarah brought our meals in decent time and we began to eat.

I spread extra butter and jelly on my toast and cut my steak into large bites. My eggs, cooked over easy, dripped yolk which the potatoes soaked up. The steak was medium well, slightly charbroiled. It was all delicious.

Sarah left to bring back more hot coffee. I felt I could drink a gallon of the stuff.

"Did you notice the horses outside?" asked Michael.

"I did," I replied. We scanned the cafe to see if we could pick out who had come in on the real horses, as opposed to our iron horses.

"I'll bet those guys over there," Michael said. "They have that cowboy look."

"I would say there's no look about it. Those are real cowboys. Can you imagine saddling up for the day and coming here to eat?"

"Not me," said Derek.

"You don't like horses?"

"Horses have teeth," Derek explained.

"So do women," replied Michael.

"They don't bite."

"Some do."

We ate our breakfast and debated the relative merits of horses and women. I think in the end women won.

"Sarah could give Maggie a run for the money, eh?" I said to Michael.

Michael looked her over again. "No," he said. "I'm staying true to Maggie."

"You suppose we can get some chain lube anywhere?" said Steven.

"Pretty early still," said Derek. "Maybe a gas station, but I doubt it."

"My chain needs to be wiped off and lubed. I looked at it with a flashlight this morning. There's dirt all over it."

"We'll keep an eye out for some place," I said.

We stayed for a few more cups of coffee, each of us in turn chatting up Sarah, who didn't mind, and then we headed out. There was a thermometer by the door that read 43 degrees. As we walked by the horses tied along the side of the building, Michael said, "Pet the nice horses, Derek." Derek ignored both him and the horses.

From Alpine we rode north towards Eagar. The sun rose from the mountains. It was beautiful country. We could see there was more meadowland than forest, but there were plenty of trees, especially farther out by the mountains. In Eagar we stopped only long enough to gas up the bikes. The gas station had no chain lube for sale, which we didn't expect anyway, and from there we headed west and cruised along towards Show Low. The clerk at the gas station said there was a Wal-Mart there. Michael said he knew Wal-Mart carried the proper chain lube and it likely was open this early.

Show Low surprised us with its sudden suburban appearance. The landscape had seemed so rural since Socorro that it was startling to see the mall and the rest of the businesses appear. The Wal-Mart loomed over the town and we pulled into the parking lot. With all the room in the huge lot we pulled into individual parking spaces and shut off the bikes. Normally we would share spaces but the lot was so big it didn't matter. We crossed the lot and walked to the store, where a crowd stood in front of the doors. The doors were locked.

"What gives?" I asked Michael.

"Must not be open yet," he said. He asked a man in the crowd the time. He checked his watch and spoke to Michael. Michael turned back to me.

"Seven. In thirty minutes. I guess they open here later than in San Diego."

"What's the line for?" said Steven. The crowd, we noticed when we had gotten closer, was not really a crowd but a line of people. Near the doors some of the people sat in chairs. Some had sleeping bags. Some had coolers with food and drink. The line started at the doors and wound its way back and along the side of the building.

"That new game is coming out today," said Michael. "I'd forgotten. Today is the first day it goes on sale."

"A game?" I said.

Michael explained it was the latest electronic game. The people were lined up to buy it.

"You gotta be kidding me, Mike," I said. "They're lined up to buy a toy?" I looked at the crowd. "These people are adults."

"Join the real world, Jordan. You must live in a cave."

There was some movement inside the store and the crowd of people nearest the doors pressed forward. Someone said something to Steven about the back of the line. Other people stared warily at us. They were afraid we were trying to cut ahead.

"Let's get out of here," said Derek.

We moved away from the doors and across the lot we saw a Starbucks coffee shop. I suggested we hang out there until after the store opened and the mad rush was done. We all agreed. Inside the shop I treated for four coffees. We sat around a pub-style table.

"You're in a fine mood," said Michael.

"The damn coffees were half as much as our steak and eggs breakfast," I said.

As soon as I said that the others began pulling out their wallets. I made them put their wallets away.

From our table we saw the Wal-Mart doors open and the line of people began to flow into the store. The line moved ahead and kept entering the store. People who had just arrived in cars and parked in the lot were going in also. Finally, there was no more crowd in front of the store, just a steady stream of people in and out. We finished our coffees, threw away the cups, and walked back to the store.

An old man, standing at the front wearing a blue vest, welcomed us to Wal-Mart. We stepped across the shiny floors, almost wet looking with waxy brilliance, and Michael led us down a main aisle. We had to move around other shoppers, most of them slouched over shopping carts. They leaned on the carts for support as they half-walked and half-rolled through the store. Wherever they stopped the aisle was blocked solid, so Michael turned to a new aisle and kept us heading in the right direction. The aisles were clogged with fat legs and fat stomachs. We passed shoppers coming our way and not one met my eyes. Their eyes were always off a bit. Merchandise filled every shelf. It was lined up so neat you could snap a chalk line to it. In every aisle I saw shoppers with dull expressions and vacant eyes staring at it all. An insistent hum filled the store, a barrage of cash registers, noisy displays, talking, and the loudspeaker blasting now and again with unintelligible garbage. The electronics department swarmed with shoppers and people pressed against the locked display cabinets. I assumed that was where the game was held. One man leaned across a counter, his jaw jutting out and his brow furrowed into tight lines. He was angrily berating some clerk.

The clerk was on the phone. There were more people who stood behind the angry man. They were all watching the clerk.

"That's not good," said Michael. "They may be out already."

Hanging from the ceiling, lit by row after row of fluorescent lighting, were all manner of signs. One sign marked the automotive section. Michael found the chain lube for Steven there. We wanted to use the back register but that station was closed, so we made our way back to the front of the store. We passed the same shoppers, or maybe they all looked the same, and found twenty registers staggered across the front. Ten were open and each one had a line. A young girl, her red vest denoting authority, rushed to wherever a register light blinked. We stood in line, shuffling ahead one step at a time as each shopper in front of us checked out. We were lucky and our register never had a blinking light. The four of us standing in line made our line seem longer than it really was, and I saw shoppers carefully evaluating which line to choose. As we passed through our register the cashier thanked us for shopping at Wal-Mart. The line we had been in shrank and within seconds it filled up again with shoppers, all of them skillfully wheeling their carts into position. We left with our single plastic bag holding the chain lube.

Outside, the sky was blue and the air smelled fresh. I felt the tension leave my neck and shoulders. My hands felt clammy and I rubbed them on my pants to dry. I took several deep breaths as we walked up to our motorbikes.

"What's the matter with you?" said Michael.

"That place. How can you stand it?"

"That place, as you put it, at least had what we needed."

"It's horrible, Mike. I wasn't kidding before, about the belly of the beast and all that."

"You know, Jordan," said Michael, as he removed the chain lube from the bag and handed it to Steven, "you can really be an asshole."

"What's your problem?"

Michael didn't answer. He walked away and headed back to the Starbucks.

"You ought to lay off that," said Steven. He was kneeled by his bike. "It's his job, you know? And he's right. Where else would you find chain lube at seven in the morning?"

"Fuck that," I said, blowing it off. But it bothered me Michael was angry.

"Walk your bike and I'll apply the oil," I said.

I crouched down and held the opened bottle upside down close to the chain and let the oil flow. Steven walked the bike far enough to make the chain go around one time, then he produced a small towel and we repeated the process, except this time I wiped the chain off. Then we did it again with fresh oil. More than enough oil flowed over the chain and onto the parking lot. It made a mess. I used up the whole bottle, nearly, and then I tossed the bottle to the ground.

"Let's go," I said. The three of us rode to the Starbucks. Derek and Steven waited on their bikes while I walked inside. Michael was sitting at a table and drinking another coffee. He liked the white chocolate drinks.

"Hey, come on, buddy. I'm sorry," I said to him.

"Don't worry about it. I hate the place as much as you do. I just don't have a choice, you know? We can't all be self-employed."

He stood and we walked outside. His coffee was still half-full.

"Here," he said. He took out his keys and tossed them to me. "Go fetch my bike."

I caught the keys and walked back across the lot. When I got to Michael's bike a lot attendant, a pimply faced kid in a flagman's vest, was staring at all the oil on the ground and at the empty bottle. He watched me get on Michael's bike.

"Shaft drive. Don't use chain lube," I said to him politely, but he didn't know what I meant. I motored the big bike back to the others.

"There you go, sir," I said. I got back on my own bike. Michael finished his coffee and tossed the cup. We started off again in good spirits. As we left, Derek yelled out to watch for elk. Michael gave him the finger.

Chapter XVI

The ride west was smooth and scenic and the four of us rode together most of the way. We went through some ragged areas filled with old trailers set back from the road. We saw a few sofas sitting in weedy yards and graffiti spray-painted on fences. But that was rare. Most of the ride was through pleasant meadows and through tree-covered flatland.

It looked early on as though the sky was clearing, but the clouds had come back as we rode into Payson. We stopped there and debated a route. We decided to head northwest and then west to Sedona. The Frommer's Guide listed a campground there, just outside town.

This country was a mix of high plateaus cut through with canyons. We moved through it all under a light sprinkle, but it was not enough to bother us. The sky remained gray and heavy. We moved along in the damp weather and stayed together. Sometimes we passed a slow truck or someone pulling a trailer. We passed one by one, taking turns, and then regrouped ahead. We were still in the high country, the elevation signs reading between five and six thousand feet, and we hit a new highway and followed that due west. This highway ran along the top of a huge plateau thick with ponderosa pine and we saw the edge of the plateau running to the south of us. When the road ran close to the edge it looked as though the earth simply dropped away. We stopped at some point to stare at the view. It was like standing on the rim of a great table and under the low gray clouds the rim looked ancient and mysterious.

The blacktopped road began to drop from the plateau and we submerged into waves of dark forested canyons and valleys. Above us the clouds threatened to downpour any second. The sky was dark and thick, but the heavy looking clouds sometimes broke and yellow sunbeams poured through the broken parts. The road fell beneath our wheels and in less than fifteen miles we dropped three thousand feet.

We turned slightly north and sprinted ten miles to a turnoff that led west again a short distance. We gained back some of the elevation, although it was hard to tell on the interstate. In only a few minutes we were in Sedona. We saw red rock formations rising all around us, towers and spires and buttes, and we threaded our way into town and down the main street. The buildings on each side of the boulevard hung signs advertising palm readings and mystic vortex tours. We passed jewelry stores with large window-front displays that advertised crystals. There seemed to be an awful amount of traffic. We wanted out of it. The road left the town and we entered the foot of a canyon. We crossed a high steel girder bridge and five miles farther in we found the campground.

The campground was in the middle of the canyon, thick with trees. A creek ran along its edge. We circled through the campground on a narrow paved road until we found a good site. Then I took the duty of walking to the ranger station to check us in. The ranger was pleasant and it was only five dollars for the site. There was wood for sale and I bought a five dollar bundle of firewood. I carried it back to the site and found Michael and Derek had already set up their tents. Steven was still unpacking.

"Did you see any showers?" Michael asked me.

"I saw some brick buildings that look like rest rooms," I replied.

"I'll go see."

I began to set up my own tent under the heavy branches of an old oak. Our site was on a little rise that looked over the whole campground. I set my tent so that the door opened toward the view. I saw Michael walking off in the direction I had pointed out.

"What do you feel like doing tonight?" Derek asked me.

I thought a bit. "How about a nice dinner somewhere? Prime rib and drinks?"

"Now you're talking."

Michael came back.

"Bad news, men. No showers."

Steven heard what Michael said and walked over. No showers was a problem. The four of us had not showered since leaving Truth or Consequences. That seemed a while ago. We stood there and talked it over. No showers meant fast food takeout for dinner and I really wanted that meal I had just talked about with Derek. I didn't have the nerve to show up at a nice restaurant unless I was somewhat clean.

I searched through my bags and found the little soaps and shampoos I had swiped from the Tombstone Motel.

"I'm hitting the creek," I said.

"No way," said Michael. "That water will be freezing."

"I don't care. I'm hungry and I want to eat good tonight."

I started down towards the creek. I heard the others talking behind me as I walked away. Halfway to the creek I looked back and saw them following me. They wore shorts, no shirts, and were barefoot. They were going in.

I worked my way up the canyon, hoping to gain some privacy from other campers. The creek flowed along a channel sculpted from water-smoothed sandstone. The sandstone had a coppery, orange-red color. The channel was filled with pools and small waterfalls. Smooth, overhanging banks rose high along some of the creek, while along other sections the bank was perfectly flat and terraced. The others followed me until I climbed up a terraced bank and I found myself head high above a deep pool of slow-moving creek. I could see the creek bottom as clear as if there had been no water. I judged it maybe eight feet deep. The others stayed at the creek's edge. Michael put his bare foot in the water. "No way!" was all he said.

I removed my shorts and shoes and looked down to the water. I paused and then I dove in. The water grabbed my heart and I thought it would stop beating. It was silent under the water's surface and impossibly cold. As I glided back to the top I broke the surface of the water, gasping, and I heard Derek, Michael and Steven laughing.

I hardly had breath to yell at them, but they took turns diving in also and the next day, when I checked out, the ranger said the entire campground could hear the screams. The four of us made quick work of cleaning up and once out of the stream we walked back to the campsite, blue-skinned and shivering. We changed clothes and made ready to hit the town.

The Frommer's Guide listed a place called the "Cowboy Club," and we found it easily enough. Michael mentioned it looked expensive while walking in but no one seemed to care. The place was decorated with cowboy gear and steer horns. We were shown to a booth by a cute hostess who was replaced by an even cuter waitress. We warmed up to the place in a hurry.

"Check out this menu," said Derek.

"Have what you want, guys. I'll put the tab on my card. We'll settle later," I said.

I was feeling very much at home and not worried about costs. Not tonight, anyway. It was the contrast between bathing in the canyon creek one minute and then sitting in a fancy restaurant the next that had me feeling so good. Life was wonderful.

We started off with large cold drafts from the bar, the names of which escape me now. But they were large and cold, I remember. For appetizers we tried skewers of grilled buffalo meat with a basket of warm bread, plus an order of deep-fried shrimp which came with a side of red pepper-ginger jam. We had salads with blue cheese, onions, pecans, and all the usual greens.

Steven ordered prime rib done with black pepper molasses, a baked potato with sour cream and butter, with little cups of au jus and horseradish.

The waitress asked, "You're sure you want it rare?"

"So rare it doesn't exist," said Steven.

Michael took note of Steven's answer and smiled.

Derek ordered a Black Angus tenderloin filet with blue cheese butter, with baked potato also, while I ordered the halibut with pistachio crust and a vegetable sauté. Michael had the same as Steven, only well done.

During the meal the waitress kept the beer flowing. We toasted the trip and ourselves. We had a grand time. The waitress presented the bill and with the tip it came to $272.00. I put it on my card, with Michael, Steven, and Derek handing me cash for their rough share. Now all we needed was some nightlife.

Outside, the night had a pleasant feel. The heavy cover we had been under all day was clearing in long, broken streaks. We could see stars and the moon highlighted any cloud that passed in front of it with a silver glow. Michael passed out four cigars he had picked up somewhere. We were in the parking lot, sitting on the bikes, in no hurry, and we smoked the cigars and watched people walk by.

"We needeth now a bar that rocketh," said Derek, drawing on his cigar.

"Me thinketh you are righteth," I said. "What sayeth the wisest one?" This to Michael.

Michael paused, drawing slowly on his own cigar, and looked up to the sky.

"The night doth calleth," he said.

"Verily, the man is wisdom itself," said Steven.

"Verily," I agreed.

Michael put out his cigar and zipped his leather jacket.

"Let's ride!" he said.

We followed him out from the lot.

Whatever magic Sedona contained, however, was hidden away from us that night. We roared through the streets of Sedona looking for a suitable bar, but it was a weeknight and the place seemed dead. We regrouped in some parking lot, trying to decide what to do.

"Don't these new age mystics ever party?" asked Michael.

"We can have a beer at that place back down the road a bit," I said. There were only three cars out in front but it was the best we had seen.

"Might as well," agreed Derek. We rode back to that bar and went inside.

It was dead, of course. There were a couple locals playing pool and the place didn't even have a cute barkeep, unless you favored mustaches. We paid too much for one round of four beers. We sat in a corner. Someone near our age wandered over to us, hearing our talk about Sedona. He had the long hair, beard, and mustache that gave him the "Jesus" look. Maybe he was one of the advertised mystics, we guessed. He muttered something and walked away after we ignored him.

"Hardly worth taking a bath for," said Derek. We finished the beers and rode back to camp.

In the morning we stood around the campfire I had started with the five-dollar bundle of wood. The air was cold but the skies were clear and the day promised to be a warm one. For breakfast we broke out granola bars and munched on those as we packed our gear. I checked out with the ranger. We left our site cleaned up and bare and hit the road going up the canyon.

We rolled along, the road bordered by high cliffs on each side, the cliffs on the right side dark and cold, the cliffs on the left side brightly lit, with magnificent spires and turrets glowing bronze under the morning sun. The road climbed steadily up the canyon. The creek flowed in the green bottom, flashing silver here and there when it appeared through the leafy trees. We rode together, gradually rising to the top of the striated canyon walls. The road climbed with smooth curves, breaking in and out of shadows, and it felt cool one moment and warmer the next. The road kept climbing and suddenly under the full sun we hit the high plateau at 7,000 feet.

As we left the canyon there was a sign showing a lookout point, so we drove along the access road and found a crowded parking lot. Michael wanted to look around, so we stopped and parked the bikes. People were everywhere, walking to and from the wide trail leading to the lookout point, all along of which were vendors selling various souvenirs, trinkets, and jewelry. Much of it looked Native American in origin. Some of it looked like cheap tourist crap. From the lookout we saw the view of the canyon slicing down from the plateau. It looked like a deep irregular saw-cut on the edge of a table. I could see the final switchbacks we had just climbed.

I lost the others in the crowd, so I walked along from booth to booth admiring the show. At one booth I stopped and picked up a pendant shaped like a stylized cross. It was turquoise, but the arms of the cross, which were equal in length, displayed different colors. The young woman at the booth explained the colors to me.

"Each color represents a direction. It's part of the Navajo belief. You see," the young woman was pointing out the colors with a slender forefinger. She had beautifully formed hands.

"You see," she continued, "there is black, white, blue, and yellow."

"And which is which?" I asked, meaning which color represented what direction.

She smiled and looked at me directly and I felt embarrassed. She was so pretty and she had caught me staring.

"Black is north," she said, pointing to the top of the cross. "White is east, blue is south. And yellow is west. Each color represents not only a direction but also a spiritual world."

"Like a heaven and hell sort of thing?" I asked, just to be saying something.

"No, not like that at all. Each world is part of a journey. A great truth is revealed with each journey. One passes through each world, as our first people did."

When she said that last part, as our first people did, she looked me in the eyes again and her gaze registered her sincerity and belief.

"I wish I knew more about it," I said, meaning it. "I feel embarrassed."

"No, no, please," she said, and by the way she spoke I knew it was all right.

I asked how much for the pendant and I bought it of course. She put the pendant in a small pouch and handed it to me.

"When I get back home," I told her, "I'll look into it a bit more."

I reluctantly left her booth, the young woman giving me a lovely smile as I said goodbye.

After a while I found the others. They had also been looking at all the assorted trinkets and whatnot for sale. They had bought souvenirs to bring back home and we compared items.

Flagstaff was just a short blast up the road, no more than twenty miles. We reached it in less than ten minutes, it seemed. As we approached we saw the snow-covered summit of Humphrey's Peak. Steven pulled to the side of the road just past Flagstaff and made me find the Frommer's Guide. He wanted to know how high the peak was. I looked it up and read out loud that it was 12,633 feet.

"That would be fun to climb," he said.

"You're a mountain climber now?" I said.

"Why not?" he said.

He got back on his bike and sped off. The rest of us had to fly to catch up. We were heading west now on Interstate 40. Steven kept the speed up. Michael's big six-cylinder Honda moved easily along and of course Derek's sport bike had no trouble either, but I struggled to maintain the pace. After two successive nights of camping, and the Sedona nightlife disappointment, I knew the others were anxious to get to our next destination and have some fun. At our dinner in Sedona we had decided on Laughlin, Nevada. There would be some nightlife there, no doubt, and the promise of it urged Steven, Michael, and Derek on. The traffic was heavy with trucks and they wove their way through it. I had to get gas and I signaled by pointing at my tank. The others followed as I took the turnoff to Williams. I was also hoping we could get some food somewhere as I rolled into the main drag of Williams. I found a gas station and stopped next to the pumps. We shared the gas hose, filled the tanks, and split the bill.

"Do you think Route 66 is big around here?" said Steven.

He was laughing at all the signs along the main drag. It must have been part of the old Route 66 before the interstate came along. Every business had signs up advertising Route 66.

"I think we get the idea," I said. "Look at all the signs."

"There's an old-time soda fountain across the street," Michael.

We looked and saw it was true, because a sign said it was an authentic Route 66 old-time ice cream parlor.

"Let's go have some old-time malts," said Derek.

That sounded good to the rest of us, so after we filled the tanks we crossed the street and sat outside in the patio and ordered chocolate malts. The malts were pretty good, at that. I had the map out again.

"Any one up for a cruise along old Route 66?" I asked. I showed the other three how the old route went. "We could take the back way into Laughlin, through Oatman. It's a ghost town."

Steven shook his head. "Not me. I want to get to Laughlin soon."

"Me, too," said Michael. "I want to hit one of the cheap buffets."

"I vote with them, Jordan," said Derek.

"Go ahead if you want to, bro. We can meet at the Riverside hotel. Just check at the desk to find us."

I thought it over. I would only slow them down on the interstate. It was a straight shot to Laughlin and I knew they were going to let the bikes air out.

"I think I will. Just leave word at the desk. I'll be a few hours behind you."

"I'll stay with you, Jordan," said Michael.

"No, go on."

"You're sure?"

"Really. No problem."

I didn't want Michael to feel he had to hold back on my account. I knew he would enjoy pushing the Valkyrie to speed.

"Let's see the shop next door," said Steven.

We finished the malts and walked over to a small shop next to the ice cream parlor. There was a display of Route 66 t-shirts that had caught Steven's eye.

"How much are these?" Steven asked the girl.

"Fifteen," she said. He bought one. So did Derek. Michael and I looked at the bandanas. The girl running the shop joked with us.

"You don't need helmets in this state, you know. Most of the guys just wear bandanas."

She looked at Michael.

"I've got a perfect one for you," she said to Michael. She selected a bandana for him.

"This is what you need." She handed him a colorful bandana to wear. It made him look like a pirate. Michael admired himself in the mirror.

"I'll take it." He paid her and kept it on.

I picked out a different one, one not so bright. I paid for it and tied it on my head.

The girl said goodbye to us and we walked back to the bikes.

"All right, old man. We'll see you at the Riverside."

"Ride safe."

I saw Michael holding his helmet in his hand. He was debating with himself.

"What the hell," he said. He left it off and started his bike and pulled out. We followed him to the interstate on ramp. At the ramp he put on the throttle and the big bike accelerated quickly. Derek and Steven stayed even with him. In just a few seconds they were mere specks far ahead of me.

I had a few miles to go before the turnoff to the old route. They were long gone by the time I reached it. As I pulled off I scanned the interstate one more time to see if I could spot them. The massive lanes ran straight for miles, fading away to the horizon. They were gone. I was glad I had decided to go the old way. I would have been dead weight on the sprint to Laughlin. I glided down the off ramp and turned onto the old two-laned road.

The old route was like a river of time. It ran with the contour of the country and lifted and dipped and had that magical feel that promised something new around every curve. I had the road alone. This was wonderful riding and I missed the others. I wished they could have seen it.

I saw boarded-up gas stations and old faded buildings of brown and gray. I imagined the life each building surely had in days past. It must have been something to see. The buildings sat now with peeled paint and cracked windows. They were like talus piles from an abandoned mine.

I passed forgotten towns like Peach Springs, Valentine, and Hackberry. A freight train came my way on track that paralleled the road. I pulled off the pavement and rode a short stretch of dirt road that led to the track. I turned off the motor and sat on my bike with the front wheel just feet from the track. The train approached, pulled by six mammoth diesel electrics that shook the ground as they passed. There was no end to the cars in tow and they passed in quick blurred segments stretching to a long line that appeared slowly from the horizon. I sat on my motorbike and watched them roll by. The train passed on and silence returned. I left the dirt road and rolled back onto the old route.

I was getting deep into the desert and away from the high plateau country. Above me the sky was a cloudless light blue and the sun was harsh and bright and the road shimmered with heat waves. The miles passed by. I rolled through a hot dusty town sprawled across flat ground and filled with diesel trucks and pickups. It was rough and ugly, but maybe it was only the approach I took into town that made it seem that way. Maybe it looks better from other angles, I thought. I passed through it sweating from stoplight to stoplight until I found the road I needed to cross over the mountains and on to Laughlin.

I found the road and it headed dead straight towards the mountains. I had the throttle turned and I kept my speed up. The mountains ahead rose higher as I approached, but the road kept dead straight until it reached the first foothills. At the foothills I had to slow for a tight turn. I began a slow climb, the road rising and curving like a thick rope piled in a corner. It was a dream to ride. I climbed up from the hot plain into cooler air. The rising narrow road constantly doubled back on itself and I leaned hard into the curves. The increasing height gave me views of a silver-gray landscape thick with thorn brush. I kept climbing and finally I reached the summit. I pulled out onto the dirt shoulder there and shut off my motorbike. I remained seated on the bike enjoying the coolness and looked out over the view. The valley far below had dark granite rock outcroppings jutting through the silver-gray thorn brush, and farther off I saw the hot dusty town I had gone through spread out across the low desert. I stared out over the town. When I looked back into the valley I saw this time a herd of wild burros walking slowly and nibbling on the brush. They looked content.

It was quiet and peaceful and in the cool air I spent some time just enjoying the view. I sat on the bike and I watched the burros. They seemed to have no particular place to go. One bush was as good as another and they slowly wandered together in the valley.

I was just ready to leave when I heard a loud sound of clashing gears and protesting metal. I turned and saw a large tractor-trailer rig rising from the road ahead like some leviathan dragging itself from the deep. The tractor-trailer approached the last rising curve. It almost broke in half as it turned and made the summit. It looked huge as it passed. The driver briefly looked me in the eyes. He used the last inch of road to swing the tractor around the summit curve and begin its descent. I watched it grind away and disappear down the falling road.

When it was gone I wondered how, coming up, I would have handled that big rig suddenly blocking the road. That would have been a surprise, no doubt. I decided it was not worth worrying about. We had never run into any elk, either. I mounted my bike and began the descent off the backside of the mountain into Oatman. The road curved even more than before. I leaned into the curves, enjoying the freedom of being alone on the road as I headed into Oatman. I noticed all the sharper turns bore fresh drag marks, as though some giant beast had dragged a claw across the asphalt.

Chapter XVII

Late in the day I rolled into Oatman and decided to stop. I sat at the polished bar at the Oatman Hotel. Drinkers crowded the bar, mostly men, and it seemed to me they were regulars. I wondered where they came from, as Oatman was stuck in the hills many miles from Laughlin. It did not seem likely any of the men crowding the bar were residents. But they were there, all right, and they kept up a steady racket of shouted banter and good-natured teasing towards the bartendress.

No one bothered me, and my walking in wearing a leather jacket and looking travel worn had produced no comments. The bartendress smiled when she served my beer. She came back between the teasing to check on me.

"Did you come the back way?" she asked me.

"Yes."

"Then you were on the old Route 66. Must have been a lovely ride today."

"It was. I got surprised by a huge truck coming over the mountain."

"It was probably trying to avoid inspection. They go that way sometimes."

She went to the other end of the bar. I noticed all the dollar bills pinned on the walls. There must have been a thousand. I leafed through some brochure left on the bar counter. It read that Clark Gable and Carole Lombard spent their wedding night at the Oatman Hotel on March 29, 1939. A few years later she died in a plane crash. The brochure claimed Gable's heartbroken ghost haunted the hotel. I was reading more about Gable's ghost when the bartendress returned.

"This true?" I asked her, showing her the brochure.

"You bet it is."

"Have you seen his ghost?"

"Many times. Not only Clark Gable, but more than one handsome man has come back to haunt us."

She winked at me as she said that and it lifted my spirits. I ordered another beer from her and thought I needed to shake my melancholy mood. That's how it is with motorbikes. You ride and ride, sitting motionless for hours, no radio, no talking, and what you begin to do is think. You think about the past, you think about the future, you relive parts of your life, and all the time you keep, unconsciously, the balance, coordination, and awareness you need to ride. But your mind thinks and goes off on its own like an ungoverned flywheel and all the time the motor hums along and the wheels turn and the wind blows and the road leads you onward.

So now I was in a pleasant bar with a pretty girl serving beer and a lively crowd and there was no need to worry, no need to think past the moment, no need to think at all. I only had to be.

When the bartendress came back I gave her a big smile. She leaned against the bar on her side and began to say something, but some loud voice on the other end yelled for her.

She turned and yelled back, "You keep it down! And clean off your damn beard. I'm not serving you until you do."

Her comments raised loud laughter up and down the bar and the chastised one pulled himself off his stool to go to the men's room.

She turned back to me. "Damn guys eat all the peanuts and leave half of it in their beards." She put out her hand. "I'm Robyn. With a 'y'."

"Jordan." I shook her hand over the bar counter.

"I noticed your bike outside. Where're you riding from?"

I gave her a quick rundown of the trip.

"So where are the others?"

"Oh, they're way ahead of me. I'm sure they have rooms already in Laughlin. Probably lounging by the pool. They took the I-Forty from Williams."

"And you the mysterious loner type? Taking the quiet back roads?"

I liked the way her eyes looked when she smiled.

"I don't know about the loner type. I think I just got outgunned on the highway."

Robyn laughed. "No," she said. "It's in your eyes. They give you away." She looked at me just a little longer than necessary. Then she was called away again to pour beer up and down the bar.

She came back.

I asked, "Do you have a felt pen?"

"Sure." She pulled a pen from a jar and gave it to me.

"Leaving a dollar bill behind?"

"Sure. Why not." I scrawled my name and date on a one-dollar bill. "Where shall I pin it?"

Robyn held out her hand. "Help me up."

I steadied her as she stepped on a stool or something I could not see on the other side of the bar. Then she stepped onto the bar counter.

"Don't let me fall."

She had my dollar bill and she was pinning it onto the ceiling above me. I was holding her legs about thigh height. She had to stretch up to pin the bill and the men up and down the bar were yelling and pounding on the bar. She stepped back down.

"There! It'll be there any time you come back."

She smiled at me and I felt my face turning red from all the comments.

"I'll be back," she said

The man who sat next to me glanced at me in a way that suggested he wanted to talk. I had been ignoring him. It was the way he sat, hunched over his beer like a dog guarding its bone.

He had a sharp profile, with a hooked nose shading a stubbled chin, and he wore an old wool coat too warm for the saloon. The coat draped past his waist like a curtain. He wore old boots made of dull, well-worn leather that protected his feet, both of which he hooked solidly over the brass rail. Except for his eyes he hardly moved. The eyes gave away nervousness, although he seemed outwardly calm.

"Not bad, eh?" he suddenly said.

"What?"

"The bartender. Not bad."

"Sure. She's nice."

"She likes you."

"For the tip, I'm sure."

"No. She likes you."

The man took a sip from his glass.

"I'm Billy," the man said.

"Jordan. Nice to meet you." When he looked at me directly I saw his eyes were very blue and seemed out of focus.

"I used to ride," he said, slowly.

"Caging it now, huh?"

"No," he replied, "don't drive anymore either." He stared at his beer.

I looked carefully at him. He seemed all right on the outside. Inside, I guessed, his nerves were shattered like a dropped Thermos. I placed him as one of the types who drifted into small towns all through the West and who lived off disability checks. They blew into town like tumbleweeds and piled up in bars and saloons. For a moment he seemed to have forgotten we were having a conversation.

Then he said, "You're lucky the donkeys aren't in today."

"I saw a herd when I crossed the mountain."

"Yeah. Most times they're in. Wander right through town. Tourists feed them. They'd tear up your seat. Chew it right off the damn bike."

"Wonderful. I'm glad they're not in town, then."

"The donkeys aren't. Plenty of jackasses around, though." He looked down the line of stools at the bar, filled with men giving

Robyn a hard time. He turned to his beer, hunched over it as before. Our talk was done.

I drank my own beer and resumed ignoring him. I looked again at all the dollar bills pinned to the walls and ceilings. There were probably more than a thousand, actually. Now I had one.

Robyn came by and I ordered again. I would have liked to talk to her some more but she was so busy. I wondered if the sonsofbitches tipped her well. She deserved it. When she finally got a chance to breathe she came by and rested at the bar in front of me.

"So, you'll be joining your friends in Laughlin?" she said.

"Sure. We'll be out at the bars, no doubt."

"I'm here till ten."

"Then I might be back." And what an ass you are, Jordan, I thought to myself. Might? This beautiful girl gives you the broadest hint and you give back might?

Robyn tilted her head and looked at me as if I needed to re-phrase what I had said.

"Ten o'clock," I said, this time firmly.

Robyn smiled and picked up my empty glass. I knew it would not do to stay longer. There is a protocol to these things. I got up from the bar stool. The man next to me never turned his head. I left and no one at the bar noticed.

The sun was still bright this late in the afternoon. I wondered what the others were doing now. Probably gambling or cruising on one of the riverboats. I noticed my seat on the bike was still in one piece. The donkeys had me worried. I took my time getting back on my bike. It felt pleasant to be outside and in the sun. A cooling breeze had picked up.

I looked at the hills surrounding the town. They were treeless and barren, gray-brown in color, eroded into buttes and washed-out gullies. Oatman was surrounded by the hills, sitting comfortably along the narrow road I had followed through the mountains. The road was stuck with telephone poles on both sides, not one of them exactly vertical, and each pole supported long looping wires suspended along the street. I could not imagine all the lines still worked. I thought they must have strung up new ones and just left the old lines hanging. Each building along the street had a wooden overhang shading the concrete sidewalk. I saw signs advertising t-shirts, silver jewelry, antiques, gemstones, and leather jackets. Most of the buildings displayed the flag from hangers fastened to the wooden posts that supported the overhangs.

Tourists walked around idly. Across the street and down several buildings I saw five motorbikes backed up against the curb. I looked away and began to adjust my bags, tightening the straps that had come loose on the ride. I readjusted Kokopelli. He was still strapped to the pillion seat bar. I looked up again and noticed three bikers leaving the building directly in front of the bikes. They talked loudly and one of them was putting on a leather jacket he may have just bought. The other held a can of beer. And the last, throwing a leg over his bike, had tattooed arms and a red beard braided into two leads hanging down.

I stared at them a moment. Then I stopped what I was doing with my bags and walked in their direction. They didn't notice me until I was near.

"How you doing, sport?" I said to the one with the red beard.

He stared at me, trying to make me out.

"I know you?" he said. He remained on his motorcycle.

"You're about to."

His eyes squinted and he got off his bike, away from me so he had to walk around it to face me. Standing near me, he had several inches in height and I guessed outweighed me by forty pounds.

He said, "You got some kind of problem?"

His two buddies had edged behind him.

"As a matter of fact, I do, sport. You were in Tombstone. That was my brother you and your buddies beat up."

"The twerp with the little doll?" He looked over to where I had walked, saw my motorbike, saw the brightly-colored Kokopelli in the sunlight.

"Well, well," he said. "You get your feelings hurt over your precious doll?" The two behind him snickered over his comment.

"Seems to me, sport, you and your buddies are pretty tough.

Especially when you outnumber someone. Isn't that right, sport?"

"Why don't you call me sport one more time and find out?"

"My pleasure," I said. "Sport."

He stepped forward and swung a big right fist from his hip. He was taller, heavier, and from the looks of his arms stronger than me and he did not have a chance. I stepped lightly to my right and used the outside of my right forearm to strike the inside of his. It feels like getting hit with a piece of pipe. His face registered the pain and surprise and I stepped to my left and brought a solid short left to his jaw. I had always been taught to aim slightly below the jaw and anticipate your opponent dropping his chin, and my punch connected hard and solid. It staggered him but he didn't drop. It didn't matter, though. I was already bringing my right foot across in a roundhouse style kick to his right knee. The toe of my boot caught him squarely and he lurched to that side. He still didn't fall. I had not expected him to. Big guys, no matter what the movies show, are hard to bring down. You can hurt them but they can absorb a lot of punishment.

I stepped back and waited. He did what they always do. Enraged, he rushed me, hoping to use his size to knock me down and smother me on the ground. I stepped left again and swept my right foot at his right shin, sweeping it back and at the same time I used both arms to push him to his left. He fell hard onto the pavement. I heard him grunt and he began to get back up. I stepped towards him, intending to catch him with another blow, but I didn't get a chance. One of his buddies jumped on my back and had his right arm around my neck. I reached up with my left hand and hooked his right wrist. With my right hand I grabbed just behind his right elbow. I bent down and twisted hard to my left and he went over my back. As he hit the street I kept my grip on his right arm, stretching it out and twisting it counter-clockwise. I put my left foot on his face. I kept twisting his arm. He began to scream and I think I might have kept on twisting his arm right out of the socket had not the other buddy of Red Beard tried to tackle me from behind. I had to let go of the screamer. The tackler had both arms around my waist. He tried to pick me up. I hooked my right foot to the inside of his right ankle to keep him from lifting me, then I pinned his arms to my waist. I bent down fast and rolled to the ground. I landed on top of him and as his grip around my waist broke I slammed my left elbow hard into his face. All of this was one smooth motion and I was rolling back onto my feet and had almost made it when Red Beard rushed me again and this time knocked me down.

I had trouble with his weight; he felt like a horse rolling over me. I was on my back scrambling backwards. I brought my right knee up to his groin and then to his gut to force him up and give me some room. He swung blows wildly at my head, but they were easy to parry. I kept scrambling backwards. I don't like fighting on the ground and it's the last place you want to be if you are outnumbered. I cupped both hands, striking his head over his ears, then I placed my right thumb into his left eye socket and forced his head to my left. I was just about out from under him when I felt a hard blow to my back. I saw it was the screamer. His right arm was dangling down straight and he was holding it with his left hand. His kicked me again viciously, his face contorted with rage, and I knew I was in trouble. I kept my head covered as I got to one knee, trying to stand and at the same time trying to keep from being knocked unconscious from the kicks.

I regained my feet, but only briefly. Someone knocked me down once more. It was the tackler, and Red Beard jumped on me again. He straddled my chest and began to throw punch after punch at my face. I used my open hands against his shoulders, taking the power out of his punches. When I fell I saw two other bikers running my way. I remembered that there had been five of these guys originally. I was in trouble and I knew it and I thought that if I was going to go down, I would go down hard. I caught Red Beard in the face with a solid punch thrown upwards and blood flowed from his nose. Someone was kicking against my legs. Red Beard's face was bloody and twisted with animal brutality. He raised his right fist, using his left hand to knock away my defenses, and he began to bring his right fist down with all his power. From nowhere a hand wrapped around his face and twisted it back. He screamed and he was suddenly rising away from me and I had room to slide up and roll to one side. I caught another kick to my back, but I got up on my feet.

I heard someone to my right yelling, "Bro! Bro!" and I turned and saw Steven grappling with one of the two bikers I had seen running towards me while Red Beard had me down. I ran over and grabbed an arm and locked the wrist hard and the biker dropped to his knees. I released him as he fell to the pavement. Steven looked past my shoulder and as I turned again, looking back to where I had seen Red Beard last, I saw Derek lowering an unconscious Red Beard down to the pavement.

Michael was behind Derek a few feet, on the ground, and getting the worst of it with the fifth biker. I started in that direction but Derek waved me off. He took two large steps towards Michael and the fifth biker saw him coming. He released Michael, stood, then turned and faced Derek. He was tall, taller than Red Beard but not as heavy, and it looked as though he knew how to fight. He stepped towards Derek. Derek waited, hands down, looking almost bored, and the fifth biker came in hard, leading with an overhand right. Derek easily sidestepped it and brought a knee up to the biker's gut, then grabbed the biker's head with both hands and twisted it around and down. The biker spun counter clockwise and fell. He tried to get up but Derek kicked his legs out from under him.

"Stay down, pal. I'll break your neck if you get up," said Derek.

Derek said this calmly and the biker knew it was true and he stayed on the ground.

I looked around. Red Beard lay unmoving in the street. The biker whose wrist I had bent sat on the ground also, hunched over and rocking back and forth. The biker with the twisted arm stood several yards off, still holding his arm. That left the two others and they raised their hands, palms facing out, to signal they were through. It was finished.

I looked from Steven, to Derek, to Michael, and said, "What in the world are you guys doing here?"

"Saving your ass, evidently!" said Michael.

"I told them about this place, bro," said Steven. "I said you'd probably stop here and it was worth seeing."

"Did you guys get to Laughlin?"

"Of course. We made it hours ago, bro. We got rooms."

"It's time to go," said Derek.

People were starting to gather around us, looking at the scene. They had come out of the tourist shops. Several of them looked at Red Beard, who seemed to be recovering slowly.

Derek saw me look at him also.

"He'll be fine. I used a sleeper hold. He'll come to."

"I can't believe you guys got here," I said.

"We can talk later. Let's get out of here," said Derek. He began walking to the bikes. While I had been fighting I hadn't heard them ride up.

I walked to my own bike and started it up. The others circled back towards me and we rode down the street and left Oatman behind.

Chapter XVIII

The road out from Oatman had little traffic and we flew along the desolate hills. We headed down towards Bullhead City and the river. Once in Bullhead City we rode from stoplight to stoplight and hit the turnoff to the bridge that led across the Colorado River. Halfway across the bridge we were in Nevada. In a few minutes we pulled into the parking garage of the Riverside hotel. It was less than a half hour ride from Oatman.

In the garage, Steven handed me a small hand towel from his bags.

"Wipe your face, bro. You're still bleeding a bit."

I had noticed a small cut above my eye in my mirrors on the ride in. I had used my sleeve to wipe it as I rode. It was not much, really. I used the towel Steven gave me to wipe it again. I handed it back.

"Keep it," Steven said. He was smiling.

"Man oh man!" said Michael. "Let's go to Oatman! I'll bet Jordan's there at some bar. He was there, all right. There and taking on half the street. What the hell!"

Michael was pantomiming riding a motorcycle. "Hey! Is that Jordan? What's he doing in the street? Fighting? Who's he fighting?"

Michael kept riding his phantom bike. He squinted. "Why, he's fighting everyone! Should we help? Steven says yes, Derek says yes. As for me, I say, let's have a beer, maybe several, first!"

Steven, Derek, and I were laughing.

"Tonight, Jordan, you're buying the beer. You got that?"

"As much as you can drink, Mike."

I looked at all three of them. They looked back at me, each of them smiling.

"Hey, guys," I started to say, but Derek and Steven cut me off.

"Shut up and just buy the beer."

Derek and Steven walked off towards the hotel. Michael followed, the three of them discussing the fight for my benefit.

"I thought your brother knew how to fight?"

"I thought so, too. Good thing we showed up. Bro looked pretty pathetic there."

"Almost as pathetic as Mike. Now that was pathetic."

"Hey! I had the biggest guy!"

"That's true. I kind of liked Mike's 'fall down and cover up' technique."

"It was certainly unique. A unique way to fight."

"Better than the 'let me fight all five at once technique'."

"Yeah. That needs some work."

I was unpacking my panniers, smiling and listening to them talk as they walked away. Before they left the garage, Michael turned and yelled out, "Room 1406!"

It took me a few minutes to unpack my panniers. I left the garage and walked into the hotel, crossed the lobby area fronting the entrance to the casino, and found the elevators. I rode the elevator up to the fourteenth floor. I noticed there was no thirteenth floor. Down the hall I found room 1406. I knocked on the door and Michael opened.

The room had two double beds and a dresser unit with a television sitting on top. Between the beds sat a small nightstand with a telephone and lamp. One of the beds was rumpled up and had Michael's gear thrown across it, so I took the other bed and placed my gear on it. I took off my boots and lay down on the bed.

"You all right?" asked Michael.

"Sure. Just a little sore."

"I would think so. Damn, Jordan. We rode up, swear to God, and we had no idea what was going on. We saw a bunch of guys in the street, but it looked like clowning around, you know?"

"Believe me, it wasn't."

"Steven saw you first. He went tearing down the street and jumped off his bike and we were right behind."

"I never saw you guys arrive."

"Yeah, well, that big guy saw me. He had me down before I threw a punch. I'm afraid I wasn't much help."

"The hell you weren't, Mike. I was in trouble."

"What happened, anyway?"

"I started it. Those were the guys who beat up Steven in Tombstone."

"Why didn't you find us? Why go it alone?"

"I don't know, Mike. I really didn't think about it."

Michael sat on the edge of his bed. "You and my uncle."

"What?"

"You and my uncle. He didn't have to go off on his own either. He could have waited for help."

"Your uncle was trying to save lives, Mike. I was just trying to get revenge. I wanted to hurt the ones who hurt Steven. Your uncle is a hero. I'm just a guy who wanted to hurt someone."

"Come on, Jordan. It's not enough five guys tried to pound you into the ground? You have to beat yourself up, too? Hey, you upheld the honor of Kokopelli! My aunt would be proud of you."

I knew Michael was just trying to cheer me up, but after the adrenaline rush was over I felt drained and empty, and I thought how stupid it all was. I looked at Michael sitting there, waiting for me to say something.

I said, "You're right. Let me shower and shave and get cleaned up and tonight we're all going to have fun and the hell with everything else."

"Now you're talking!" Michael said. Then a moment later, "And you're buying, right?"

"What happened with your uncle's money?"

"That? A few beers, a tip or two..."

I threw a pillow at him and went into the bathroom. After a long hot shower, I did feel better. I looked at myself in the mirror. Except for the cut above my eye, and some sore spots on my legs and back, I was fine. The sore spots, I knew, would turn green and purple and stay sore for a time, but what the hell. It could have been much worse.

Michael removed the small first aid kit in his bags and he fished out a bandage for my cut. It gave me a rakish look, we thought. He talked about the fight some more. I let him talk. I think it had scared him. The big guy who had grabbed him as he ran up to help me had easily lifted him and thrown him to the ground. I knew from experience how it feels to have that done to you; if you are not prepared it is deeply disturbing emotionally. We all feel to some extent, especially after we become adults, that we can handle ourselves and to be shown otherwise, to have that feeling of sureness about yourself broken, forces you to re-examine how vulnerable you are. Some, of course, never can face it and they hide behind a façade of toughness that really only signifies fear. They act tough and give off a "don't mess with me" attitude, but deep down they are terrified. Others learn how to handle themselves, but then also learn that no one is invincible and that although you may have tipped the odds in your favor nothing can be guaranteed. You can always tell the difference. The tough ones have to fight to protect what is not there. The others are quieter and have a sad look in their eyes.

So I let Michael talk and when I got a chance I said, "You did good, you know."

"No, that guy was all over me. Derek had to save me."

"And you guys saved me. You jumped in there. You did your best. You saved my ass."

"Thanks, Jordan. Don't get in a habit of needing my help, though." Michael was drawing himself up to his full height, strutting around the room and swinging his shoulders. "I can't always be there."

"I'll keep that in mind."

"By the way, you catch the floor number?"

"Yeah. No thirteenth floor."

"Which makes the fourteenth floor the thirteenth, technically. I tried to get different rooms but no luck. The place is packed."

"At least you got the lucky room."

"I didn't mention anything to Steven or Derek."

"They won't notice. We're the superstitious ones."

We left 1406 and knocked at the room opposite in the hall. The number read 1408. Derek answered the door and waved us in. The room was the same as ours, except it again had that college dorm look, with stuff scattered here and there and Steven's panniers upended and emptied over one of the two double beds. Steven was getting dressed and Derek went back into the bathroom. We could hear him using the hotel-provided hair dryer.

"Hey, bro, Mike. Grab a beer," said Steven.

On the dresser were two six-packs of beer, or what was left of them. I pulled two beers off the plastic rings that held the cans and passed one to Michael. I would have sat down but there was no clear space on either bed. In one corner was a chair with their helmets set on it. Michael placed them on the floor and sat down on the chair.

"You wrote me about this place, bro."

"I did?"

"Sure. The Losers' Lounge. Best bar in the Southwest, you said."

I remembered. It had been years ago, at the start of my traveling.

"That's right. I had just begun my bike tour. As I recall, I was thrown out."

"You wrote that you got laid every night you came in."

"I recall that, too. Every night but the last night. That's the night I was thrown out."

"Over what?" asked Michael.

"I don't recall that part, actually."

Derek came out of the bathroom. He had heard us talk.

"No doubt you had a great time, though," he said, smiling.

"No doubt. Although I'd like to be able to remember it. I remember it being a great bar, though. Every drink a buck."

"Let's hope they don't remember you now," said Michael.

"No chance. It's been years."

"How many years, bro?"

"Had to have been just past a year before mom died. I came back, you were with me at the apartment less than a couple years, then you've been at college, what, ten years?"

"Try four."

"All right, then six years total? That's all it's been? That can't be right."

"That sounds right," said Steven. He was putting on a shirt, pulling it over his head. "You know," he said, "I barely remember living with you at the apartment."

"I couldn't forget," I said. "I came to your school as your legal guardian. No one took me seriously."

"I remember that. The other kids thought I had it made."

"Little did they know."

"You got that right." That last comment he directed to Michael and Derek. "It seems I was out of high school in a flash"—Steven snapped his fingers—"and into college and mom was gone, and you started the business. Things changed so fast."

"The one thing you can count on, I guess."

"Then let's hit it before the night passes," said Derek.

"Hold on a sec," I said. I pulled the last two beers from the plastic rings and tossed one each to Steven and Derek. "To the trip!"

"To the trip!" they replied, along with Michael. We drank our beer down, tossed the cans into the wastebasket, and left the room.

After the elevator took us down we crossed the lobby floor that was covered with that red and orange carpet casinos love so much and we looked for the entrance to the dinner buffet. We ate a decent meal at a ridiculously low price, I think it was under $5.00 each, and then we left the buffet and looked for the Losers' Lounge. We walked through the crowd that milled around the rows of slot machines. The crowd was thick and we had to pick our way through. We passed old ladies fiercely guarding their change cups, smokers sitting on stools and piling cigarette after cigarette into black plastic ashtrays, low rollers who played multiple slot machines and who glared at us as we walked by in case we had any ideas about playing one of the machines they had staked out for themselves, young couples giggling and paying more attention to each other than the spinning dials in front of them, bored wives who had lost their husbands somewhere and did not care, and the low-lifers who couldn't make it past the doormen of the fancy casinos in Las Vegas and always end in Laughlin instead.

We walked under the bright lights and heard sirens and bells announcing unseen winners. There was row after row of brightly chromed slot machines. All of it reminded me of some subterranean mine complex, only instead of miners these were gamblers working for the silver that poured forth from the lit machines. They pulled on the handles with the same expression the old-time miners must have worn, when any swing of the pickax might be the one uncovering fabulous riches. The main difference, I thought, was that the old miners at least had a chance. These new miners, feeding the insatiable machines nickel after nickel, quarter after quarter, dollar after dollar, saw their money disappear like spit into the desert sand.

We walked through the crowds and could not find the bar. Michael had to ask one of the cocktail waitresses, dressed in sequins and peacock feathers, for directions to the entrance. She grabbed Michael's arm and, leading him, led all of us to the right spot. She gave Michael a smile, so Michael tipped her, pulling out a couple dollars from his shirt pocket. He had stashed a few bills just for such use, claiming it was the sign of the veteran. It would not do, he had told us, to make a show of pulling out a wallet. The key was to be discreet.

The entrance was manned by two large bouncers dressed in black tuxedos, one on each side of a red velvet rope corridor leading in. They were checking identification. Steven filed in first, then Michael, then Derek. As I stepped through the bouncer to my right looked at me. Then he blocked my way. There was no smile on his face.

"Jordan Wryte," he said.

My jaw must have dropped. I stood there speechless. The bouncer could not have seen my license yet; I was just pulling it out. He stared at me, not saying a word. Then a big smile broke across his face.

"I know you. I've been working this door ten years. I remember people. Especially people that give us some excitement now and then." He stepped back to allow me to pass. "I'm sure everything will be fine tonight. Have a good time."

He let me pass, still holding that impossibly big smile across his face.

I found the others inside, waiting for me.

"What was that about?" asked Derek.

"That bouncer recognized me."

"No way," said Michael.

"I swear he did."

"I saved all your letters, bro. Maybe you ought to read the ones from Laughlin, refresh your memory a bit."

"Maybe," I said. I saw a table clearing out near the dance floor. "Grab that table."

We approached the table, moving through the bar, but not too fast, wearing the bored expressions important to bar veterans. The table was ours and we sat down and a waitress appeared. She wiped off the tabletop and set down napkins. She asked for our orders.

"I'll get the first round," said Michael.

"I said I'd buy, remember?"

"No, you're off the hook."

The waitress stood there impatiently. The place was busy.

"Four beers!" said Michael.

The waitress began to rattle off a number of different beers, the way they do when they are in a hurry and want your order quickly.

"First one is fine, miss," said Michael. The waitress vanished among the tables, threading her way smoothly through the crowd.

"Hey, check this out," said Steven.

He passed around some tourist brochure. The brochure had

all the slang names the old timers used for liquor.

"I'm ordering shots!" said Steven. He signaled a different waitress and ordered something. She came back with twelve shot glasses and was setting them down for us just as the first waitress came back with the beers. The first waitress glared at the second, who simply ignored her.

The first waitress announced to Michael, "That'll be $8.00."

Michael leaned over to me and said, "I thought you said everything here was a buck?"

"Things change," I said.

Michael gave her a twenty. The waitress grabbed it and said, "Thank-you." And walked off again.

"Hey!" said Michael, but she was gone.

I was laughing. "Nice tip. I think Steven started a range war."

"That rookie!"

Steven had finished paying for all the shots. The twelve shot glasses and the four mugs of beer covered the tabletop. It looked like the day before prohibition.

Derek said, "How much were all the shots?"

"Don't worry about it. Wasn't no twelve dollars, though."

I happily ignored him. "What are all these?"

"Who cares?" said Michael. "Drink up!"

We each grabbed a shot glass, clinked the glasses, and drank the contents in one gulp.

"That's good bust-skull!"

"More of that phlegm-cutter!"

"Another round of tonsil-paint!"

We finished the shots and we each grabbed a mug of beer. We toasted the trip once more and leaned back into our chairs. All our shot drinking had attracted looks from a nearby table filled with women. They smiled at us whenever we looked over.

"That'll be our reserve if we strike out elsewhere," said Derek. He reached for his wallet and pulled out two hundred-dollar bills. He slapped them on the table. "Guys, I've had a great time on this trip. Use this till it's gone, then everyone's on his own."

He got up and wandered past the tables. He circled the crowd along the edge of the saloon like a seemingly disinterested bird of prey, ready to dive at a flash of interest.

Steven watched him go. "Reserve, hell. I'm ready to rock." He stood and approached the table of women near us. Michael and I watched him talk to one, then a second, and then a third. He came back to the table.

"Why do they give you signals, then say no to dancing?" he said, exasperated.

Michael was smiling. He leaned in towards Steven. "Listen up, rookie. You never ask more than one girl at a table of women for a dance."

Steven looked at me. I nodded sagely.

"The second-choice theory," I said.

"That's right," said Michael. "If the first one says no, the others you ask next realize they weren't your first choice. Pride won't let them say yes. It's an automatic turndown. Fully automatic. Reflex action." Michael moved his hand, palm down, over the table to help illustrate.

"It's just a dance!"

"Oh, no. It's much more than that," I said.

We saw Derek out on the dance floor with some brunette. She was dancing close to him.

"So you're the expert on women, eh?" Steven said to me. "And when was your last big success?"

"I get out from time to time."

Steven looked to Michael for confirmation.

"He does," said Michael. "I wouldn't say he's particularly successful at it, though."

"What is that supposed to mean?" I said, offended.

"I'm just saying that if you put your last three women together, you might, you know, get a full set of teeth. I'm just saying." Michael had his hands out, palms facing me, and kept repeating, "I'm just saying."

"Hey!" I said.

Steven was laughing. I couldn't help but laugh either, but I still managed to get "You liar!" out.

I drank more beer and when I put the mug down I said, "It's the time thing. The business and all that. Women hear I have a business and they read into it and want more than I can give right now."

Michael was nodding.

"And you think it's easy for me? I used to go to nice bars downtown and when the inevitable question came up and I said Wal-Mart that ended it damn quick. The lawyers and doctors get all the action there."

"So what do you do?" said Steven.

"Find the dive bars, of course. The more cheap, the better. I'm most times the only guy there that has a j-o-b. I'm like a god at those bars. It's all relative, my young friend."

"Including the women," I said. Michael and I clinked glasses.

"Well, I'm not wasting time," said Steven. He got up and left the table and began to work the crowd. A few minutes later we saw him out on the dance floor. Both he and Derek were good dancers.

"They'll be having fun tonight," said Michael.

"You know it," I agreed. "I always did."

"Is the place the same?"

"Looks the same. They've updated the pictures a bit. The band was more rock and roll. But this band is good, too."

Michael looked at the framed pictures hanging on the walls. There was a picture of the Hindenburg and the Titanic, a picture of Neville Chamberlain, a picture of the Buffalo Bills football team and a picture of the prosecuting team in the O.J. Simpson trial. There was a movie poster for some film called Howard the Duck and pictures of Al Gore and Hillary Clinton. There were pictures on the wall behind the bar and up above, in the balcony area, we saw more. As we looked up the people sitting near the edge looked down on us. Someone waved.

"I get it," said Michael. "All losers. I thought the name came from the unlucky gamblers."

"No. This bar celebrates the losers in life."

"Then we fit right in."

"Everyone does."

We lifted our beer mugs in toast. The waitress, the second one, came by and took our order for another round of beer. The first waitress seemed to have abandoned us. I ordered four more beers and used Derek's money to pay. I put the change in one side of my wallet to save it.

The lounge was filling past legal capacity. All the tables were filled and the aisles that ran around the tables were crowded with people standing about hoping to get a seat somewhere. The waitresses moved through the crowd with a practiced ease. Most of the time only their trays showed and they held the trays above everyone's heads as they worked their way through.

The lights dimmed. The overhead light bars that held swiveling lights of different colors were now working. The lights hit the crowd like small spotlights. The band was loud and between songs the crowd noise was constant, filled with the incomprehensible chatter of hundreds of people drinking and having fun.

Michael said to me, "Did I ever tell you my river boat story?"

"Not that I recall."

"It's a story my uncle told me."

I raised my beer glass. "To your uncle." Michael raised his glass also.

"It was back around the middle of the eighteen-hundreds when they first explored this area. A captain or lieutenant, Ives was his name, he explored the river here starting from the gulf. He took a steamboat upriver all the way to the Grand Canyon. Must have come right by here."

Michael paused to drink from his glass.

"He was a lieutenant. The boat kept running aground. They had to push it sometimes, all the crew jumping in the water to pull or push the boat up the river. The local Indians would watch and laugh at them. They knew the river and they always gathered at the spots they knew the steamboat would have trouble. The crew had to jump in the water and push the steamboat, and each time the Indians stood on the bank and laughed at them. All those Indians on the banks, just laughing at them. Must have been very entertaining for them."

"So what happened?"

"They made it. He never quit. Ives explored the area by foot, then declared the whole area was worthless. The boat was named the Explorer. I remember that part. They found it eighty years later, buried in the mud of the Colorado delta."

"Here's to the Explorer," I said, raising my glass once more. Derek and Steven had not come back yet, so Michael and I had taken the extra beers.

"Yeah. I don't know why I like that story so much. It's better when my uncle tells it."

"It's a good story," I said. "Your Lieutenant Ives wouldn't recognize the place now."

"No, he wouldn't. What we learn tomorrow makes us fools yesterday. Jordan, you read much?"

"Chemistry books, journals. I have to."

"I do. I used to read biographies by the dozen."

"No more?"

"They end badly. My uncle always sent me books, mostly classics. I'd read them and imagine how the characters would be today."

"Like how?"

"Like Hemingway's bridge-blower, or Chandler's detective. I'd imagine how it would have been if those characters met, if they'd understand the other, that kind of thing."

"Would they?"

"Those two? You bet they would. They'd understand each other perfectly."

"I don't know about any detective, but I personally detect we are out of beer again."

The waitress, as if she had read my mind, reappeared and all I had to do was nod and in a moment she was back with four more mugs. I paid this time with my money.

"Mike, you all right?"

"Sure. Don't mind me. Sometimes I get a little moody."

"It's just the beer. I think you need more." I pushed two of the full mugs towards him. Michael downed one in one long draught. Then he slammed the glass down on the table.

"Fucking-a!" He was back to normal.

Derek and Steven came back to the table. They were dripping

sweat.

"What a place!" said Steven. He reached for one of the mugs of beer and drank it down. Derek did the same.

"No wonder you had so much fun here!"

Derek stood and clinked two empty glasses together until our waitress came back. He held the glasses above his head.

"I declare this a *no-empty* zone! By default, any empty glass must be replaced with a full one at once!"

The waitress was smiling. Derek scanned the table for his money and I pulled the rest of it from my wallet and handed it to him. He gave it all to the waitress.

"Verily, thou cometh and goeth, but the beer shall remain!"

The women at the nearest table looked at us and began to applaud Derek. He acknowledged them with a small bow, then put his arm around the waitress and whispered in her ear. She listened to him, smiling and nodding. She left and returned with more beer for us. Then she went to the other table and distributed shot glasses to all the women. They raised their shot glasses and we raised our beer glasses in salute.

Derek slumped back in his chair. "Men, I'm having a great time." He looked at each of us in turn. He raised his glass again. "Thank you, all."

"What have you been doing all this time?" asked Steven, meaning Michael and me.

"Discussing philosophy," I said.

"Sounds boring."

"Drinking Derek's money" said Michael.

"Sounds fun."

"Enjoy it while it lasts. It'll go fast," said Derek. He looked over at the table of women again. "Well, you likely won't see me for the rest of the night." He stood and then leaned down to Steven. "If the *Do Not Disturb* hanger is on the doorknob, do not disturb." He winked and then walked to the other table and the girls made room for him.

"That damn sign will be on the door for sure," said Steven. "I might be sleeping in your room."

"Thanks for the vote of confidence," said Michael. "What

makes you think there won't be a sign on ours?"

Steven ignored him. "Bro, I've been thinking."

"Here we go," I said.

"No, really. I've been thinking about your trip, the four-corner thing. We don't have a theme for this trip."

"Do we need one?"

"Sure we do."

"How about the South by Southwest tour?"

"No. I've been thinking. We can hit Death Valley from here, and from there we can stay at Lone Pine."

"And?" I said. "What's in Lone Pine?"

"Mt. Whitney. Get it? It'll be the lowest to highest tour."

Michael leaned in across the table. "You don't mean to climb Whitney, do you?"

"Sure! Why not?"

"Well, for one, you need a permit. And for two, I'm not climbing up some damn mountain."

"Oh, come on!"

"No. The problem with mountains is that they're always some place high. Find me a mountain somewhere low and easy, I'll join you. Not Mt. Whitney."

Steven looked to me for support.

"He's right. You need permits. You can't get on the trail unless you have one," I said.

There was a fuss at the table near us, where Derek sat with the women. He was standing and reciting poetry, his arms outstretched and his voice strong.

"...the slings and arrows of outrageous fortune, or to take arms against troubles..."

Derek finished and bowed. The women all clapped and cried out for more. Derek sat down again, feigning exhaustion with his effort. He had an arm around each woman sitting at his sides.

Steven, at our table, yelled at Derek, "a *sea* of troubles!" He dipped a napkin in his beer and wadded it up. He threw it at Derek and hit him in the back of the head. Derek raised a hand in acknowledgment without turning around.

Steven turned back to me. "Just think about it, bro, will you?"

He stood and scanned the room. "Just think about it."

He left our table and disappeared in the crowd. Michael and I watched him go.

"Hell," said Michael, "we might be sleeping in the hall tonight. The women seem to fancy your little brother."

"He's a good-looking kid. So the high to low thing doesn't appeal to you?"

"I thought this was our last night."

"You pressed for time?"

"No. I can spare a few more days."

"So what do you think?"

"It's up to you. Steven wants to go. Derek won't care."

"I suppose not."

The waitress was back with more mugs of beer. She was following Derek's instructions literally. Anytime an empty mug sat on the table she replaced it with a full one. I lost count and had to hope she was keeping track of the money.

Michael caught a woman's eye and got up to dance. He came back sweating and happy.

"Come on, old man. Get out there," he said.

His last dance partner had some friends and I took turns dancing with each of them. The dance floor was so crowded one could hardly move. We just sort of stepped in place, bumping against other dancers and being jostled around. Each time I came back to our table people had filled it and I had to keep chasing them away. I got tired of it and gave up the table. Michael had become a permanent fixture at the table where his dancing partner sat, anyway. I spent time leaning against one of the railings that circled the bar.

The band had taken a break. They returned to the stage. The lead singer announced they were going to slow it down a bit and made some joke, but it was hard to hear what he was saying. A slow song started and I heard a voice close by say something.

"I'm sorry?" I said.

"Would you like to dance?" the woman near me said.

"Sure."

We walked out to the dance floor and I led her deep into the crowd of dancers. She raised her arms and put them around my neck. She pressed up close. I had my arms around her waist. We moved together slowly with the music. When the music stopped we stood awkwardly on the dance floor waiting for the next song. She seemed not to mind. We danced to several more songs and talked little. It was too loud for talking.

The band played a long set and when they took another break the woman I was dancing with smiled at me and said she had to go.

I smiled back at her. "I enjoyed dancing with you," I said.

"Me, too," she said.

She walked off the dance floor. She attracted attention from the tables as she threaded her way through. I watched her leave. From the dance floor I looked for the others, but I had no luck. I asked someone the time and was surprised how late it was. Time had telescoped into itself the way it does in bars and I decided to take a walk by the river. I left the Losers' Lounge and walked through the smoky casino again, past all the flashing lights and sirens and bells, across the ugly carpet and past the green felt tables still crowded with gamblers, until I found the glass doors leading out.

Outside the cold air hit me like coming up through deep water and breaking the surface. I followed the concrete walkway to the riverboat landing and walked down the ramp that led to the floating dock. The riverboat was not there. There was no one else around. I leaned against the wooden rail and looked out across the dark river. There was a mist rising from the river. All along the river were hotels brightly lit with neon lights and the mist, rising and swirling, blurred the neon into an artist's palette. The air felt cold and fresh. I stayed for quite a while, until I sensed my mind was clearing, and then I decided to head back to our room.

I took a different set of elevators up and everything was backwards coming to the room. While I stood in the hallway I heard Steven's voice and then a woman's voice laughing from inside the room opposite mine. The door to my room was propped open with a pillow and no light showed. I guessed Michael was asleep and did not want to bother with letting me in. He had not given me one of the key cards to the room. I entered and kept the lights off but I could make out his still figure on one of the beds. I crashed on the other bed.

Chapter XIX

In the morning I awoke to the sound of the television. I became aware of it slowly, the meaningless sound penetrating my mind, becoming more distinct until finally I was awake. I opened my eyes and felt things were different. I sat up and looked around.

The room was a mess. Gear was scattered on the floor and there were clothes piled on the chair and table. The blankets on the other bed were thrown aside. The bed was empty. I heard the shower run. I looked around the room for my panniers but they were gone and I realized then that I was in the wrong room. I still had my clothes on from last night and my shoes were on the floor. I picked them up and walked to the room door and opened it. I looked at the number. It was number 1408. Number 1406 was across the hallway. I left room 1408 and crossed the hallway and knocked on 1406. Michael opened the door.

"Up finally, eh?" he said as I brushed by him.

I grunted. I saw Steven sleeping in my former bed. I sat down in the chair. The air smelled of perfume.

Michael was smiling.

He said, "I found Steven's key card and checked on the other room this morning. We didn't know where you were last night. I saw you sprawled asleep on one bed, Derek on the other. You two looked like a couple of gunslingers who'd shot each other dead."

"I felt dead. I heard voices in here last night."

"Oh, yeah. You did, at that. We had a great time. A very great time."

"Don't rub it in. I thought Derek would be in on that."

"You didn't see what happened? He passed out in the bar. Fell over the table of women he was at. The bouncers made us leave. We carried him up to his room and put him to bed. Three of the women came with us."

"Three?"

"I looked for you but you were gone. Last I saw you had some doll on the dance floor and then you were gone. We had a date lined up for you but you missed it."

"Unlucky me," I said. Something stirred in my brain, Michael's comment about the date, but I could not recall what. Then a moment later I remembered Robyn and the 10:00 date I was supposed to have kept.

"I'm just blowing it all over," I said.

"Well, she wasn't that good looking, to tell you the truth. Why don't you shower and we'll have breakfast? Steven will be a while, I think."

I looked at Steven. He had not moved on the bed. He had the covers piled on himself and all I saw was the top of his head sticking out from the covers.

"Sure. Check on Derek, will you? Let him know. He's already up. We can eat, the three of us, while Steven sleeps in."

We took the elevator down to the casino area and found the breakfast buffet. No matter where you wanted to go it was always necessary to walk through the casino. Tired gamblers from the night before still fed the machines, while others, fresh from a night's sleep, laughed and screamed whenever coins fell tinkling into the metal trays. We had only just come back from the first trip through the buffet when Steven joined us. He looked tired but cheerful.

"Where'd you spend the night, bro?" he said.

"Your room. By mistake."

"Mike tell you about our night?"

"He did."

Steven was happy. He took a turn through the buffet and came back to our table.

"I lost my stone necklace," he said to no one in particular.

"You gave it away last night," said Michael. "Gallant gesture and all." Michael mimicked Steven, "Here. You can remember me with this..." Michael held out his arm in a dramatic pose. Derek and I laughed.

"Which stone did you have?" I said.

"The blue one. It was azurite, I think. I don't even remember doing that."

"You remember more than I do," said Derek. Michael had filled him in on his evening.

"By the way, was there any change?"

"As a matter of fact there was." Michael handed Derek a ten-dollar bill. "The waitress hunted me down. She gave it to me before we left."

Derek was looking at the bill. "That's all?"

"Well, I tipped her, you know."

"I see." Derek put the bill away.

"I'll get breakfast," I said. "I'd meant to buy last night."

"Did you think about my plan?" asked Steven to me.

I recalled now his talk of Death Valley and Mt. Whitney from last night. I let Derek in on it. He was not at the table when Steven had first brought it up.

"It'll be roasting there," Derek said. He looked at me. "Your bike is the only one air-cooled."

That thought had crossed my mind. I asked Michael what he thought.

"You should be all right. Just keep moving, but don't push it," he said.

"All right. I'm game if you all are. I'll plan a route."

We ate breakfast and went back to our rooms. It took less than a half hour to pack up and we met down in the garage at the bikes. The panniers were strapped to the bikes and we started the bikes up and rode slowly from the garage. Just north of Laughlin we found the highway that led west to the blacktopped road that pushed north to Las Vegas. We ran north a short distance and turned west again at a small town named Searchlight. In a few miles we crossed into California.

The road was leading us to the Death Valley turnoff. We crossed a mountain summit at five thousand feet and began to drop again. When we hit the turnoff we had fallen to one thousand feet. The turnoff, at the truck stop town of Baker, where we gassed up the bikes and bought water, took us due north towards Death Valley.

The road followed a flat plain broken up by islands of furrowed hills, wrinkled and brown in the sun. To our left tall mountains rose thousands of feet. The mountains looked gray and orange-streaked. They were rocky and looked mostly impenetrable, but sometimes we saw canyons cutting into them. The canyons were fronted by huge fan-shaped debris piles. We stayed on the plain with the islands of small furrowed hills. Basalt deposits appeared. The basalt was colored deep black, cubed and rectangular with sharp angles. It made long jumbled piles against the hills. The road followed the flat plain and we saw a sign that read "Badwater" and we knew that was the road we needed. We turned west and the road headed towards the tall mountains.

As we hit the mountains the road found a canyon entrance, but instead of climbing it dropped into a hidden gorge. On either side of the gorge strange formations of gray rock and yellow sandstone appeared. Long black lava flows lined the road. The road dropped, winding its way down, and hit bottom.

It turned north and ran along the edge of another plain. This plain was far lower than the other we had traveled and on the far side of this plain was another towering mountain range. The plain was flat and desolate. It got even lower as we went north. The air had been warm all along the ride and now, with the sun straight up, it was suffocating. The air hung heavy and it blew hot against our faces and heated our lungs.

Michael was leading our group, then suddenly he pulled up. We followed him off the side of the road. He dismounted and took off his helmet.

"The hell with this," he said. He strapped his helmet onto the back of his bike. His hair was wet with sweat.

I took my helmet off also. I strapped it onto one side of the pillion bar and motioned for Steven to give me his helmet. I strapped his onto the other side of the bar. It looked sloppy but it was that or he had to wear it. There just wasn't a spot to carry the helmet on his sport bike. Michael took Derek's helmet and did the same.

Steven and Derek put on sunglasses. I took mine off to clean them with my bandana. The bright sun reflected off the rocks and made my eyes hurt. I put my glasses back on after cleaning them and I felt my eyes relax.

"How's your bike holding up?" Michael asked me.

"It seems all right."

"If we get stopped we'll be fined."

"I don't give a rat's ass."

"Neither do I."

I looked out across the flat valley. Heat waves radiated in the distance. The valley floor was tinted white, the whiteness shimmering in the heat waves.

"Let's get moving."

We rolled along the road. There was no traffic either direction. The road stayed to the east side of the valley. It hugged the base of the mountains we had just descended and curved in and out. To our left was the flat hot plain, salt colored and barren, and on the far side the tall gray mountains rising abruptly, twisted and furrowed, cut through with canyons that all emptied to the plain. We followed the road for miles.

The road cut right, then came around to the left in a wide loop like a bay road fronting a small dry inlet. A large parking lot appeared with a small building holding rest rooms. From the parking lot there was a ramp to a wooden deck that led out to the salt flat. Steven signaled to us and we followed him to the paved lot. We parked the bikes and took out the water bottles we had bought at Baker and Steven led us down the ramp that led to the wooden deck. The deck jutted out like a pier over the salt. From the end one could walk out onto the salt flat itself. Before the deck ended a posted sign read:

177

Badwater Basin
282 feet / 85.5 meters
Below Sea Level

Steven had walked to the sign and we followed him. We grouped around the sign.

"This is it, eh?" said Michael.

I pointed back behind us and said, "Look at that."

High up on the black colored cliff rising from across the road a second sign hung from a jutting boulder. It simply read: Sea Level.

"Check out the salt rings," said Derek.

On either side of the deck the salt flat stretched out. The dried salt was formed into small raised hexagons. Posted signs read this area was off-limits. But at the end of the deck the salt had been pounded smooth by other visitors who had walked out to the middle of the salt flat.

"Let's head on out," said Steven. He was excited about being here. He stepped off the end of the deck and began walking. The surface was hard as concrete, white as bone, and ran smooth and straight to the middle of the salt flat. Steven walked along oblivious to the heat and we followed, sweating and cursing. After a few minutes Michael stopped.

"Screw this!" he said. "I'll meet you guys back at the bikes." He turned away and I could see the sweat stains down his back.

Derek and I followed Steven out. We arrived at the middle, or near it. I judged we had walked a bit less than a mile. In the heat it felt like ten. My shirt was soaked through. There was no breeze. The three of us stood there saying nothing. In every direction the salt flat stretched out level and white. The mountains towered above the plain on each side. The mountains were gray and brown with streaks of black. The sky was the lightest blue imaginable.

"Awesome," said Steven. He spoke in a low voice.

He pointed to an area that looked as if no one had walked on it before.

"Let's check that out," he said, and headed that way. Derek and I followed him at a slower pace. In a few minutes he was ahead of us. I stopped walking.

"I'll just wait here," I said.

"You and me both," said Derek.

We stood there in the sun, surrounded by the bright white expanse. Steven's figure diminished as he discovered the pristine area he wanted to explore. The sun reflected off the salt, bright and harsh. I knelt down and picked up a few crystals. The salt was loose here, not trampled and worn smooth. I tasted the crystals.

"Salty?" asked Derek.

"Very."

"A margarita would be nice about now."

"I need a break, I think."

A minute passed between us. Steven bent down in the distance, looking at something he had found. I began to think that if I ever wanted to clear the air between Derek and me that maybe now was the time.

"Derek," I said.

He turned and faced me.

"Steven told me about what happened to your family."

"Did he, now?"

"I just wanted to say I understand. I understand how you feel."

Derek was silent. He looked off to the distance. He turned back to me.

"You understand, do you? I don't think you do, Jordan. I don't think you do at all."

"I've lost someone, too."

"Lost? You've lost someone? Jordan, you're a fool. You've no idea."

I felt my anger rise.

"Why don't you tell me, then?" I said.

"You want to know? You want me to tell you how it was, the murder of my mom and Beth, the animals who did it, ...what I went through?"

Derek stopped. There was a catch in his voice. He looked up at the sky.

"There was a tape...Let me ask you, Jordan...have you ever

wanted to die? Have you? I do, Jordan. Every single goddamned day."

"You can't mean that, Derek."

"This from the man who just finished telling me how he understood. What do you understand, Jordan? Tell me. You can't understand wanting to die? Maybe you haven't lived enough. You, with your planned-out life and opinions on everything and everyone."

"You don't know that."

"Sure I do. Anyone else would have said he was sorry about what happened. Oh, but not Jordan; he has to say he understands. It's your way of keeping the upper hand."

He walked a few steps away from me and stood with his back turned. He came back, stepping up close.

"Remember that girl, Jordan?' he said. "That girl in Tombstone? Did you understand her, too? Did you pass judgment? Want to know what she said about you, Jordan? She said you were boring."

I felt my anger spill over in a way it hadn't in years. Even when fighting Red Beard I had not felt it. But I felt it now and I dropped my right shoulder a fraction and swung my right fist hard at Derek's jaw. I caught him with a glancing blow and I felt myself lifted high and then completely over. I landed on my back in the salt. I rolled back to my feet.

"Shouldn't fight angry, now, should we? Didn't your instructors teach you that?" Derek was circling me, his hands up, taunting. He stepped forward in a sliding half-step movement and kicked out his right foot with a side kick. I stepped to my left and used my right leg in a knee-high roundhouse. His side kick, coming down, deflected my leg partially. Still, it caught him and staggered him.

He recovered and moved in quickly. We stood grabbing each other like wrestlers. Each of us worked for an almost imperceptible advantage in balance and position. I got it first, using my left hand to lift his right elbow and ducking under it and behind him. I lifted him and arched back, a wrestlers' suplex move, and Derek fell heavily onto his neck and shoulders. He rolled to his feet, his eyes furious. He came at me again. He stepped inside my straight right and brought his left elbow against the side of my head. I felt a body blow next that hurt and I dropped to my knees. Derek launched a vicious kick to my head and I absorbed it with my crossed forearms. He fell and I swung one leg across his body and grabbed his foot and held it to my chest. I was working for any kind of leg bar but he was too strong. He rolled with the pressure I was trying to place on his leg and I lost my grip. He rolled away and got back on his feet just as I did. We faced each other warily, still circling like maddened animals, both of us breathing hard and the coarse salt crystals covering our clothing. Sweat ran down and dripped off our faces.

Steven ran up to us, yelling, "Knock it off! Goddamn you two! Knock it off!" He got between us, his arms outstretched. He looked from one of us to the other. "Stop!"

Steven looked at me, his eyes pleading. "Go! Go on back!"

I started to say something but he stopped me. "Go on! Go!" he said.

I turned and began to walk back to the motorbikes. I looked back once and Steven and Derek were still there, talking. I made the long walk back to the wooden deck and walked on the planks to the concrete ramp leading up to the parking lot. Michael saw me coming.

"Holy shit! What happened?" he said.

I just shook my head and kept walking to the restrooms. I didn't trust my voice. In the restroom I ran water onto my hands and splashed it on my face. It took a few minutes to clean up and when I came back out I saw Steven and Derek were coming in. They were still out past the deck.

I walked to my motorbike. I took off the extra helmet and I set it on the ground. Michael came up.

"Well, I can kinda guess," he said.

"I'm sure you can," I said. I paused a moment, looking out over the salt flats.

I said, "Mike, there's a motel in Lone Pine called the Lone Pine Inn. I'm heading there. Let Steven know that's where to go, will you? Let them know. Then catch up to me on the road."

"Come on, Jordan. Stick around."

"No. Just catch up to me, will you?"

"All right. I'll let them know."

"Thanks," I said. I started up my bike.

"Hey!" said Michael. "How the fuck do I get out of this hell hole? You've got the map."

I pulled the map from the left side pannier and handed it to him. "Furnace Creek to Stovepipe Wells. You can't miss it."

Michael took the map. "You don't need it?"

"I've got the route memorized."

"See that you follow it. I'll catch you on the road."

I motored out of the lot and hit the road. As I left I noticed Steven and Derek had just reached the wooden deck. Michael was standing, waiting for them. In my mirror I saw him look back at me.

Chapter XX

I pushed it on the bike. I found the road to Lone Pine and headed west. The road climbed from the valley. Posted signs gave the elevation. In long smooth straights and long smooth curves I rose from the flat plain. The signs read 1000 feet, then 2000 feet. I kept pushing the bike and passing traffic. I never slowed or waited. I passed far to the left or I straddled the line and split the lanes. A truck driver coming the other way gave me a long blast on his horn as I approached, but I made it back to the right lane in time. I saw him in my mirrors getting small. The air felt cooler as I climbed. The road signs said 3000 feet, 4000 feet, 5000 feet, and then I was at the crest and working my way across. At the divide I saw another valley ahead, flat and green looking. I could see the road winding its way down several thousand feet to meet it. Across this valley were more mountains. They erupted fiercely from the valley floor, high and angular, granite blue and tinted white all along the highest edges. I finally eased back on the throttle and glided down. There was a motorcyclist far back. I could make out only the headlight. The light was gaining on me. As it came close I saw it was Michael. He pulled alongside and once we hit the flat valley he signaled to pull over at a turnout.

"You must have been really moving!" he was saying as we

pulled over. "I kept expecting you just ahead. You must have taken a shortcut."

"Or maybe the 'ol White Knight here has more in it than you think." I patted the gas tank.

"Yeah, well, better put the brain bucket back on. We've been lucky so far."

We put our helmets on and cruised across the flat valley into Lone Pine. On each side of the road there was gray and green chaparral. A few thick-trunked mountain mahogany trees appeared, and on the edges of the blacktop small wildflowers bloomed white and red and purple. The road led us to the main highway through town and we turned north. I found the motel, low and shake-shingled like most of the other buildings in town, and I asked Michael if he would mind separate rooms. He said no, although it doubled his cost. I unpacked my bike and went inside my room. It felt damn good to rest alone but in a couple hours I got up from the bed and joined Michael outside the motel. We had planned to eat together. I saw a yellow sportbike sitting near another room.

"They're both here," said Michael. "Steven went somewhere to get permits to climb Whitney. I told him I'm out. These mountains go straight up two miles. Gave me goose bumps crossing that summit."

"Beautiful, wasn't it?"

"Beyond beautiful, Jordan."

We ate at a small diner we found just down the road. The food was nothing special and I had bought a newspaper that we shared. Michael was patient until we had nearly finished. Then he brought up the subject that had been bothering him.

"You going to tell me what happened out there?"

"I'm sure they filled you in."

"Don't act like that, Jordan. Not with me. Steven said you and Derek had fought. Derek just sort of shrugged it off. He seemed pretty upset, though."

I looked at Michael. I said, "Did Steven ever tell you about Derek? About the murders?"

Michael shook his head. I told him the story. When I finished he let out a long breath.

"I never knew any of that. It explains a few things, though. That's a lot of pain to carry." Michael paused. Then he said, "That's not what you fought about?"

"No. To tell the truth, I'm not sure what happened."

I was looking at Michael. I did not like the expression on his face.

"Something on your mind?" I said.

"Maybe." He seemed to be considering something. Then he said, "Jordan, we've been friends a long time."

I nodded.

"And if there was trouble anywhere, problems, whatever, you'd be the first one I'd want around. You're the best man I know to send in. But you're also the worst man to send in."

I remained quiet.

"You've changed the last few years." Michael said. "I miss the old Jordan a little."

"You too, Brutus?" I said.

"Come on, Jordan. Don't be like that."

"Steven hasn't said anything to me."

"Steven idolizes you. You were his hero growing up. You still are. But you've tightened up somehow. Maybe it's that business you're trying to get off the ground, I don't know."

I didn't say anything for a minute. Michael stayed quiet, looking at me across the table. Then he looked down.

"I'm sorry, Jordan," he said. "Maybe I should have just kept my mouth shut."

"Hey, no worries, eh?" But I didn't fool him. I was feeling as low as I had felt in a long time. We paid for our meals and walked out the diner. The air was cold. It had gotten dark while we had been inside eating. We stood by our bikes in silence.

"I think I'll find a bar somewhere. Maybe I need a dose of the old days," I said.

"Want company?"

"Not right now."

Michael nodded and got on his bike. He pushed the starter button and the big Honda rumbled to life. He rolled off the lot without looking back. I watched him enter traffic and accelerate away. I got on my bike and reflected for a few minutes. Then I turned it over and I wheeled it through the lot slowly. I hit the main drag and turned the throttle to feel the pull of the motor. When I had passed the traffic in front of me I slowed down and cruised the boulevard. There was a sign in red neon that read Saloon to my left and I u-turned and made my way back. There were other bikes out front, no sportbikes, and I backed to the curb and flipped out the kickstand with my heel. A few men in leathers stood on the sidewalk. One of them said, "Hey, nice ride, man," as I got off the seat. I took off my helmet and nodded at him. I put the helmet on the pillion post. There would be no need to lock it. I saw that all the bikes were Harley's. I guessed that this bar was the type that had segregated parking: Harleys in front, cars and all other makes of motorbikes in back. I smiled to myself, thinking that it would not have stopped Michael from parking in front. He would have backed his Honda in and, the funny thing was, the Harley riders would have accepted him. For some reason the six-cylinder Honda had their respect. But the hell with Michael, I thought. I walked inside.

A long bar ran along the wall to my left. I found a stool and sat on it. The bartendress took my order. She came back and set down a pitcher of beer and a mug. I poured the beer from the pitcher into the mug. The beer sloshed over the top of the glass. There was a small stage in the back and I saw that a band was getting ready to play. It was not yet nine o'clock. The band had five members and the stage was so small two of the guitarists stood on the floor in front. The lead singer was a woman.

I saw the usual mix of people a small-town bar attracts. The bikers I had seen out front were now inside. They had two tables pushed together. All of them wore leathers and I guessed they were an informal club on a ride, probably made up of attorneys and bankers. The bikes out front were expensive. Some of the riders wore sunglasses inside the bar, trying for that tough look. They were just missing it. They were missing it by quite a lot. Hell, I was in a mood, I thought. Well, why not. What was Mike's problem, anyway? I suppose he had a right to say what he wanted. The hell with that and the hell with him. I really didn't give a damn. I finished the pitcher of beer and ordered another.

The band started up and the music was loud rock and roll. The bar countertop vibrated with the bass. Some woman asked me to dance. I danced a few songs and then came back to my barstool. When she asked me again later I turned her down. But I saw another woman walk in and I saw her and her girlfriend take a table across the bar. I motioned to the waitress and I asked her to take two of whatever they were drinking to their table. A few minutes later I saw the woman and her girlfriend scanning the bar, trying to guess who had sent the drinks. I gave a nod and they smiled. The band took a break and when they resumed I walked over and asked the first one to dance. She smiled and said yes and we danced a few songs. The girl I had turned down watched us. A slow song came up and we finished the set with it. I walked her back to her girlfriend and she said something about do not forget to ask again, or something close to that, and I went back to my stool. The bartendress brought another pitcher of beer. I asked her to send a pitcher to the table full of bikers. I was full of generosity for everyone.

The lead singer for the band took the microphone and announced a free drink to the person there who had traveled the farthest. People started shouting out names of states and cities. I shouted out San Diego, but there were people from all over. Some guy from Rhode Island won. After he won some guy came out of the bathroom buttoning his pants and yelling Melbourne and he won a free drink, too. I guessed Lone Pine attracted people from all around the world for the mountains here.

The Melbourne man sat near me at the bar and I bought him a beer. He looked surprised, smiled and said, "Thank you, mate!"

I raised my glass. "Cheers! To sheep-fuckers down under."

His smile changed a bit and he raised his own beer slightly. Then he looked away.

After the lead singer gave away the free drinks she motioned for the other band members and they joined her at the stage. They started to get ready for another set. I caught the eye of the woman across the bar and I walked over. A chair got in my way and I tripped walking by it. I made it to her table and asked her if she would dance the first song with me, but she hesitated. She looked at her friend and her friend was laughing. She looked back at me and smiled, no. I reached for her hand but she pulled away and then some guy was at my side speaking to me. I turned to face him but before I spoke a leather arm was around my shoulders and someone was leading me away saying, "He's all right—he's with us—he's fine" and I was seated at the bikers' table. They were all laughing and clapping me on the back. Someone poured me a glass of beer. The bikers raised their glasses.

"We got your back, buddy!"

I drank the beer and when the waitress came by I ordered another pitcher. Before the waitress left I stopped her and told her to better make it two.

"There you go!" one of the others shouted.

Someone asked me about my bike. I had to think hard over the year and all that. But it didn't matter, it was a Harley and that's all that counted.

"Fuck them Jap bikes!" someone said.

"Pot metal pieces of shit!"

I stood, holding a full glass. I drank it all the way down without stopping. I slammed the glass on the table and sat down.

"Next!" I yelled.

Another man at the table did it, then another. The third one choked on his beer, spraying it over everyone. He was laughed at and taunted by the others. Then they started on the bikes again. I held up my hand.

"Wait!" I said. "I have a story." I stood for maximum effect.

"Gentlemen," I said, "let me relate the true story behind Harley-Davidson."

"You can't tell me shit about Harleys, man," a voice said. Someone else said, "Let him tell the damn story!"

"Did you know," I paused to steady myself, "that the earliest motorcycle was invented by a man named Hernando Brutay?"

"Fuck that. There ain't no Hernando Brutay."

"Shut up, Frank. Let him tell the story," someone said. Everybody was smiling.

"Thank you," I said. I continued. "He invented the motorcycle, see" —I held the back of the chair— "but it didn't have a kickstand. People rode it but when they got off the bike, the fucking thing just fell over!"

"No shit? So what happened?"

"He gave up on it. Left it rusting in a field somewhere. What people don't know is that a man named Ed Harley found it in the field and he took it to his good friend Ed Davidson." I stopped and drank from my glass.

"There ain't no Ed Harley, either!"

I ignored the doubter and resumed the story. Everyone was at the table was smiling.

"You see, Ed Davidson" —I pointed at the doubter— "had invented the kickstand years earlier, but there was nothing to put it on."

"On account the motorcycle hadn't been invented yet?" someone said.

"Right!"

"So he put it on the motorcycle?"

"Right again!" I said. The table was laughing, guessing what was coming.

I continued. "So now they had a motorcycle with a kickstand, but they needed a name for it. They saw the name 'Brutay' on the bike, so Davidson said how about: *Ed-2 Brutay*?"

The table cheered at my story, all but the guy who had questioned the names. He was saying, "What the fuck is that supposed to mean?" and someone else said, "Latin, asshole. Read some Shakespeare sometime," and we all raised our glasses and drank a toast to Harley-Davidson. I sat back down but I missed my chair and fell against the table behind me and onto the floor. Several hands grabbed me and pulled me back up. There was a scuffle going on and suddenly I was out in the cool air. The Harley bikers had come outside with me.

"That fucking dick," I heard one of the bikers say. "We were just having fun. He didn't have to throw us out."

Someone asked me how I felt, meaning could I ride, and I said words to the effect that on my worst day none of them could keep up with me, and there was more backslapping. I got on my bike and turned it over and they all rode with me back to the motel. I rolled up to my room door and all the bikes were loud. They were gunning the throttles. Michael's light came on in the room next to mine and he walked out barefoot wearing only shorts. He saw me in the crowd and walked over.

"What the fuck?" he said.

I got off my bike and nearly tripped again. One of the bikers saw Michael's Honda parked outside his room.

"That must be an early model Brutay!" he said, and everyone laughed but Michael, who stood there not knowing what it was all about. The bikers said goodbye and rolled on out the lot. I could hear the bikes a long way off, and then they finally faded away.

"I'll see you in the morning, Mike," I said, and walked into my room. I fell onto the bed, sat up and took off my shoes, then fell back again. I was asleep in seconds.

Chapter XXI

Someone was knocking on the door. I must have heard it subconsciously because I was dreaming it, the door knocking steady and loud, until I awoke and I knew it was not a dream and someone was at the door.

I rolled out of the bed. By the light just barely coming through the curtains I saw it was early. I opened the door and looked out. It was Steven.

"Bro, let me in," he said.

I opened the door enough to let him pass. I shut it behind him and walked back across the room. I laid down again. Steven was carrying paper bags and he was putting them on the table by the chair. I smelled coffee.

"Time to get up, bro. I've got coffee, bagels, cream cheese."

"Why?"

"We're climbing today."

"Like hell we are."

"Oh, no. You're climbing." He brought over a paper cup of coffee. It smelled good. It was the only thing to make me sit up. I took the cup and removed the lid and took a sip.

"You gotta be kidding me, Steven. Go with Michael, or Derek. I got in late."

"Yeah. Midnight. You woke us up with your biker pals. I got

two permits on cancellations. I was lucky to get those."

He was preparing the bagels. He offered me two.

"I've got a small backpack. I have water for us, chocolate, sunscreen. We're all set."

The bagels were warm and soft. The cream cheese made them wonderful.

"What friggin' time is it?" I asked.

"Not quite dawn."

I took a few minutes to drink the coffee and eat. Steven waited patiently.

"Let me shower, then," I said. I got up and took a hot shower. I came out from the bathroom and steam rolled out into the room. Steven had the television on. I dressed, picking out what I thought best to wear. I had thermals, a t-shirt, and a wool long-sleeved top. One part about motorcycling is that you get good at choosing cold-weather clothing. A leather jacket only does so much. Sometimes you need more under it.

When we left the room the air outside was head-clearing cold. I could see my breath. I had no idea where to go, so I let Steven lead. I followed him out the lot and we rolled down the main drag a short ways. He turned west towards the mountains up a narrow road. I saw a sign that read: Lone Pine-Elevation 3730 ft. Past that was another sign with an arrow pointing ahead that read: Whitney Portal.

The road led up past some oddly shaped hills covered with boulders. The hills looked familiar, as though I had seen them before. They made me nervous and I did not know why. I had never traveled the area before. The mountains ahead towered above us. I wondered how the road could go any farther, but it did and we started to climb very steeply.

The valley dropped below us, spreading out darkly but for the town lights in the distance. We continued to motor up the steep climb. Across the far side of the valley the sun's first yellow rays flashed over the eastern mountains. The oddly shaped hills below glowed orange and cast strange shadows. We kept climbing through the heavily forested side of the mountain. It followed a wooded draw up and in. I could not see the town below us anymore. It was cold and I was glad I had my gloves on. I wondered if I would need them on the hike. We came to a loop in the road and it doubled back to itself. Parking lots were off to each side. The lots were almost full. Steven pulled in front of a parking space and backed in. I shared the space with him.

I got off the bike and took off my gloves. It was still cold but I thought the hiking would warm me up. I asked Steven where we were.

"This is the Whitney Portal," he said. "Look at that sign." He was pointing at another elevation sign that read: 8311 ft.

"We've gone up nearly five thousand feet already. I can really feel it," I said.

"Wait till we start hiking."

Steven looked excited. He fished around in the small backpack. I saw he had supplies packed in it.

"You want me to carry that?" I asked.

"I got it. You just try to keep up."

"How far do we have to go?"

"You don't want to know."

There were plenty of people in the lots, some with full backpacks, some with daypacks like Steven's. Most of them were heading towards a certain area and we followed them. We passed a small store. A sign on the building read SHOWERS $3.00. Some of the backpackers were standing and drinking coffee. Their packs rested against the building. The packs were all different colors.

Past the small store we saw something that looked like an unfinished patio. Coming closer I saw it was a walkway framed with heavy beams. All the hikers walked through it. It was the start of the trail. We joined the crowd and walked along the dirt path. It led up a long slope and then cut back across the face of the mountain. We crossed a stream. The trees and scrub oak were very thick. The parking lots below us were visible only in patches. Then they completely disappeared. There was no sign of the store or of the cars. The other hikers thinned out on the trail according to their different walking speeds. We passed several hikers, most of them with heavy packs on. A white-bearded old man using a walking staff bounced by us like we were standing still. He nodded at Steven as he passed. Still, we kept up a fair pace and I thought that coming on the hike wasn't going to be so bad after all. I was glad I came.

We passed a stream again, crossing it single file on a series of split logs placed there for that purpose. Steven stopped and took off his pack. He pulled out two half-gallon plastic bottles of water. He offered me one. I unscrewed the top and took a long drink. The water was fresh and clean and tasted as good as any I had ever had. I handed the bottle back.

"You sure you don't want me to carry the pack?"

"No. I'm fine. It's only ten pounds or so. Nothing like some of these others."

He meant some of the other hikers who carried such heavy loads on their backs.

He re-shouldered the pack and started again. The trail never stopped climbing. We walked through thick pine forest topped by a white granite monolith looming above. We heard voices from other hikers and most of the time we were not alone. A lake surrounded by trees appeared to our left. We passed it and then we came to a flat area large enough to hold many tents. This was a designated campground, we assumed, and hikers had pitched their colorful tents here and there. The tents were zippered closed and we guessed the owners were likely on the trail. We walked through the campground and another series of switchbacks appeared. Halfway up these switchbacks we saw the summit of Mt. Whitney. It looked golden-orange and white in the morning sun. We stopped and gazed at it. Several other hikers also stopped. Most of them had cameras out.

"What do you think, bro?"

Steven looked at me, smiling, and I saw the sweat on his face.

"I think I'll never make it. I was feeling good until seeing this."

The summit, glowing in the morning sun, made me feel weak. I felt good along the trail until now, but I had not known what I was in for. Seeing the summit, the height, the distance, I realized now the effort I would need to reach it. We still had thousands of feet to climb.

"Ah, what the hell," said Steven. "Let's just enjoy the hike and see what happens."

He was happy and his enthusiasm was contagious.

So we kept going. I found it more and more difficult to catch my breath and my heart was pounding. I stopped now and then to rest, but only briefly.

We passed another small lake lined with boulders. Some people were fishing from the shore. The trail was much rockier and the trees began to thin out. The trail had steps blasted out of the rock in many places and my legs were feeling the strain of constantly climbing. We drew even with the granite monolith we had seen above the pine trees and I knew we must have climbed very high. Nothing but rock surrounded us now. There were no more trees.

There were fewer people on the trail. We saw some hikers far ahead, looking like specks of bright color on the trail above, and sometimes, as we turned a switchback, we saw others far below. Steven kept a decent pace and I did my best to keep up but I was sweating heavily and I had to stop whenever my heart threatened to pound out from my chest. We came to a small meadow and we stopped to take a break. The meadow contained a stream. The sun-brightened water ran lightly across the meadow, the meadow blooming with reddish-colored primrose, and above the meadow was the snow, beginning halfway up the blue granite mountainsides, unbelievably white and clean, so bright it hurt to look at it. The snow hung heavily from the mountainsides and covered the peaks. Steven pulled off his backpack again and produced some chocolate bars. We ate our chocolate bars and rested. There was no breeze and the morning sun, not yet directly overhead, felt warm on our faces. A few other hikers passed by.

Before we started again we removed our warmer clothing and stuffed it in Steven's backpack. From the meadow the trail was very steep and we worked up the path slowly, not talking much, both of us breathing hard, our legs driving us up. The trail leveled briefly and then climbed again. There were more switchbacks and I joked to Steven that I was tired of *up*. He just grunted and kept going. There was a wonderful stretch across a moraine of jumbled rock and large smooth boulders that we had to walk across, and then up and around a granite cliff. We crossed more smooth boulders. Then we came to a still and quiet lake hanging off the side of the mountain, cobalt blue in color, matching the color of the cloudless sky above, and here, sitting on a ledge overlooking the lake, we sat for a break and rested. We had been hiking for hours.

The lake was very still. We sat, looking out over the water and across to the steep mountainside that made the opposite bank.

"I wonder how deep it is," said Steven.

I looked at the lake and the mountains rising before us. I thought that it looked like a huge cul-de-sac. I wondered aloud where the trail went. Steven looked around also. He was staring at a massive slab of mountain west of us. It was perhaps a mile away.

"It has to go up that," he said. He pointed at the mountainside. I looked but I could not see a trail.

"I can see people on it," Steven said.

I looked harder. Then I saw, very faint, tiny bits of color on the lower part of the mountain.

"Are those hikers?" I said

"Yeah. They're working their way up. I can see part of the trail. It switchbacks all the way. I can see a dozen hikers."

I could not see any part of the trail and only a few hikers. They showed as small pinpoints of color against the white mountainside. I could see them only if I looked hard. If I looked away it took me a minute to find them again.

"That has to be at least two thousand feet up the face of that," I said.

"You game?"

"No. I'm done. My legs feel like bags of lead shot."

Steven gazed at the mountain.

"Go ahead," I said. "If you want to, go on."

"You don't mind?"

"Not at all. I'll just head back."

"I'd like to try it. I might not ever get a second chance."

"Nonsense. Give it a shot."

Steven was quiet. I could tell something was on his mind and I gave him time. Then he said, "Bro, about me in the business..."

I waited.

"It's not that I don't want to. I just want to travel some. I want to do some of the things you did, you know?"

"I understand."

"Do you?"

"Sure, Steven. But I really hope at some point you'll be my partner. Put that degree to use and all that."

"When I get back I'll think about it, bro. Who knows? Maybe I'll feel differently then. I don't want to let you down. I promise I'll consider it. Besides, I don't have much of my money left to travel on anyway."

"You have all of it."

Steven looked at me, puzzled.

"After Mom died and I sold the house, I put half away. We lived off the other half, but I dipped into the savings to help start the business."

"You used my half to start the business?"

"Sure. And to pay for your school. Over the years I've been able to put it all back. It's all there."

Steven did not say anything. He was quiet for a long time and we sat there eating chocolate bars and sitting on the ledge. It felt like we were kids again, sitting on a tailgate somewhere and idly throwing stones.

"I had no idea, bro," he said.

"Well, it's the truth. There's a graduation card with a check inside sitting on my desk. I was going to give it to you at the poker game. I'll hand it over when we get back."

"You know, Freud had something to say about that."

"About what?"

"The truth."

"He's dead, isn't he? And what would he know about chemistry, anyway?"

Steven laughed. He looked at the mountain where the trail went and then he stood. I stood, also.

"Well," he said, "I'm going to give it a shot."

"Tear it up," I said. We shook hands.

"I almost threw you out this morning," I said to Steven. "The coffee saved you. But I'm glad we did this."

"Me, too, bro."

I turned and started going back down the trail. I had gotten a few steps when Steven called out. I stopped and looked back.

"Thanks, Jordan. For everything," Steven said.

I waved and watched him turn, and he began walking up the trail towards the switchbacks.

Chapter XXII

The walk down the mountain was far less demanding and I could enjoy the sights better. The landscape looked different coming down. I hiked across the granite outcroppings and over the smooth boulders coming down to the tree line. I passed the lodgepole pines, the first ones twisted and stunted but growing slender and tall as the stands thickened around me, then the dull-green, scraggly looking Jeffrey pine and the white pine that looked like Christmas trees. There were hikers still coming up, most of them with heavy-looking backpacks, breathing hard and not speaking. They stopped to let me by. I gave them an excuse to stop and rest. The granite monolith rose above the trees again and I knew I was dropping fast. Near the streams and small lakes I noticed the cottonwoods and birch growing dense and thick. There were other plants and shrubs that I did not know the names. Several times I heard water flowing but I could not see it through the trees. The trail dropped along switchbacks and meandered a long course weaving in and out through the trees. I looked for the portal but I could not find it. I walked along a dusty section that followed the side of the mountain for quite a distance, then it cut back to another long drop. I saw a few bright flashes of metal and I knew I had to be getting close to where the cars were parked. Finally the trail cut sharply down. I saw the wooden portal and I passed through it. A hiker with a large backpack sat resting under it. He looked tired. I asked him the time and when he said three o'clock I felt very tired also.

I walked by the store once more and through the lot to my bike. I pulled out my leather jacket from the pannier. Steven's bike was next to mine and I wondered how he was doing on the trail. He still had my wool long-sleeve in his backpack. If he got cold going up he could use it. I motored out of the parking lot and to the road. The view of the valley was wonderful going down. I was less nervous than when we had first come up.

When I hit the main drag I turned left and found the fast-food place I had seen earlier. I ordered a hamburger with fries and two shakes. It felt good to sit down and eat. My legs were still very tired and I had a few blisters. I had that heavy feeling you get when you have exercised very hard and just want to hit the sack and crash. All the beer must have sweated right out of me. The other people in line had given me plenty of room, I noticed. But I felt good and the hike had been purifying in its way. I looked forward to a hot shower and sleep.

The motel was only a mile down the street. I pulled in the lot and parked near my room. The door next to mine was open. I looked in to say hello to Michael.

"How was it?" said Michael. He was on the bed, watching television.

"It was great. Steven's still on the trail."

"How far did you get?"

"Some lake. A peaceful lake just before the real climbing starts."

"You look beat."

"I am. I'm crashing in a minute. It was beautiful up there."

"I'll bet it was."

"You see Derek today?"

"He's out getting a bite."

"How is he?"

"Quiet. I think he just wants to put things behind him."

I nodded. "I'm going to crash."

"You want to join us for the last night out tonight?"

"Knock softly on my door if you guys go out. If I'm awake I'll join you. If I don't answer it means I'm still asleep."

"Will do," Mike said.

I walked out his room and over to mine. Inside, I sat on the bed and removed my shoes. I was almost too tired to get up and undress but I did, then I took a long hot shower. I came out of the shower, dried off, and fell on the bed. The bed sheets felt cool and fresh and I stretched out in luxury. I fell asleep in minutes.

I never heard anybody knocking.

Chapter XXIII

It was the morning of the last day. I was outside strapping the panniers to my bike. It was cold and crisp outside. I'd had plenty of sleep and it felt good to be up and packed. Sometime late in the night I heard the bikes pull in and I knew the other three must have made a good night of it. Michael was up also. He worked on packing his bike but he was moving slow and with deliberateness.

I was far ahead getting ready, so I walked across the street to a donut shop and brought back donuts and coffee. I put the box of donuts on my bike seat. I handed a cup of coffee to Michael.

"Thanks," he said. He looked like he needed it.

"The three of you have fun?"

"Yes. We did, at that."

I could see his breath as he spoke. He sipped his coffee.

"After this vacation I'll have to have a long rest," Michael said.

"You guys find a good bar?"

"Same one you found, apparently."

"How's that?"

"They were still talking about you. You definitely made an impression."

"I don't remember much of it, actually."

The door to Steven and Derek's room opened and Steven

stepped out. He shut the door behind him. He had his panniers and tank bag in his hands. I walked to his bike.

"I've got coffee and doughnuts," I said.

"Thanks, bro. Damn, what a night." He finished strapping on the bags. "Derek's just now getting up. He says he'll catch us on the road."

"We can wait if you like."

"No, that's all right. He's still got to shower and pack. He'll catch up to us."

We stood around the bikes and ate donuts and drank coffee. Michael and Steven talked to me in low tones about the night out. After I heard about the night out I asked Steven how far he had gotten up the mountain.

"Maybe two or three more miles. It seemed like those switchbacks were never going to end. I got near to the top of that divide we saw, but it was getting icy when I hit the snow. I could see for miles. It was really something to see. I wished you had been there."

"Me, too. I never would have made it up those switchbacks."

When we were ready to go Michael took the box of donuts and the last coffee to the room Derek and Steven had shared. He came out a minute later.

"He says thanks."

I made one last check of my bags. Kokopelli still rode on my pillion post. I removed him and handed him over to Steven.

"Your turn. Bring him home," I said.

Steven laughed and strapped him to his bike.

Michael said, "Well, let's hit it, men." He pressed the starter button and his motorbike rumbled to life. Steven and I did the same. We rolled out the parking lot and into the street.

The road south was newly paved and our tires tracked smoothly over the asphalt. I looked at the mountains rising steeply from the valley on my right. The morning sun made them glow. Several of the peaks were sharp and jagged. The mountains reminded me of some ancient stone fortress protected by dragons. The flat valley to my left contained lone patches of water here and there. Down the road I saw a river flowing a short distance before it disappeared. The sky was cloudless and blue.

The mountains became smaller as we traveled south. There was no more snow on the peaks. The mountains turned brown and silver-gray and became more rounded and furrowed looking. The valley narrowed and I could see ancient lava flows, black and cold looking, running down the hills to the left. Then the land flattened out wide from each side of the road again. The freshly painted yellow line stretched out straight for miles. We were not riding fast, to give time for Derek, and we cruised along at a steady pace. In the very far distance I saw small mountains and hills rise from the flatness, crowding in close to the road again. It looked as though we would be winding our way through. After that, I knew, there would be buildings, homes, businesses. It all would get busy. We would be back into traffic and freeways and home.

I saw a single headlight in my mirrors coming fast. In a moment Derek joined us. He slowed down slightly and then accelerated again, raising his front wheel and passing us. Then he lowered the wheel and crouched low on the bike, riding parallel to Steven. Then both bikes screamed and Steven and Derek became smaller and smaller as they raced down the straight stretch of road. In a few seconds they were just small dots far ahead.

Michael and I kept a steady pace. I figured we would find them miles ahead waiting somewhere. There was no use trying to keep up, not even Michael's bike could catch them at that speed. The ride was too nice anyway. I was not looking forward to it ending. I wanted it to last.

We traveled the long straight stretch of road. The hills ahead became clearer and sharper. We came to the first hill and the road rose slightly and curved to the right in a long sweep. It wound its way through the pass in smooth easy curves. On a curve heading down and to the left I saw traffic backing up. I had to brake and slow down. I noticed a car on the shoulder turned around and facing the wrong way. A man was standing by it. He was turned away from me. I saw that the front of his car was damaged. The left headlight was smashed and the hood was crumpled back. I saw other people on the side of the road. Some of them were running.

I used the right shoulder to pass the slowed traffic and just ahead I saw several more cars pulled onto the shoulder. I pulled up and got off my motorcycle. I couldn't see any other cars that had been in a wreck. Then I heard people yelling. There were two small groups of people gathered forty yards apart, and I heard Michael behind me say "Oh, God!" and he grabbed my arm and pointed. I looked and saw a motorcycle on its side way off on the shoulder. I felt my legs go weak and I began to walk towards the far group of people. Then I began to run.

I reached the group and people moved aside. Steven lay face up on the sandy ground. His eyes were closed and blood came from his mouth and nose. He was still breathing. I knelt down beside him. I could hear his breathing, shallow breaths that made the blood bubble. I was afraid he might choke on all the blood. I put one arm around his neck and head and held him up. I didn't know what to do. I heard people saying things. Someone said an ambulance was coming. Then someone said there were two of them and I didn't know what he meant. I held Steven and hoped he would not choke. I heard people saying things and I did not know what to do.

A hand pulled on my shoulder and I felt myself being pulled up. I didn't want to let go of Steven, but there were suddenly several hands on me. I saw a stretcher placed down in the sand. It was three paramedics and two of them lifted Steven onto the stretcher and the third was holding me away. He said something but I could not hear him. They carried Steven across the sand to an ambulance. They were moving fast. They put him inside and shut the doors. It left with its siren on.

There was a second ambulance still there. I wondered if that was what the person had meant by two. I stood there staring at it and someone walked up to me.

"Your buddy wants you to come," he said. He had a hand on my arm and guided me to the other group. Michael was there.

"I saw them take Steven away," he said to me. He was looking at me, asking me.

"He was still alive," I said.

Michael nodded.

"Derek's hurt bad," he said.

I only just noticed the other bike in the dirt, the men kneeled down, the other stretcher, and on the stretcher Derek, lying on it and not moving. I felt everything come into focus, as when you turn the focus knob on a projector and the image becomes clear. There were three paramedics again. They were working on Derek. One was cutting off his pant legs. His left leg was wrapped in towels. The towels were red. Derek was unconscious. The paramedics were working fast and not speaking. Suddenly they lifted the stretcher and people moved out of the way. They carried him quickly to the other ambulance. They put him in and shut the doors. The ambulance drove off with its siren on. I heard the siren a long way off before it faded.

A man stood by Michael and me.

"Were you with them?" he said.

"Yes."

"I saw it happen. That car right there. Swung wide on the curve and hit both bikes."

I looked where he pointed. It was the car I had seen with the smashed headlight and crumpled hood. There were three police officers questioning the man who had been standing near it. Two police cars were parked close. Another officer was walking towards us. He had gray shoulder patches sewn on. The patches read Ridgecrest Police. He spoke first to the man with us.

"We'll need a full statement, sir. Can you come to the station with us?"

The man nodded and said, "Officer, these young men were with the two who got hit."

The officer turned and faced us.

"Did you two witness the accident?"

"No," said Michael.

"Better come down to the station. We'll need your help."

"Where are the ambulances going?" I said.

"Of course. I'm sorry. Ridgecrest Regional Hospital." He pulled out a notepad and scribbled on it. He handed it to me. He had written an address: 1080 South China Lake. He handed

Michael a business card.

"Afterwards, come by the station."

Michael looked at the card and nodded. I was watching the three police officers. They were handcuffing the man they had been questioning. They put him in the back of one of the patrol cars.

Chapter XXIV

It was no good at the hospital. We went to the emergency room first, but we were told to check intensive care. That was wrong and we returned to the emergency room, this time someone had the correct paperwork, and we were told to wait. A doctor came out to the lobby and asked who we were. When I gave my name, he checked his clipboard and asked if I had been related to Mr. Steven Wryte. I knew then what was coming and when the doctor said he was sorry I sat down and said nothing. I heard Michael speaking to the doctor. The doctor left and Michael sat next to me.

We waited three hours more. A nurse came out with forms for me. I had to fill them all in. There was a line on one form for the name of the deceased and I wrote in Steven Wryte. In my section, under relationship to deceased, I wrote: Brother. I returned the forms to the window where another nurse sat. She took the paperwork from me, scanned it briefly, and told me to wait again. She stapled the forms, put them all in a tray, and continued with what she had been doing. I returned to my chair.

In a while a second doctor came out. He looked tired.

"You are family of the young man"—he looked at his paperwork— "Derek Connor?"

"We were traveling together."

"You are not family?"

"No."

The doctor looked distressed.

"By law, you understand, I cannot release any information except to family."

I explained to the doctor.

"I see," he said. "I can tell you the young man is seriously hurt. He is not conscious and he may lose his leg. There will not be more to report until perhaps tomorrow."

I told the doctor that Michael and I were going to the police station. We would have the police call the doctor. Maybe the police could locate any family. The doctor gave me a card with a number to contact. Michael and I thanked him and we left for the police station.

The police were friendly but businesslike. They interviewed us in a small room and we filled out more forms and wrote statements. A detective came into the small room and said there would be a criminal investigation of the accident. I gave him the doctor's card. The detective said I would be contacted shortly. The body would not be released until the preliminary investigation was completed. There would be an official cause of death report, blood tests for drugs and alcohol, an analysis of the accident scene, and an examination of the motorbikes and the car involved in the accident. He gave me a card also and said he would be contacting me soon.

We walked out the police station and Michael and I stood by our bikes. I sat on my bike but I did not start it.

"What do you want to do, Jordan?" Michael said. He spoke softly.

I waited a moment.

"I'm not sure."

"We can stay here a few days if you'd like."

So we did, and we visited the hospital but we were never allowed to see Derek. Immediate family members only, we were informed. He was still in critical care but the doctors told us they expected him to survive. They had not been able to save the leg. The police located a relative of Derek's, a cousin named Allison, and she came out on the third day. Michael and I took Allison to lunch and she told us Derek had no immediate family left. She stayed another day and gave the hospital permission to release information to Michael, who said he would stay a few more days to help out. The hospital let Allison and Michael go see Derek on the fourth day, but the police had called me by then and released Steven's body. I had to leave for San Diego to make arrangements and I did not get a chance to see Derek in the hospital.

In San Diego I arranged for my answering service to call every customer I had and explain how it was. Michael came down three days later and was a great help. He had gotten an extra week off, he said, which turned out to be a lie, and he helped run the business and kept me free to do all the things I needed to do. I called the same funeral home that had handled my mother's funeral and they were very kind and helped with all the details of transporting Steven. I called the university and the academic counselor was wonderful. At the funeral many of his classmates came down. I heard some funny stories about Steven I had not known before and I was pleased he had been so well liked. Many of his classmates also knew Derek and a few traveled up to Ridgecrest to see him.

I rented a small cargo truck and traveled to Santa Barbara. I met with the academic counselor at the university, who allowed me into Steven's dorm. It didn't hold much, some IKEA furniture, his clothes, books, mostly chemistry text books but also a book of poems, Tennyson, with the last page marked, and other odds and ends. I packed up all his furniture and gathered all his belongings and his mail. I closed his bank account and handled all the insurance matters. The motorcycle was totaled and I collected the payoff. There were some unpaid bills, hospital deductibles, some utility bills, the balance of his rent. I set up a mail forwarding address to my business, since I did not know what else might be coming. It seemed each time I thought I had things covered something else came up. There are so many interconnected lines in our lives, I suppose. Before I left for San Diego I met once more with the counselor and one of his professors.

"We're going to record Steven as having earned his degree,"

the counselor told me.

I said I was very pleased to hear that. The professor asked if I knew Steven had been pursuing a minor in philosophy. I said I had not.

"Steven was very bright. Very perceptive. He admired you very much, by the way."

I shook hands with both of them, then drove back down to San Diego. It was late and getting dark when I arrived in front of the business. I locked the truck and planned to unload it the next day. Michael was sitting outside in an office chair with his feet up on a bench, next to several barrels of various chemicals marked FLAMMABLE, smoking a cigar. He watched me unlock the gate and walk into the yard.

"How'd it go?" he asked.

"Fine," I said. I went into the office and brought out a second chair.

"Got another cigar?"

Michael pulled one from his pocket and gave it to me.

I struck a match, lit the cigar, and tossed away the match.

"Want to tell me what's going on?" I said.

"How's that?"

"Like why you seem to have all this time off from your job?"

"Yeah. Well, there's been some changes."

Michael explained to me Walmart management had gotten funny about his extra time request.

"I was supposed to go home and decide what's important in my life. They called it a 'decision day'. I told the sonsofbitches I didn't need a goddamn decision day. They had the whole management team in the office with me, almost, all of them looking deadly serious. The store manager said he was letting me go. I said he could kiss my sweet ass. I walked out."

"You've worked there a long time, Mike."

"Since I was a kid, pushing carts in the lot."

I looked at Michael. He had sounded tough and flippant about losing his job, but I saw a scared man sitting next to me, wondering what he was going to do, a man worried about starting over.

"Why didn't you tell me before?"

"Come on, Jordan. You're not Superman. You have enough going on."

We sat there in the yard quietly smoking our cigars as the sun went down and the first few stars came out. It was a warm summer night and it felt nice to be sitting outside.

"Jordan, you remember that time in Tombstone at Big Nose Kate's? When we all sat at that raised table by the window?"

"I remember."

"Man, I loved that. It felt like we were invincible. Just us against the world. Looking back, it was just us. We were all we had."

I nodded, remembering.

Michael was quiet for a minute, then he said, "It wasn't his fault, you know. Or yours."

I took a long draw on my cigar and exhaled the smoke out.

"I know that, Mike."

I looked over at Michael. He was watching the night sky.

"I guess I have a new partner, eh?" I said.

Michael looked at me. "You mean that?"

"I do."

"I don't know anything about this stuff," he said, indicating the barrels around us.

"I'll teach you. First lesson…throw the matches away from any barrel marked FlAMMABLE."

Michael extended his hand in the dark and we shook hands. From that point on he was a partner in the business and he worked hard at it.

After a month making deliveries and helping me compound products, Michael took an interest in formulating. He worked at creating simple products at first and moved on to more complex formulas as he became comfortable.

We expanded the product line and the business grew. We added a salesman. I still slept in the office to keep expenses down. And things did not always go smooth. Michael created a new hand soap for mechanics, using a combination of d'limonene solvent, polymer thickeners, and borax, and he tested different percentages over and over until he felt he got it right. When he put it out for the first time he mistakenly used the dye I used for the Laser degreaser, and he used too much. The soap stained people's hands and we got angry calls for a solid week. I had nightmares of people approaching me, holding out their hands and pointing. One night I awoke in a cold sweat. One of the faces looked like Steven.

Michael fixed the product and it became one of our biggest sellers. I took to calling him the Lieutenant but I don't think he got it. He continued to work hard, working late hours and coming in most weekends. He asked for a week off during Thanksgiving, saying he wanted to take a short trip. I reminded him he was a partner and not an employee and could do as he liked. He was gone a little more than a week and never said where he had gone, but he seemed happy. By the time the new year came around I had few worries about the business. For the first time I knew, without a doubt, that it was going to be very successful. I was no longer a bathtub compounder.

And Michael had a surprise for me near Christmas. He had me meet him at Dirk's. Walking in I saw him with a slender girl standing at the bar. As I got close she turned and gave me that dazzling smile I remembered from Magdalena.

"You remember me?" she said.

"Of course. How could I forget? Hi, Maggie."

I put out my hand and Maggie glanced at Michael and then brushed my hand away. She gave me a hug and held it.

"I'm so sorry," she said softly. She held me close and then let me go. "When Michael told me I couldn't believe it. It must have been awful."

I said nothing and Michael spoke up.

"I finally talked her out here. It took some doing."

He was smiling, looking at Maggie. She was smiling and looking back at him, and I could see how they felt about each other. I was happy for him.

"Well," I said, "we need to celebrate." I ordered a pitcher of Guinness for Michael and me. Maggie said she would prefer a chardonnay.

I poured two glasses of beer and lifting mine I said, "To all of us being on the same side of the bar."

We touched glasses and drank.

"That's where I went those days I was gone," Michael said.

"I gathered that."

"He showed up with a big grin and surprised me while I was working."

"I was nervous as hell."

I said, "Why wouldn't you be? You were excited the first time. Those same guys there by any chance?"

Maggie laughed when I said that.

"Oh. You should have heard the talk after you four left. It took them an hour to settle down."

"I'm glad they weren't there when I came back. It's a little different being alone without anybody to back you up..."

Michael paused and Maggie glanced at him and then me. They thought they had hurt me by talking that way but I wanted them to go on.

"I thought we'd be mixing it up over your attention," I said. I smiled at Maggie to show her it was all right.

"She was by herself when I surprised her. I had the whole bar with just her and me."

"You got lucky," said Maggie to Michael.

Maggie looked at the pendant I was wearing. She reached out to examine it.

"A souvenir from the trip," I said.

"It's pretty. The colors match your bikes," she said.

Michael and Maggie were holding hands and I was happy for them. They looked good together. I stayed another hour and we talked, and then I left them there to make a night of it together and I drove back to the shop.

Chapter XXV

A letter arrived in January from Ridgecrest. After all the delays the trial was to begin. Both Michael and I had given depositions months earlier, but there were delays and continuances and all the legal crap that goes on. We had to wait until we got the word. Now it had come.

"You need to go, of course," said Michael one night. "You know I've got it covered."

"I know," I said. We shook hands and I traveled up to Ridgecrest and took a room. I met with the prosecutors and they gave me an update of how the case stood.

"I'm afraid we can't use the toxicology tests," the first prosecutor said.

"Why not?"

"They were challenged. Not the results, but the custody chain. Somewhere down the line it was broken and the judge will not allow the results as evidence."

The other prosecutor, the younger one about my age, said, "But we still have the witness and the surviving victim. Their testimony will be the strongest part of our case. And we have the arresting officer's testimony of the driver's condition at the accident scene."

"Will I be called?"

"No. It's all going to come down to what people saw and what the hard evidence shows."

I attended every day of the trial. I had my first close look at the man charged, sitting at the defendant's table with three lawyers. I guessed his age to be mid-thirties. His wife sat in the first row in court. She attended every day also. All the technical details of the accident were presented. There were estimations of probable speed, the positions of each vehicle, an analysis of road conditions and the weather, all of it presented by experts. Much of it was challenged by the defense attorneys. The police officers on the scene were brought to the stand and questioned at great length. The defense attacked the field test conclusions with experts who stated the field tests were at best only 60% reliable. Factors such as shock and unseen injuries might produce the same test results at the accident scene, they claimed. Who could walk a steady line under those circumstances?

The first eyewitness took the stand. After the prosecutors were finished with him, the defense team had him on the stand the rest of the day. The defense had a computer-generated animation that conceivably explained everything the eyewitness claimed he saw, but in a way that showed the defendant not at fault. The animation showed how the accident might have appeared to the witness from different positions and angles, and it showed that what the witness thought he saw might not have been what happened. The witness wavered on his testimony. I could not blame him.

On the third day of the trial the prosecutor stood and called Derek Connor to the stand. During the previous days I had not seen him and now he came through the courtroom doors, using a cane and walking to the witness box. I saw the end of the prosthetic leg when he stepped up to the box. The prosecutor asked questions and Derek answered them straightforward and concisely. He finished with Derek too quickly, I thought. Then the defense had their turn. They hit him with everything they had, but it was like throwing marshmallows at a steel door. He answered every question patiently and in detail. The defense kept cutting him off. They asked the same questions different ways and at different times but his answers were always the same: Steven and Derek were leaning into a left turn. They were traveling at sixty-five miles per hour. Steven was just ahead of Derek. The approaching car was coming up around the curve at very high speed. It lost its grip on the road and drifted into their lane at the last second. Steven was hit at the rear wheel. He had missed clearing the car by twelve inches. Derek was hit in the middle of his bike.

When they finished with him he was excused by the judge. He walked down from the witness box and past the defendant's table. As he passed the first row of spectators he saw me. We looked at each other and then I nodded. He nodded back and continued out the courtroom. It was the last time I ever saw him.

The following Monday I received a call from the prosecutors. We met at their office.

"We've agreed to a plea bargain," one of the prosecutors told me. "Vehicular manslaughter. He'll get one year."

I knew he felt bad, but without the toxicology tests there was no basis for a gross vehicular manslaughter charge. The man had no priors and the defense was argueing that the sportbikes had come across the yellow line and not the car.

"We don't know how the jury may react. They have on one hand a middle-aged driver with a clean driving record and on the other hand two young men on fast sportbikes, one of whom was riding with only a permit."

I said I understood and I thanked them for all their work. I shook their hands, said goodbye, and traveled back to San Diego. I filled Michael in on everything. He listened in silence until I was finished.

"I can't believe it."

I told him about seeing Derek Connor.

"How did he seem?"

I hesitated, searching for the right word. "Calm," I said. Then I said, "Resigned."

"Definitely one of a kind, I'd say," said Michael. "It wasn't fair what happened to him. To any of us."

"No."

Three months later there was a settlement with the insurance company.

I was sitting in the yard one evening, enjoying the first few days of spring. In the corner of the yard was a small storage shed. Everything I had picked up in Santa Barbara was in there. A few pieces of mail had arrived in the weeks following and then stopped. Everything was in the shed. It was time, I thought, to start going through it all.

I unlocked the door and pulled out a few boxes. I sorted it out, deciding what to keep and what to throw away. Most of it I trashed. There was a letter with feminine handwriting on it, and I debated over opening it. Something was inside, so I ended up opening it. It was from the girl Steven had so gallantly given his leather necklace at Laughlin. The note was a bit harsh, something about if you were not going to call than this meant nothing and some other dramatic words. She had returned the necklace. I kept the necklace and threw away the letter. I finished going through it all. There was a notebook Steven had kept, a sort of journal he had scrawled notes into. Some of the notes were chemical notations, no doubt just study notes, but there were also general observations he had made. One section was underlined. It read: From error to error, one discovers the entire truth.

I read the underlined section again and I thought: Only if we know them as errors, perhaps.

I sat near the shed, holding the notebook in my hand. I thought about the trip and all that we had done, and more, so much more, and through it all hearing Steven's voice, "Hey, bro!" and I began to cry. I sat alone in the yard and cried, and later, as the evening passed into night, I locked the shed up for good and went back inside the shop.

Two months later Michael caught me as I was mixing a tank of degreaser. We had four tanks now.

"What's with your bike?" he asked me.

"What do you mean?"

"The tank's missing."

"I'm getting it painted."

He looked at me oddly but did not question it. A few weeks later I called him into the office. He came in as though he knew what I was about to say.

"I'm going to take some time," I said.

"I thought you might."

"I want to work out what's fair with the business."

"Hell, Jordan. You draw the least of any of us."

"I don't have rent to pay like you."

"You just keep drawing what you get now. I'll put it in your bank account each week."

"I might be gone a while, you know."

"It doesn't matter. We'll be here when you get back."

The following day I left.

I left early on a clear windless morning and I traveled north on the interstate through crowded towns like Temecula and San Bernardino. I passed through the fast-growing town of Victorville and through the ghost town of Red Mountain. I approached Ridgecrest and before that town I cut across the highway and circled back. I parked my bike on the side of the road and walked out across the sand and the rocks to the spot where my brother had died.

I had the stone from the leather necklace in my hand. I dug down a few inches and put down the azurite. It looked so blue against the sand.

"Here's to crossing the bar, Steven," I said. I covered the stone with sand and walked to my bike. I straddled the bike and looked down on the gas tank where the artist had airbrushed the design from the old woman's cloth weaving, the whole design super-imposed over the image of the great trickster himself. I turned back across the road and headed north. There were miles of open road ahead.

Also by

David Grant Urban

A Line Intersected

Each orb with flame and embers the Devil seared;
Above the screams he spoke thus:
Malign me not, blind man, for I have made you see

After Michael Collwood's wife is murdered, he loses everything else in his life. There is only one path left for him to follow: find his wife's killers and exact brutal ervenge. His sole ally in his quest for justice is an old homeless man who loves literature and believes he is living in 18th century England . *A Line Intersected* rips open corruption and evil under the perennial blue skies of San Diego.

Fiction

"David Urban is a dark poet. With seductive grace and powerful prose, *A Line Intersected* transfoms the postcard vistas of San Diego into a barren landscape of murder and betrayal. Urban isn't messing around with this terrific debut novel."

-Tim Maleeny, bestselling author of *Stealing the Dragon* and *JUMP*

About the Author

David Grant Urban is an award-winning author based in San Diego, California. To receive updates and more information please go to:

www.davidgranturban.com

CPSIA information can be obtained
at www.ICGtesting.com
Printed in the USA
JSHW021210280523
42285JS00004B/18